MAKE A WISH BUT NOT FOR MONEY

By

Suzanne Strempek Shea

Make A Wish But Not For Money

PFP, INC
publisher@pfppublishing.com
144 Tenney Street - Georgetown, MA 01833

August 2014
Printed in the United States of America
© 2014 Suzanne Strempek Shea
First PFP edition © 2014

ISBN-10: 0991427564
ISBN-13: 978-0-9914275-6-7
(also available in eBook format)

Front Cover Image "Heart in Hand"
courtesy and © Michael Cohen
www.michaelcohentiles.com

Author Photo © Helen Peppe

Also by Suzanne Strempek Shea

Fiction

Selling the Lite of Heaven

Hoopi Shoopi Donna

Lily of the Valley

Around Again

Becoming Finola

Nonfiction

*Songs from a Lead-Lined Room: Notes — High and Low — from My
Journey through Breast Cancer and Radiation*

*Shelf Life: Romance, Mystery, Drama and Other Page-Turning
Adventures from a Year in a Bookstore*

*Sundays in America: A Yearlong Road Trip
in Search of Christian Faith*

*140 Years of Providential Caring: The Sisters of Providence of Holyoke,
Massachusetts* (With Tom Shea and M.P. Barker)

*This Is Paradise: An Irish mother's grief, an African village's plight,
and the medical clinic that brought fresh hope to both*

Praise for Suzanne Strempek Shea's Work

Fiction

Selling the Lite of Heaven

"I barreled through this bighearted and precisely drawn story, marveling at the author's gifts and accompanying myself with the laugh track of my own involuntary guffaws. And the second time I read *Selling the Lite of Heaven*, I loved it even more. Suzanne Strempek Shea has created a multifaceted, unflawed gem."

— Wally Lamb, author of *She's Come Undone*

"Shea's witty yet warm rendering of a community where strong mothers rule and meek daughters find creative ways to rebel is satisfying on many levels." — *Glamour*

Hoopi Shoopi Donna

"She's what Amy Tan is to Chinese-Americans, Isaac Bashevis Singer to the Jews, Jimmy Breslin to the Irish, Mario Puzo to the Italians, Terry McMillan to African-Americans — She's Suzanne Strempek Shea." — *Rocky Mountain News*

"Shea has a distinctive voice — comic, bittersweet, a bit old-fashioned — and a distinctive sense of place. In her novels, the author has quietly created a quirky American version of English village fiction, wry and closely observed. — Amanda Heller, *Boston Globe*

Lily of the Valley

"It is a gift to take the ordinary and make it extraordinary, to reveal the lives we see unfolding every day, and add a charm and warmth to them that those of us who move around them sometimes forget to notice. But this is the way Suzanne Strempek Shea does it for her readers." — Ann Hood, author of *Comfort: A Journey Through Grief*

Around Again

"Shea brings uncommon depth and richness to her narrative, which powerfully conveys both the adolescent push for independence and the adult need for connection." — *Booklist*

Becoming Finola

"An engaging tale, deftly crafted and plotted, with plenty of Irish whimsy, charm, and blarney." — *Kirkus Reviews*

"Shea returns to fiction in another delightfully enchanting tale about the unorthodox ways dreams can come true . . . Sophie is a beguiling heroine, a plucky, lucky American minx who becomes the sort of Irish lass that would have made Maureen O'Hara proud." — *Booklist*

Nonfiction

Songs from a Lead-Lined Room: Notes — High and Low — from My Journey through Breast Cancer and Radiation

"This is one of those books that changes our life forever. I am deeply grateful that I got a chance to read it, and will recommend it to everyone I know." — Anita Shreve, author of *Fortune's Rocks*

"When bad things happen to a talented, insightful, witty reporter and virtuoso novelist, her notes delivered a brilliant silver lining. I'm not the same person I was before reading *Songs from a Lead-Lined Room*, Suzanne Strempek Shea's brave, honest, enthralling, darkly funny story. I couldn't put it down, and I'll never forget its lessons about friendship and good intentions gone awry. I loved many books, but never before have I come away with the conviction that I've just read the one that's been missing from the world."

— Elinor Lipman,
author of *I Can't Complain: (All Too) Personal Essays*

Shelf Life: Romance, Mystery, Drama and Other Page-Turning Adventures from a Year in a Bookstore

"With her sparkling humor, reporter's eye for detail, raconteur's love of anecdote, literary passion, and affection for humankind, Shea fashions a fresh and rousing tribute to the grand and quirky tradition of bringing books and readers together, with insight, finesse, and enthusiasm."   — *Booklist*

"Book enthusiasts who pine for a friendly, like-minded community will love this light, funny memoir."   — *Publishers Weekly*

Sundays in America: A Yearlong Road Trip in Search of Christian Faith

"Do you believe in miracles? You will after you read *Sundays in America*. This book will lift you up. If you've stopped going to church on Sundays, it will lasso your lost faith. If you never left, it will remind you why you gather, why you pray, why you are part of the flock. Suzanne Strempek Shea writes with soul, straight from her heart; this book was just what I needed to read."   — Luanne Rice,
author of *The Lemon Orchard*

"*Sundays in America* is unlike any other book you'll ever read. While born and raised Roman Catholic, Suzanne Shea invites us to accompany her on a year-long pilgrimage to weekly services in non-Catholic Christian churches . . . Like all pilgrimages, this one will enlighten you and change your life too; and I might add, you will not find a pilgrim guide more fun to be with than Suzanne Shea."   — Karol Jackowski,
author of *Ten Fun Things to Do Before You Die*

This Is Paradise: An Irish mother's grief, an African village's plight, and the medical clinic that brought fresh hope to both

"We hear about the triumph of human spirit a lot. But Mags Riordan personifies the idea. In This Is Paradise, Shea takes on her extraordinary journey and shows us the power of a mother's love."
— Ann Hood, author of *Comfort: A Journey Through Grief*

With endless thanks to Elinor Lipman,
whose name was spotted in my palm by a reader back in 1991,
and who ever since has been a life-changing friend and mentor.

Acknowledgments

I'm so grateful that my lifelife includes the names Tommy Shea, Elinor Lipman, Julie Strempek, Maureen Shea, John Talbot, Peter Sarno, Roland Merullo, Elizabeth Searle, Susan Tilton Pecora, Michele Barker, Roberta DuComb, Mary Ellen Lowney, Tanya Barrientos, Holly Angelo, David Bergengren, Janet Edwards and the late Flo Edwards. I'm honored to be able to use on the cover of this book an image of the tile "Heart in Hand" by Western Massachusetts potter Michael Cohen. Special thanks to Mary Lee Wile all other readers who have asked me, "When is that book about the dead mall coming out?" Here it is, with all best wishes.

1

To find the place of all knowledge, first find the Flaming Pit.

Enter the mall at that sign.

Take a left, past the wide oaken doors of the brick-faced restaurant with its faint steaky smell and its three sunken dining rooms, each lower than the previous and staggered around a massive propane-powered open fireplace. Walk past the adjacent Pit Pub door lit by a pair of Medieval-ish mace-and-chain lanterns burning with orangey lightbulbs haywired to mimic flickering wicks. Then past the fluorescent-tube brightness of Fast Foto and its lab-coated cashier flipping through a hairstyle magazine, the nearby developing machine rolling its gears in vain, depositing no sets of four-by-six images onto the tray that has been angled toward the window for the interest of the absent passersby. After that, pass the first dark store window, and the second dark store window, and the third and the fourth consecutive ones, as well as the matching empty ones on the opposite side of the corridor.

Unless you are thirsty for a frosty cup of the namesake specialty, or are craving a dog with the works, don't stop at the Orange Julius stand floating in the middle of the stone-dead mall hallway like an island of '70s kitsch, its only inhabitant a tired and thin and pale middle-aged woman in a peaked paper hat and orange-and-brown polyester pantsuit, who glances up at you with surprise, then, fast, shifts her eyes downward to the frankfurters tumbling on the endlessly rotating grill. Move along the next uninterrupted stretch of darkened windows, three or four of them papered with a stretch of yellowing rainbow-colored letters inviting you to FEEL THE EXCITEMENT! Notice that, without realizing, you have begun to walk to the beat of the instrumental version of "Do You Know the Way to San Jose?" echoing from the scratchy ceiling speakers. Keep going until you come to the waterwheel that doesn't turn the water that's not beneath it. Note the cheery metal street signs that direct you to Main and Spring and Pleasant, which are not really streets but the mall's three armlike halls of shops that split at the Town Common, where the trio converges and where a gazebo, dry cement pond, flagless pole and much square yardage of once-emerald AstroTurf have been arranged to mimic the center of an old New England village.

This bucolic theme has been inserted anywhere space allows. Around the common, where your footsteps take on an increased echo, the mall grows a second story despite there actually being no shops reaching that high. Shutter-edged windows of false building fronts have been painted with silhouettes — a woman reading a book, a girl holding a doll, a baker sniffing a loaf of bread from which wisps of warm aroma float — suggestions of life in a place that now has little. Faded plastic ivy and grayed morning glories cascade from planters beneath each sill. One planting has attracted an oversized fake monarch. Another includes a nest occupied by a hope-bearing stuffed bluebird. High above, weather-beaten skylights allow a hint of the real and genuine sun to cascade.

Cinemas I and II are to your right, down Pleasant, but you should continue straight on Main. Though it might not appear so, the busiest section of the mall is ahead. This is Main Street, after all. The Music Man is located here, just before his brother the Tax Man. The Village Barber across from them. The Village

Stylist next door. And, two blank storefronts down, just after a small stand of plastic maples shading a concrete bench and an ashtray on a stand, and just past Experience Travel and Bunny's Card Nook, look for the one large shop shared by Lens Is More and Affordable Attorney. You have arrived. To find the place of all knowledge, enter the next doorway. The one across from Mom and Sis's Craft Shoppe. Turn in at the sign for Irene, Queen of the Unseen.

Her parlor sits at the end of that alley-shaped space. When the mall opened forty years ago, these four hundred square feet were the proud home of The Tie Rack, and the owner of that business thought it perfect to select a space shaped long and skinny, roughly the proportions of the headache-inducing choices of neckwear that hung from scores of pegs nailed floor to ceiling. To Irene Cervelli, occupant of this space for the eighteen years since the then-starting-to-struggle mall relocated her shop and those of the scattered remaining tenants into a central location, the length of the store creates drama. A prolonging of your journey to reach her, and the answers and insight you seek. From the lip of the mall corridor, you must walk a good sixteen paces, each one bringing you closer to the curtained half-circle window cut into a big black far wall. There is nothing between you and that window but the long stretch of gray industrial carpet beneath your sneakers, and, finally, the purple upholstered high-backed chair on which you will sit to ring the bell that alerts Irene to your presence — though someone with her gift surely already knows you are there.

She indeed had to know you would be there well before you were walking past the dried-up waterwheel, before you pushed open the door at the Pit. Before you parked your car, before you steered it off Berkshire Road and took your pick of the thousands of vacant parking spaces. Before you even left your garage. Before you had your decaf and second Winston.

Before you opened your eyes and focused on the blank white wall across from your bed, then at the unpalatable lump stirring next to you. Before you were reminded yet again that you were not where you wanted to be in your life and you wondered for the millionth time just where you were supposed to be. The palm reader certainly knew all this about you. Knew everything. Because isn't that what these people do?

You finish the walk to the far end of the space, and you pull the cord marked "RING BELL." After a few silent seconds, the curtain parts. Not in the middle, like on a stage, but only from the right. A hand secures it to an unseen hook, and then most of the rest of this Irene woman appears as she rolls her chair to the center of the half-circle cutout. She is not what you had anticipated — though what would you know about such things, as this is your first time visiting a palm reader. What you know is from psychic people portrayed in movies and books, and from your cousin who long ago had her fortune told at a harvest fair up in Buckland. That palm reader, who told your cousin she would bear two children — one, a boy who would bring happiness, the other a girl who would carry misery (and because of that, after your cousin's first son, your cousin sent her husband for a vasectomy) — that palm reader wore a plain silver ring on a big toe that bore a tuft of hair and curled like a monkey's digit. You cannot see this Irene's toes. So you aren't able to check if this is a shared palm-reader characteristic. You can see only everything from the waist up. That much of her looks like anyone else, like any other rather well-kept fiftyish white woman. A face that if you had to select it from a chart would be called oval. Dark eyes set low, resulting in a big, wide forehead, a span of flat flesh that, due to its acreage, draws your eyes right to it before anything else. But, considering her work, maybe that is where all the thought-cooking and future-figuring happens. Her hair is done in a rather nice short, choppy style not unlike that of the news anchor who came to speak at your church's ladies' club and mentioned how she gets that nice short, choppy style created for free at a fancy shop in Longmeadow that, in return, gets its name run at the end of the news program. But the anchor's hair was blonde, and this woman in front of you, her hair is black. And she is wearing a fuzzy green sweater with a minimum of jewelry. No rings, no earrings, no watch, only a thin golden chain looped around her neck and disappearing behind the green knit so you won't know what, if anything, it bears, unless you ask, and you feel you would have to be acquainted with her at least a tiny bit in order to do that.

All in all, this palm-reader woman, this Irene, looks no more or no less like somebody regular, somebody normal, somebody everyday who might rush from work and take the seat next to you at your nephew's youth wind-ensemble concert and start quickly flipping through the program to find the point to which the night already has progressed. Certainly she does not look like anybody in a film, which is what this feels like to you — the actual coming here, the doing something like this, the thinking the scary things you are thinking about your life and your yet-unknown future — it is all something that happens to actresses portraying troubled housewives on the Women's Entertainment Channel, something else you regularly tune to. This is not something that happens to the likes of you. Even simply the sitting down and facing this Irene woman and having her face you and extend her hand, palm up, and ask, "Ten dollars, please," which you quickly find in the clear plastic purse in which you keep your coupons and grocery money, and you place the two five-dollar bills in her hand, and she nods and smiles her thanks and tucks them into an unseen place to the right of the half-circle cutout, then reaches out again, one hand, then the other, and asks you to do the same. You hold yours out, and you see they are shaking.

Next door, the Affordable Attorney is sharpening her pencils with a whining electric gizmo her mother gave her for Christmas. Next door to her, the Village Barber blows a puff of air into the blades of his rusting beard trimmer, and, next door to him, the Music Man strums a plaintive G diminished and closes his eyes. Outside, the maintenance man is sidestepping along the walkway of the thirty-foot-tall Orchard Mall sign. Sure, two inches of snow fell the night before, and another two or three are being forecast to begin around the supper hour. But, on this same day, a new season has started. And, thanks to his work, there it is, announced to the world in three-foot-tall letters:

S

P

R

I

N

G

But you and your focus are here. Inside the mall, at the far end of store space sixty-three, where this Irene woman is taking both of your hands into the surprising warmth and comfort of her own.

The feeling is instantly good and calming, and that alone is worth the money you have given over. Her accent, American, regular local Western Massachusetts, is nothing exceptional as she begins the reading by saying softly and calmly, "Make a wish." There is a pause. Her eyes roam the counter, looking for who knows what. "Make a wish," she repeats. In a few beats she adds, "But not for money." You consider the exception she has posed. Then you do as she asks. You make a wish. Silently.

You know to do that much. Like the ones made over birthday candles, or before the toss of a coin, or on the occasion of a necessary lie, you keep this wish quiet. Afraid almost to tell it to yourself.

Regret pours over you cold and quick, like one of those buckets of ice or whatever it is they dump on coaches at the end of big football games. The regret of coming here, of finally biting the exotic lure of the tiny ad you've spotted in the *Pennysaver* every Thursday for years: "Your Life Is in Your Hands. Visit Palm Reader and Teller of Fortunes Irene, Queen of the Unseen. At Orchard Mall: 'Main Street Recreated.'" The paragraph and its all-important all-capitals float beneath a drawing of one hand cradling another and lines of light beaming from both. The lines had to be the knowledge held in there, knowledge that needed somebody like this woman Irene to translate it, like it was in another language and you could see the words but had no clue as to how to read them. Somebody like this woman Irene, she understood. And there you are, because you have your questions and finally, finally, you want some answers. Even if you haven't the strength to ask.

The only question so far is from this woman Irene. "Would you open your left hand?" You do. "This," she continues, "is the hand of inheritance. What you arrived here on earth carrying." She speaks slowly and with some hesitation about it, showing the talents, the inclinations, the powers that were yours at birth. Your right hand, she says a bit more loudly after clearing her throat, "This one tells me what you will do. Or what you already have done with those things." And with just these bits of information, for the first time in your life, you look down at your palms with real interest.

On the left one, near the top of your wrist, is an ink smudge. A mottled childhood stove-touching scar marks the edge of the thumb. They are all that stands out for you. They, and the fact that your palm is beginning to look old. Like this woman Irene's, hers, like yours, having opened and closed a zillion times. But on this day, this morning, with your hand in her hand, it becomes something quite different. The San Jose song is over, and something else has started up. Not music this time, not any other sound, but something more like an energy that fills your ears and the space around you, and you wonder, can this woman Irene hear it, too, as she peers closely into your skin and her eyes widen. As she spots something other than the ink and the scar and the faint crossroadish crease between your second and third fingers, just above the well where you could hold your turnpike toll money or catch rain at the start of a long-awaited shower.

"There is hope." This woman Irene whispers almost like the idea is a shock, and with her eyeballs now an inch from your hand, and you can feel the hot bursts of the T and P. She continues quickly but evenly, "Margaret, Margaret, you must go to her now." And even though it is what you really had wished you'd be told by this Irene woman — by somebody, because it really is much easier to do what you are told than to go to all the effort of having to make the decision yourself — you are startled. Along the edge of your shirt collar, your hair actually stands like they say it does in these cases, and you are yanking your hands away, and you are breathless and shoving back the purple upholstered chair and covering the sixteen paces to the corridor without knowing you've walked one step. Because you can't fathom what just happened. What she just told you. What she knew. How true it is.

And neither can she, the woman who said the words, who heard that new sound, too, and knows something has happened for the first time.

Spring has sprung the morning this woman Irene starts getting it right. And changing everything.

2

Her finger in a socket, and her toes set afire, and a comet
shooting down her spine, and the force of Niagara pouring
over the all of her, and her breath gone as if she'd been tackled
by the ankles and then had her head placed next to a ringing
gong of the elephantine size used to open the Olympics when
they are held in a country where they regularly use such things.
For Irene, Queen of the Unseen, all this at once is what the
realization of the gift of prophecy is like.

It is as simple and astounding as this: she sees — actually
sees — that other woman's dilemma. And that other woman's
destiny. And knows, as strongly as she knows anything, what
should happen next. She can't doubt it. Mistake it for anything
else. The San Jose song is over, and something else has started
up, not music, not noise, something more like an energy that
fills her ears and the space around her, and she wonders if the
woman whose hand is in hers has heard it also as this woman
Irene peers closely and sees something beyond the ink mark
and the scar and the faint crossroadish crease between second
and third fingers. As if the feature at Cinemas I and III suddenly is playing in a square in the center of that palm, this woman
Irene can see the colors of her client's frustration and hopeless-
ness, the shape of the Barbie's Dreamhouse dreams her husband has flattened with his fists from nearly the first of their
eleven and a half years together, the robin's egg color of the
old-fashioned wheel-less Samsonite case that for seven weeks

now the woman has kept packed and stowed beneath a beach blanket in her trunk. This woman Irene sees the skyscraper enormity of this other woman's fear of both staying in her marriage and leaving. And the height of the stack of cash she'd withdrawn from the bank two days earlier. But this woman Irene does not want any of that cash. What she wants is the woman to go to the place that is playing in her palm, to the green-sided house with the patio slider that is being pushed aside by yet another woman, one who has her sister's off-center chin and is beckoning her to this house of safety and change far away. Margaret is the sister's name. Margaret. With her eyes an inch from the woman's palm, this woman Irene says what she knows, "Margaret, Margaret, you must go to her now."

Then that woman who's come to her window does that sudden running off, and this woman Irene can do little more than sit and stare down the alley of her shop space and try to focus on something stationary as she matches to the beat of the Muzaked "Muskrat Love" her fortunately recovered ability to breathe.

Her experience and her reaction might be different had she always felt this day would come. Had she slid from the womb of a mother whose mother and whose mother's mother owned such abilities, today would be cause for celebration: the power she'd been told of as a child finally arriving — late, for sure, but better late than never. However, this woman Irene had come into this world via a mother whose foresight was limited to little more than knowing there would be someone standing on the porch when the doorbell rang. This woman Irene could predict rain, but only because she'd just hung her wash. The sudden closing of a business because she'd just purchased a gift certificate there. A friend's child suddenly getting a newfound interest because this woman Irene had spent the weekend combing stores for the accessories for the one that had been entrancing him for the past year. But the path a stranger needed to take to remove herself from a dangerous man and a loveless union? No way.

That's because this woman is no Queen of the Unseen. This woman is not even an Irene. This woman billed as this woman Irene is actually this woman Rosie, who, up to the second her skin touched that of the first client of the day, was hearing in her head a line she might catch when home for a sick day and overdosing on soaps: "Today, the part of Irene, Queen of the Unseen, is being played by Irene's friend, Rosie Pilch."

Rosie has all the time in the world to play — so would you if six and a half weeks ago you were among seventeen clerks at First Bank's main branch suddenly handed an empty Staples carton, asked to clean out your desk, and escorted to the parking lot by a Human Resources staffer who nodded at your Obama bumper sticker and noted with a jab in his voice how there had been no layoffs at First Bank during the three Bush administrations.

Home is where Rosie Pilch has kept herself for six and a half weeks, waking as she had for the past twenty-seven years, opening her eyes at 6:15 to the increasingly louder chirps of Northeastern birdsong coming from the clock she'd been awarded for upgrading her annual Nature Conservancy donation from twenty-five to forty-five dollars, rolling onto the floor to execute a slow trio of spine-lubricating yoga poses, locating toilet and shower and sink and hair dryer and curling iron and closet, dressing in the company-required panty hose and her own choices of low heels and monochromatic natural-fiber suit before sitting down to a pair of buttermilk Eggos and real maple syrup and black tea and multiple vitamin-bearing minerals beneficial to those in the peri-menopausal stage, then giving a fast rinse to plate and cup and silver, and taking a sponge to the surface of the kitchen table, where she would sit for the rest of the morning.

"Oh, you know, a while," she's told people who've asked how long she'd been at First Bank. Twenty-seven years seems too large a numeral to voice, something that might choke her if she tried. OK, her father had made tires for thirty-nine years. Thirty-nine. Twenty-seven standing at a bank window wasn't thirty-nine breathing lampblack at Uniroyal, but her father had been allowed to choose when he ended his employment, retiring with a fun party at Saint Stan's and driving off with Rosie's mother in a midsize RV inside of which hung a map noting each of the country's national parks, each of them being her parents' destinations over the decades on the roads ahead. Rosie's final day at work was decided by someone else: an anonymous group of executives over in Boston who haphazardly took a chain saw to most departments at First Bank's main Western Massachusetts branch, severing them in what the letter distributed to Rosie and her seventeen laid-off co-workers said was a necessary cost-cutting measure for these difficult times. "We sincerely wish you all the best and thank you for your X years of faithful service." There actually was an X — they hadn't even bothered to personalize.

For those twenty-seven years, Rosie had been a teller. She accepted deposits, doled out withdrawals, registered payments, handed out a particular year's Christmas Club membership gift of spoon rest or trivet, all with a genuine smile and desire to make someone's day better via the interaction. Whether the bottom line was two digits or seven, each customer received a warm greeting and a compliment on hairdo, attire, accessories or, failing those being anything about which she could find something positive to say, the uniqueness of a signature ("Hey, I love how you make your Q's!"). Her customers forfeited their places in line just to have the chance to stand at Rosie's window, which always offered a dish of diabetic-friendly hard candy, and in warmer weather was decorated with real flowers from her garden, held in seasonally themed vases she made at Tuesday night clay class. Her co-workers bowed to her when it came to the deft and creative organization of holiday parties, showers, birthday celebrations, retirements, and the exact words to write on the card accompanying a fruit basket sent to someone in a difficult situation for which there was no ready-made verse. Like being diagnosed with something awful. Or like being laid off. Her drawer always balanced, her bosses always praised. Rosie arrived home each weeknight and the occasional Saturday afternoon with aching feet and stiff legs, but also a definite pride in how she'd added to the weather of the world that day. Not saving it or anything, but doing enough to maybe make a bright difference with the job she'd landed the day after accepting her associate's degree in business from Springfield Technical Community College in 1983. A lifetime ago.

Twenty-seven years later, saddened and shell-shocked, Rosie has sat at her kitchen table these six and a half weeks of mornings, ready to go but having nowhere to be, waiting for the paperman to tuck this morning's edition through her mail slot, something he does not do for any other customer, but then no other customer on his route looked in the town's street directory a decade ago just to find out his birthday, every July 1 since marked by her with a handful of the latest type of scratch tickets. And when the newspaper does arrive, Rosie knows that it is 7:00 a.m., and that forty-five minutes of her now-empty day have passed. And that the great hope of a fresh classified ad section has arrived.

Sure, she can check that online, but there is something soothing about the act of opening the newspaper — maybe it is the paper itself. After all those years filling out slips, inserting them into machines, handing them to customers, the paper under her fingertips feels familiar, as does the pen in her right hand, ready to circle anything of possibility, an act that cannot be accomplished on her computer screen. This morning, as she has for the last six and a half weeks, Rosie opened the door to the front porch enclosed with weathertight windows installed just last summer courtesy of a First Bank savings plan. On the floor below the front storm door mail slot, the folded *Daily News* slept in its sleeve of orange plastic that oddly colored the front-page photo of crocuses popping from the snow. An omen that things would blossom soon? Maybe so. Because off to the left of the plastic bag, next to the hefty hand-built umbrella stand she made over several Tuesday nights the year before, lay something else that had been dropped through the mail slot, this one so many days ago, and accidentally kicked aside when Rosie was knocking snow off her boots one night after returning from the grocery store. Now that it had been spotted, the plain white envelope surprised Rosie with her name on the front in blue felt-pen ink that had been run due to the snow. The *i* in Rosie was dotted by a star, as it was at the start of the letter folded inside, the one wrapped around the set of two silver keys clipped onto an Orchard Mall lanyard.

> *Rosie:*
>
> *Sit down. I am off to Toronto — to become Mrs. Sticks Belanger! Eloping! Me! Who would have predicted that? (HA!)*
>
> *Listen — We're off to Canada and won't be back anytime soon so . . . do me a favor? I have nine months left on my lease before the mall closes for good. I know it's not going to make you a million, but why don't you take over*

for me? You have the time, you could handle it no problem. Really. You know it takes no skill, just talk to them — that's all they really want. Say something nice and hopeful and send them on their way. I know you'll do great. Thanks a million! I'll be in touch!

Love ya,
Irene

There on the enclosed porch, Rosie looked at the two keys resting in her palm. Then she looked at the palm itself. It was still soft and pleasant smelling from the guarana-berry lotion of the morning's post-shower routine. She thought of the jobs for which she'd applied and was perfectly qualified. Teller at a First Bank competitor. Office assistant at an armored-car company. Receptionist at a lending firm. She'd had three interviews in six and a half weeks, but had been offered little hope, being either overqualified, underqualified or simply one of many adrift in the same boat. One interviewer confided that the hire would be in-house, posting was just a legal formality. Another concluded his sheet of questions with the uplifting fact that he himself would be laid off in a matter of days.

For the past six Sundays, Rosie had phoned a toll-free number for the Massachusetts Division of Employment and Training, entered her Social Security number and PIN, and poked keys to answer a brief string of questions about her employment search and availability in order to receive that week's unemployment check. She didn't even have to leave the house. And here, on her porch, in her hand, was a reason to step out that door. And the promise of money. Who knew how much, but it was still money, extra cash for the next nine months. Lots of things could happen in nine months — the very least of which being this year would finally end. In the meantime, she at least would have somewhere to go, something to do, and pocket change. All thanks to Irene, who for five years had carpooled with Rosie to clay class, and then afterwards to the Ground Round for a couple of those specialty drinks mixed up to taste like some type of ice cream, and who for four years had been dating Jean "Sticks" Belanger, a former American Hockey League center of some renown, now a scout of some influence, who one day four years ago on a scouting trip to Springfield had wandered into foundering nearby Orchard Mall and through the doorway of Irene, Queen of the Unseen.

Irene read his palm that one time and instantly became a hockey fan. Scoured the sports pages for any mention of that Belanger guy. Studied Dummies' and Idiots' guides to the sport so she'd know a face-off from an offside. Went online to find his photo, then to find a map of Canada so she could study precisely where he'd come from. Found the little town of Locksley up there in the horizontal spread of Ontario, looked at the names around it and imagined them being second nature to Sticks. Had he skated Mud Lake, traveled to Cobden, rambled all the wilderness in the wide white spaces between the scattering of towns? Irene wrapped herself in knowing him without knowing him.

Over that season, Sticks reappeared at the half-circle cutout half a dozen times for half a dozen very long readings before the afternoon he said "Wanna get outa here?" Only the way he said it was "Oooota here." This man had an accent. How much better could it get? They celebrated their new life as Mr. and Mrs. Sticks Belanger while Rosie Pilch marked hers as Irene, Queen of the Unseen.

Rosie had been to Orchard Mall before, of course. It had opened back when she was in high school, and was an enormous big deal at the time. She'd taken a trip there with her parents the first week, mainly because all the ads kept repeating that free things were being offered on each one of the days of the first week, and Rosie's parents, like most people, were interested in free things. They came home with their share, all chintzy, utilitarian stuff of the type that a grown-up Rosie one day would hand to her customers: an Orchard Mall pot holder and an Orchard Mall notepad and an Orchard Mall sewing kit and an Orchard Mall pill holder and an Orchard Mall key chain and an Orchard Mall coupon file and an Orchard Mall rain bonnet and an Orchard Mall car emergency kit that amounted to a metallic space blanket to warm you if your car got stuck out in a blizzard, and a cardboard that unfolded to the size of your back window, where you were supposed to place it in an emergency so everybody could read its big message of

HELP
ORCHARD MALL

as if the mall in those days needed assistance. Certainly, the young Rosie had thought Orchard Mall was very cool, what an idea, all those stores in one place, with a roof over them, yet. Her parents said how convenient, no time wasted driving from the cobbler to the hairdresser to the dress shop to the drugstore, park once and get all your errands done. To get to Orchard Mall, the family drove down Main Street and all those places so inconveniently located in a variety of buildings standing in the open air. The Pilch family's avocado Plymouth Fury III rolled past the little town common that marked the official entrance to downtown Indian Orchard, and then along a street lined with businesses that had been the community's lifeblood: pharmacy, bank, greengrocer, butcher, baker, clothing store, cobbler, shoe store, dime store, stationer, pet store, barber, dentist, doctor, most of the people and services and stores being duplicated at Orchard Mall, where the car edged into a line of hundreds of others occupied by people who'd also driven down Main Street shaking their heads, asking who'll go here anymore, saying what a great idea a mall is, somebody should've thought of it ages ago.

Since Rosie first met Irene when paired at clay class for the end-of-night wiping down of the worktables, she would stop in to see her whenever she had an appointment at Lens is More or needed to stock up on cards at Bunny's. Raised Catholic, Rosie had been told by the nuns who educated her that anyone who professed to know the future or anything like that was doing the work of the devil. That, of course, made Rosie and her classmates all the more eager to peek beneath the canvas walls of the tents set up on a town ball field by a traveling carnival the year she was in fifth grade. Eddie Libera said he saw only a table with a candle before he was pulled back by his ankles by the very large hands of a very tall man on break from the tent bearing a sign for the Genuine Freak Show. The very tall man shoved Eddie away and shouted something foreign and sharp at Rosie and her friends, who were hiding behind the cotton candy man's nearby truck, and they ran for their banana-seat bikes and never looked back. Rosie's next contact with anyone who professed to know anything other than the here and now was forty years later. On those visits to Orchard Mall and Irene's spaces, she'd sat in the purple chair and chatted through the half-circle cutout window just to catch up, not really caring to avail herself of any particular ability Irene advertised. Even so, in the course of their talking, Irene often would take Rosie's hands in hers. She'd repeat the info about the left holding the abilities and propensities you arrive with, the right being what you go on to do. And islands. Always, she'd speak of the islands she saw in there. Meaning change that can be seen as unwelcome but that can lead to better things. "Islands like Bermuda?" Rosie had asked the first time, because when she was a kid, her neighbor Frances had come back from there with a small bottle of its pink sand, and Rosie since had a dream to go there and see a whole beach of it, but Irene answered, "Nope, go down the hall if you want a travel agent. These islands on your palm are disruptions. But good ones. If that makes sense." And Rosie would wonder how that could be so. She'd been disrupted along the way, if you wanted to call it that, once, and hadn't enjoyed it. Though her life had fallen back onto an even track over the decade since the night Dale took her out for lobster and announced that after three and a half years and having given Rosie a diamond via earring, bracelet and necklace, everything short of diamond belly-button ring and actual diamond ring, he wasn't sure about his feelings for her, and didn't she want someone who was totally sure about something huge like that? Rosie had sat there in her plastic bib, that metal claw-cracking thing in her right hand, yet-to-be-cracked claw in her left, and had watched as Dale stood and said he was very sorry, and then backed up and bumped into a neighboring lobster diner's chair before he turned and left.

Hadn't she wanted someone totally sure about his feelings for her? Most days of the years that followed, she was too busy to ponder that, going about her daily obligations and sailing along on new relationships that over the ten years had her docking for varying amounts of time in the ports of the insurance agent and the flooring salesman and the quesadilla place line cook and the volunteer at the equine-rescue farm. And now the toy-company bookkeeper who would be hers for keeps. "Those dents there," Irene regularly informed her through the half-circle cutout as she held Rosie's hand sideways, "two big relationships. Two. I'm certain." The first, Rosie knew, meant Dale. The second, and final, Rosie knew, stood

19

for Scot.

Scot, the first thing on her list.

Included in the First Bank severance package were six sessions of free private counseling to assist former employees in their transition to whatever it was they were transitioning to. Rosie's therapist, a chipper young man who even in the winter wore those pants that can be unzipped around the knee to instantly become shorts, Woody-Woodpeckered, "How does that make you feel?" to each of the realities she repeated on her first visit: "I'm unemployed. I worked there twenty-seven years. Then I was gone, just like that. I won't see my customers anymore. I might not see my co-workers anymore. I won't be helping anyone. Oh, and I won't have an income." The therapist suggested that she use another kind of litany to express her reality. One that stressed the positives in her life. He handed her a sheet of paper on which "I am OK because" was typed at the start of each line in a stack of ten. Her homework was to complete each of the "becauses." And to read from that list every time anxiety hit, which was often, beginning with those mornings at the table.

She took the sheet of paper home and sat again at the kitchen table. Though that kitchen table was in a home she owned, soon would have a plate of food set on it, food that would be fed to a fine and healthy body, a body that wasn't living in a house surrounded by war or famine or pestilence, Rosie completed each and every one of the ten lines only with "he loves me." And every morning, once she was washed and fed and dressed and sitting there at the kitchen table more aware than ever that nothing was happening in her life, she took the paper from its place between the salt and pepper shakers and, though she knew it all by heart, unfolded her litany: "I am OK because he loves me. I am OK because he loves me. I am OK because he loves me."

And, just like that, she was. OK.

Scot with one *t* had been introduced to her by her aunt, of all matchmakers, shortly after, as a response to the president's request that more Americans become volunteers, he began offering free computer-literacy classes to any senior citizen willing to come to the Senior Center on Saturday mornings to look over his shoulder as he navigated his iBook G4.

When Rosie's aunt first mentioned Scot and kept saying how kind he was, Rosie eventually asked what he looked like, and her aunt answered, "He's so kind." But Rosie went to the class anyway, on the premise of having to transport her aunt home. Scot was indeed kind. Rosie watched him guide that woman Sophie from up her street through the all-important shutting down of the computer, then begin the round of applause Sophie from up the street deserved for successful completion of the task. He indeed seemed kind and, to answer Rosie's question, was around six feet of skinny, wore outdated bleached black-denim jeans, those black karate shoes you can get in health-food stores for about five dollars, a vintage work shirt with breast-pocket stitches that announced Hank of Central Ford, a Saint Anthony's crown of yellow hair kept long enough to ponytail, and on his thin, pinkish, forty-six-year-old face two pairs of glasses he switched constantly, depending on how far away or how closely he needed to look. He put on the silver distance pair when he noticed the fuzzy, new, pre-retirement-age female shape that turned out to be Rosie there in the corner joining the clapping for Sophie from up her street, and he called to Rosie a genuine "Welcome!" which was startling because that was how she right then felt.

Two weeks later, on the first day of spring, they took a Saturday drive to the Cape, where they hung an impulsive right at the sign for First Encounter Beach. They walked on the hard-packed sand the low tide had paved for them and admired the unfurling waves, and Scot told her how he used to think that during the winter they froze in big curled wave shapes like if you'd photographed them, and like it was her last moment on earth, Rosie grabbed him for a kiss, and neither regretted the action. At a coffee shop down the road from the parking lot, they bought bowls of chowder and ate at a nearby picnic table monitored by a steroidishly large seagull standing at the other end, awaiting the oyster-cracker handouts they felt blackmailed to give. They drove the two hours home listening to a spring-training Red Sox-Yankees game that the spring-training Red Sox did not win. Then they went to the second-floor apartment Scot rented from the secretary at the Senior Center, and Scot inquired if Rosie were warm or cold — he could adjust the thermostat — then motioned, due to mentioning the word already, that the thermostat on his waterbed had been giving him trouble. "Oh," said Rosie, who knew nothing about electrical things but still said, "Do you want me to take a look at it?" and he said he did even though he suspected she would be no help. And there on the fish-print sheets that were Scot's attempt at a decorating joke, they floated for the rest of the afternoon and were in no rush to look for land.

Scot worked at the nearby headquarters of toy manufactur-er Milton Bradley and regularly proposed new game ideas to the company, even though his job there was in bookkeeping. The first game of his that Rosie was asked to test-play, the evening of that day at the Cape and on the fish sheets, consisted of a handful of cards on which Scot had painstakingly drawn mem-bers of an extensive imagined animal world. The winner of the first hand of what amounted to the card game "Go Fish" got to select the rules for the next round, and the winner of that one got to select the next set of rules. The whole thing was rather mindless, not to mention pointless, and Scot had given it the unfortunate name "Play a Round." But Rosie stayed there past the end of Letterman, complimenting Scot on his imagination and drive.

"I took this job for a reason," he explained on that night three years back. "I have my life all mapped out. Every day and every year. It is going to be wonderful!" Scot spoke like that, complete with exclamation-marked exclamations about his future. He might as well have been on a pulpit. His enthusiasm was so heartfelt and contagious Rosie wanted to shoot to her feet and cheer him on, surprising herself by hoping his map would call for the services of a navigator. In her life, things always just happened. Sure, she'd always been neat, organized, but she'd never sat down and actually said, "First I'm going to do this, then this, then this." Scot had thought to, and she found that enviable and (Dare she think it?) attractive in a retro sort of way after the round of fun but navigationless men she'd dated since Dale. Here was somebody who would plot the future, who would take his beloved to the top of some vantage point and motion toward the valley and announce, "Here's where we're going to live and raise our family and make our future." Someone who would take care of whoever was in his life.

Losing her job at First Bank had been a big horsefly in the enjoyable ointment that had been planning their engagement. Because with Scot, you didn't just get engaged, you planned it out. The past two late Novembers, on Milton Bradley Employee Travel Club bus trips to New York for the Radio City Music Hall Christmas Show, Scot and Rosie had used their free hours to visit Manhattan's Diamond District, where Rosie, at Scot's suggestion she initially thought was a joke, tried on eternity bands served up to her on long velvet trays like rock-candy desserts. They actually were to purchase a ring on this coming November's trip, and were planning to unveil it dramatically to local relatives at Christmas, then to travel to his parents' in New Jersey for New Year's, and upon return move all his great amounts of stuff — computer guts, mock-ups of games, books, CDs, map-sized charts of his possible life paths that covered many of his walls — from his apartment and into her little brick cottage at the edge of the municipal golf course. The Jack-and-Jill would be held in February, the ladies' shower in March, the stag in April, and they would be wed in the blooming, promising, picturesque month of May. It was all planned out. Including the payment plan for parties, reception, honeymoon. Then came the layoff. Then the sitting there at the kitchen table, Rosie reminding herself that she was OK, because Scot loved her.

Another suggestion the therapist in the zip-off pant legs made was that once Rosie was finished reading her list, she get out of the house as often as possible. It was not good for her to stay home, he said, and on session two had made a speech about the effect of what's around us. Even colors on a wall. He asked, hadn't she ever seen that *60 Minutes* piece on the inmate-calming Dunkin-Donuts-pink paint used in the jail? Hadn't she ever heard about all the depression and alcoholism in parts of the world that are so isolated or dark much of the year?

"Our surroundings dictate our moods more than you can imagine," he explained as she considered for the first time the pinkish hue of his office walls. "You might enjoy your home under normal circumstances, but right now it is reminding you that you have nowhere to go."

Rosie heard his words the morning she got the note from Irene and decided to become her successor, crouching in the mall hallway that first day of spring to fit one of the silver keys into the garage-door-style gate that kept Irene's space safe during the off hours. The lock didn't cooperate, and Rosie was all but ready to flee. What was she doing here? Then, click. The gate edged up a few inches. Invited her to push it up and out of sight. Which Rosie did, feeling a finality as it snapped into place overhead.

The space was dark, but she wasn't alone — a few tenants down the hall were doing the same gate-raising and preparing for the day. She'd introduce herself later. For now there was courage to sweep up as she walked to the far wall, used the second key to unlock the door to the left of the half-circle cutout window and brushed her arm along the wall in search of a light switch. Fluorescence flashed, then stayed on, revealing Irene's backstage, no more than eight by sixteen feet, neat and spare: the padded wheeled office chair in which she sat on her side of the window. The closed curtains to that window. The little travel pack of Kleenex offered to customers who, and this is not exaggerating, sometimes began to weep when Irene told one of her stories of their glowing potential, or, more often, when she simply looked into a palm and gave her trademark line: "There is hope."

Tacked to the right of the cutout is a newspaper clipping reporting a Gallup Poll that had found fifty percent of Americans believing in psychic powers. Most of those who'd participated in the survey actually had been through college, where they'd probably played at some point with Ouija boards you'd find on the same toy-store shelves as innocuous time-passers Candy Land and Scrabble. Rosie has seen this before, because Rosie is the one who gave the clipping to Irene. Clipping pieces from the newspaper is one of Rosie's hobbies. She reads for information and entertainment, but also with an eye for which stories might suit a certain friend or family member. Going online and forwarding links just doesn't have the same thrill. And the act of actually writing on a note card — even something as short as "Right up your alley!" — to accompany the story, then filling and sealing an envelope, using one of the billion address labels she received as solicitations from charities, and selecting a stamp perfect for the recipient or story theme (LOVE her usual choice) long has been a regular part of her day. Rosie had mailed the Gallup Poll story to Irene a good two years ago — this she knows because she always jots publication and date at the very top of each clipping — and now it hangs to the right of the cutout window. Irene had kept the information to herself, did not stick it to the other side of the wall for all to see, she'd told Rosie, because once people were in her space, they were there for a reading and did not need to be sold. But Irene liked the reminder that what she was doing was A-OK with more than half of her fellow Americans. That they didn't know she hadn't a clue about what their tomorrows would bring wasn't addressed in the poll. But below the story sits Irene's help in that department: a sheaf of newspaper horoscopes stacked in a box that once held a fresh supply of checks from First Bank. If stuck for something positive to tell a client, Irene glanced there:

"A surprising source will provide assistance and boost confidence."

"Complete the task you've started and rewards will follow."

"You've been afraid to make that move, but the time is right!"

A space heater to the left of the window sits at foot-level, near a trash can empty of debris. The back-door emergency exit bears a sign on its handle that warns that a mall-wide alarm will sound and the local fire department will be contacted were it opened. Irene had furnished the far end of her space with floor lamp and small upholstered chair for relaxing during idle times or lunch. An end table holds a worn copy of *Palmistry for Beginners*. Rosie picks it up and flips to its diagram of the world of the palm, where fingers aren't simply thumb and pointer and offensive middle. They are proud gods named Jupiter, Saturn, Apollo, Mercury. Their marks are referred to as whorls, loops, peacock's eyes, hooks, branches, crescents, tridents, stars, islands. They top hands bearing shapes labeled spatulate, square, conic, philosophic, mixed, even psychic. Skin quality, nails, finger angle, favored gestures, all these are supposed to be taken into account in a reading — at least according to the book, which follows the palm diagram with this warning: "Though astoundingly accurate prophecies have been delivered by palm readers over the eons, one should bear in mind that palmistry is first and foremost an enjoyable practice that simply can aid our attempts to fathom life."

Rosie exhales but hasn't realized she's been holding her breath. On this day, doing something enjoyable, helping with fathoming, sounded good. She shuts the door. Places her handbag on the floor. Removes her coat, slips the puffy blue silk scarf from around her neck and ties it around her head, gypsy-style, as Irene never had, but that doesn't mean Rosie can't. Then she tugs it off. Folds it and pushes it for safekeeping into one of the arms of her coat. Slings the coat over the chair. Swaps the glare of the fluorescents for the dimmer switch on a table lamp to the left of the half-circle cutout. Takes a seat in the wheeled office chair. Puts her elbows on the counter and folds her hands. Smooths her hair and then folds her hands again. Stares at the closed curtain and waits for the bell to sound.

She taps her foot to release nerves, but doesn't know what to do to stop feeling plain silly — what if someone she knows came by right now, saw her here (if they had the ability to see through the curtain), saw her doing this, pretending to know what the future might hold. Rosie doesn't know you, but when she hears your approach as the first person to enter the space on this first day, she is ready to run. But you're not going to know this because she's not going to allow that. Rosie has stage experience — or altar experience, if you will. Every December for four years, her entire high school life, Rosie played the Blessed Virgin Mary in her church's Christmas pageant. With a presence the church bulletin raved could be found only on Broadway, she mastered the expressions for which she had no true experience, including the incomparable surprise you might register when you are doing your virginly laundry one regular morning and an angel appears — poof, like the turning on of a bedroom ceiling light at 4:00 a.m. — to say you have been chosen to become the Mother of God. She'd acted then and she's acting now. As she hadn't regarding being the Mother of God, she doesn't know a thing about what she's doing here, either.

But you don't know any of this. You just know what she tells you once you pay ten dollars and extend your hand and she begins to stare into it. You just know what she tells you: that you must go to Margaret, which is what you have wanted someone to tell you for years now.

As you make the final step of the sixteen to the exit of the palm reader's space, you turn back for a second to make sure you didn't invent her. That you didn't imagine the right-on advice she gave you so matter-of-factly in answer to your unspoken wish. But she's still there, and even though she's silent, you can hear her message as if she's next to your ear.

You head off to do what she urged, rushing past the optician with the outdated frame selection, past that discount card place. A guy in the music shop quickens his strumming as you, the only thing moving in the corridor, rush by. You don't stop to toss a penny into the dry waterwheel pond. Your wish already has come true. You have received the answer you sought. To leave the lump in the bed and move on to the life you deserve. Ahead, the lights of the Flaming Pit mark the doors you took to enter the mall. You fly to them, and through.

3

The actual Irene, Queen of the Unseen, has no mysterious inborn gift. The spark for this career of forecasting was a regular everyday stranger-girl on a train, a girl walking from seat to seat one light-starved December Thursday afternoon forty-five years ago, when Irene was a newly hired office worker in Boston recently sprung from a two-year secretarial college.

She was reading the evening paper's Ann Landers column, in which a woman was asking if it was just she or would Ann, as well, think it strange that her new husband kept his late wife's ashes urn on the toilet tank. Irene liked to guess Ann's answers, which usually were that the writer should wake up and smell the coffee or seek counseling, sometimes both. She looked away from the page to decide the answer, and that was when she noticed the girl asking if she could take people's pulses. This girl was explaining that she was a nursing student, that the pulses were her homework. How by the end of the weekend she had to fill two entire sheets of looseleaf — front and back — with data collected from that many wrists. She repeated this explanation to each rider in the car. Most complied politely, extending their arms, maybe pulling up their sleeves a bit or, if they didn't, allowing the girl to gently do that for them. She crouched in the aisle as she found the correct spot on the wrists, fixed her fingers there, and stared at her Timex's second hand as she did her counting, beats against seconds. In this manner, she took the pulses of countless old ladies, businessmen, children. And, most interesting to Irene, this girl took the pulses of the six not-bad-looking college boys seated in three consecutive rows.

"You're fine," the future lifesaver told the first boy when she concluded her counting and handed his wrist back.

"You're more than fine," she assured his seatmate in what clearly was more than a medical assessment.

This appealed to Irene. Not the future in medicine, in helping people, in maybe saving a life. What she liked was the idea of having a valid excuse to automatically get in close and take the hand of her pick of men in three consecutive rows. Or anywhere. Irene was twenty, and currently lonely, and available — and crafty when she wanted to be. Plus always was ever-hopeful for romance. She put her own thumb to her wrist and felt the beat quicken from all the possibility.

That weekend, she tried it out. Irene knew how to take dictation. Write in shorthand. Could run the mimeograph, and calculate the postal scale, and transfer phone calls without disconnecting anyone. Made coffee so well that the men in those big meetings asked for the secret so they could take it home to the little woman. Irene knew how to do all those things, but she didn't know a thing about pulses. Her best talent was that she could tell a good story. All her life, people had said as much to her: "You can tell a good story." And they weren't kidding. From nothing, from the thinnest piece of air, the smallest thread, the tiniest fleck of color, Irene could fabricate the history of a dynasty in an empire that never existed, the day-to-day details of a vacation in a place she'd yet to visit. She could outline and fill in the intricate tangle of relationships of the people in an automobile that just passed, could make up the background to a crumb of overheard conversation, two women walking through a park, shaking their heads in disgust: "He has no job and no visible means of support." Give Irene those ten

31

words, and in return she'd give you that anonymous soul's entire world.

Irene got ready to reach out her hand to the quiet guy seated next to her on the couch at the boss's Christmas party, the guy Angie from Personnel had christened Goodlookin' Doug from Legal. Irene regularly had admired him getting icy cups of Tab from the hallway vending machines each afternoon, all big-necked and sideburned and sleepy-eyed, resembling Joe Namath in a rounder, less nose-led sort of way, and at least one month ago she had asked Kelly from Legal who was the new guy and what was his name and was he available, and Kelly from Legal had responded, "Get in line." Even so, the night of the party, it was Irene who found herself alone on the couch with Goodlookin' Doug from Legal and his holiday-color effort of green turtleneck beneath red V-neck sweater. And when Angie from Personnel walked by and broke the ice by introducing him to Irene from Workmen's Comp, Goodlookin' Doug from Legal just smiled and lifted his bottle of Michelob. His unoccupied hand was flat on the blaring black-and-red hound's-tooth check of his polyester trousers. His hands were long and bony, flat backs with thickets of dark hair running wild from the base of each pinky and disappearing into his sweater cuffs, where they went on to probably thrive unchecked over acres of taut skin. The shape of his hands, Irene eventually would learn, made up the "philosophic" type belonging to intellectuals who appear impractical and easily distracted from the niggling minutiae of everyday life. But this first night, all Irene knew was her goal of holding Goodlookin' Doug from Legal's hand. At the least. So she took a breath and leaned toward him and said, "I can read palms."

He was looking away as she said that, in the direction of the harvest-gold fondue pot that had just been brought out by the boss's wife and set on the coffee table to an overdone round of applause by the receptionists from Personnel. The wife stood there in her handwoven, burlap-looking caftan and feigned shy embarrassment, then motioned to the platter of Vienna bread chunks and the long-handled skewers and invited the receptionists to begin their turn at the dipping craze that in this holiday season of 1965 was all the rage.

"Huh?" grunted Goodlookin' Doug, not to the boss's wife, but to Irene, so Irene repeated her announcement. She added, "Want me to read yours?" The face of Irene from Workmen's Comp was eager to please and close and kind of pretty in an unprimped way, and Goodlookin' Doug from Legal was bored in the absence of the rest of the guys from his corner of Legal, seven jerks he was starting to realize weren't going to show despite promising they would, so he shrugged and grinned and held out his left hand, which Irene accepted and took in hers, gently, like it was an orphaned baby animal that needed feeding by eyedropper and other types of careful tending by a human.

The hand of Goodlookin' Doug from Legal was warm and had a weight Irene hadn't expected. He extended it palm down, so Irene turned it over, pushed his fingers flat and awaited the muse. She drew a breath and focused on the first mark that caught her eye, two lines that converged near the nicely vacant ring finger and that led to a deep and upward-swinging crease.

"See this? The upward direction? This means you right now are at the beginning of a new and different journey that will bring you untold excitement . . . "

In reality, the only place Goodlookin' Doug from Legal was headed was to thirty-seven more years in that same department, not a single one more remarkable than any other, excepting the one during which he got to occupy the fancy fifth-floor office of a boss directed to a bedridden pregnancy. He would retire exactly at age sixty-five, sideburns grayed, Namathian eyelids drooping farther than ever, neck thinned and its skin turkeyed, no longer much of a catch, his lifelong reluctance to spear just one single woman for a dip into the warm gooey fondue of longtime commitment meaning no definite companion for the golden years he would fill with walks along the perimeter of fairways, collecting lost Titlelists and Spaldings to take home and wash, pack in egg cartons and resell from his trunk in golf-course parking lots.

But, decades before all that, there on the couch at the boss's Christmas party, the future stretched only as far as holding the hand of this woman telling him the encouraging, hope-filled things she rightfully thought that he — that any of us — would want to hear regarding the big, blank, possibility-laden slate that is the future. After Irene went on for about ten minutes, taking whatever bit of doggedness Goodlookin' Doug from Legal did possess and using her words to reinforce it with steel, clad it in iron, paint it with marine-grade rustproofing and gild its edges in 22-karat gold, he turned his palm back down so it met hers, and he looked at this woman who saw such great things ahead, the woman to whom he suddenly wanted to show other qualities in the here and now, and he asked, "Wanna get outa here?"

From that night on, all Irene needed was inspiration. A starting point. Something that would spark a story. That, and a hand in hers. From there, she could go on to comprehend futures from scars, lines, bumps, ridges, prints, grasps, temperatures, skin tones. You provided the raw material, Irene would return you a wealth of information. A line with an indentation beneath it became an exclamation point that heightened the importance of an exciting project. A swirl was seen as a question mark that meant the bearer would face many questions along the way. Crease marks that formed valleys were stop signs for negativity. Her subjects walked away peering cross-eyed into their flesh — if they walked away, that is. Though they had no special powers of their own, the men whose palms Irene read (and the palms of men were the ones that interested her the most) were certain that Irene would fit fine into their immediate futures. If only for the one night on which she had taken their hand during some happy hour and had seen an entire fascinating future life right there in a square half-inch of pinky tip.

Sometimes this got her a meal. Or a date. Several times, long relationships. One time, a husband. All from nothing more than her imagination and some guidelines in a paperback from a Kenmore Square secondhand shop, its cover a drawing of a big hand, the many meaningful areas outlined and mapped as colorfully and carefully as the fifty states on a diner placemat. *Palmistry for Beginners*, the same book that sat in her space in the mall, even back then was worn and had the impressive look of age, and she had imagined it had been passed down through the generations, even though the publication date was only two years before she found it. Irene bought an indelible marker and traced the lines of her own hands, looking at them dozens of times a day to memorize not only the areas, but what they could mean. There was a surprising lot of information to be learned, and over the years Irene picked and chose and made up her own stew of things to add, hunt for and examine, embellish with meanings she felt fit the bearer. She perfected her delivery with every reading, beginning with the one for Doug from Legal, progressing to those she did for pay at flea markets, fairs, festivals, to the ones she'd been offering six days a week for forty years at a mall that was once the big kite-shaped, eye-blinding diamond in the crown of Western Massachusetts retailing.

Upon its grand opening in 1970, Orchard Mall was the region's first fully enclosed shopping mall, boasting climate-controlled comfort, fifty-five stores, triple cinemas and something called a food court. Offerings now run-of-the-mill for retail spaces were groundbreaking in those days, and crowds from throughout the region flocked to experience the novelty of purchasing anything you could desire — wedding gowns, lawn tractors, cologne, parakeets, haircuts, orthopedic shoes, cotton candy, sympathy cards, Swiss Army Knives, eye exams, beef jerky — all under one roof. "Main Street Recreated" read the slogan glowing on the sign that directed traffic off busy Berkshire Road and down the slope to a shopper's Holy Land.

From the bright April morning the mayor and the city council and the mall manager and the winner of the congeniality award from the Miss Teen USA Western Massachusetts pageant squeezed matching pairs of shining Fiskars through the thick red ribbon strung across the entrance next to the Flaming Pit, the curiosity that was Orchard Mall and its recreated Main Street started sucking the life from downtown Indian Orchard and surrounding communities. Mom-and-pop pharmacies, shoe stores, hardware stores, pet shops, clothiers, hairdressers — none could compete with either the dazzle or the low prices boasted by the mall's chains. Within a few years, "For Rent" signs began to appear on that actual Main Street, in store windows that for as long as a century had displayed bathtubs, footwear, typewriters, prams, books, corsets and cocker spaniels while, over on Berkshire Road, all those things and more became the stuff of a single destination.

Going to the mall? Boyfriends asked their girlfriends this. Kids asked their parents. Women asked their neighbors. And Irene's cousin Kenny asked her one Friday in 1970, on the phone, just as she was closing up shop for the day.

Back then, Irene's place of business was a sunroom where

she saw clients after her day of taking dictation in an office in downtown Springfield, a new job that relocated her ninety miles west to the more affordable end of Massachusetts. She got free use of a louver-windowed space stuck onto the right side of an aunt's house on a nice side street in Ludlow, just past the dairy bar with the neon cow whose tail swayed via pink tubes of light. Due to the private nature of Irene's work, she kept the sunporch opaque with an even application of spray-on Christmas snow coating the glass, allowing in a warm glow of sunlight and keeping out nosey eyes. That Friday in 1970, she picked up the phone from which her uncle had disconnected the session-interrupting ringer and substituted a blinking light.

"Want to go to the mall?" Kenny asked.

"Well, sure, but I don't really need anything special."

"Not to shop — to work," he clarified. "There are some small extra spaces they've yet to fill. My friend is the rental agent. I can get you a deal. Not on the main concourse, of course, but up on one of the little side avenues. You'll get plenty of traffic. People are scouring every inch of the place. It's a madhouse. Have you been?"

Irene had. She'd visited daily the first week it was open, mainly because a different free gift was being offered that first week every twenty-four hours. She came home with an Orchard Mall pot holder and an Orchard Mall sewing kit and an Orchard Mall pill holder and an Orchard Mall key chain. She thought it was handy to have all those stores in one place. And it seemed friendly and homey with all those people enjoying ice cream near the fountain, chatting on benches while watching their kids run figure eights around the fake maples. Did she have a premonition that she would land there? No, Irene had no premonitions, had no powers. But she was able to guess the rent probably was impossible.

"If you want to be there," Kenny said, "I can make it happen. Just leave it to me."

So, what the heck, she did. And Kenny called one night a month later to say the peanut brittle man had been closed down by the Board of Health after four violations in only the first six months of the mall's existence, leaving vacant his peanut-sized space just past the cinemas. "You're in!" he announced, and she was, Kenny having bargained for an affordable lease, and Irene one Tuesday afternoon a month later moving the contents of her sunporch into the trunk of her car and into recently vacated store space twenty-nine.

As Kenny had cautioned, it was far from the J.C. Penney and the Sears and the Steiger's and the Forbes & Wallace that his mall friend referred to as anchor stores, but it was near the barber and the optometrist and, really, when you thought about it, maybe you didn't so much need a new polyester pantsuit or weed whacker as you needed a haircut and the ability to see.

Forty years later, the barber and the optometrist are still there. As is the mall. Though just barely.

Two thousand and ten finds Orchard a ghost town the locals call the Dead Mall. "Take a right at the Dead Mall." "Oh, I live out past the Dead Mall." "That store used to be at the Dead Mall. Now it's at the Mountainside Mall in Holyoke — oooh, don't you love that place?"

Over the past fifteen years, most of Orchard's retailers have relocated there, to the posh state-of-the-art three-story Mountainside Mall in Holyoke, just off the Interstate. That hulking complex, with its ice-skating rink, wave pool, petting zoo, hotel, spa, and television station, is gearing up to celebrate the opening of its 250th retail tenant. A shining replica of a steam train delivers shoppers from stations in the suburbs, and, to accommodate all those who choose to drive, the mall recently won an appeal in court to extend its parking lot into a corner of an adjacent cemetery containing dead nuns.

"Orchard Mall? Who goes there anymore?"

For one, Rosie does. She is there. And because she is there, he asks what he always asks:

"Busy?"

Across the hall, the *M* of the sign for Mom and Sis's Craft Shoppe, the point on which Rosie has set her eyes in an effort to stop the twirling of her immediate world after seeing that woman Margaret in that other woman's palm, is being blocked by the square midsized-compact-ness of Ed Horrigan, who's asked his question even though he knows better. There is no one at all between him and the sixteen paces that lead to the half-circle cutout in which Rosie is sitting as still as a life-sized replica of herself that, were she someone famous, the mall could charge people to stand next to for a photograph.

Ed Horrigan, conversely, is moving, progressing toward her, motion being his key to each day as he zips from one task to the next, a fairy godfather dispatching people to happy places, serene places, exciting places, snow-frosted mountains, isolated beaches, exciting cities, promises — no, make that near-guarantees — of peace and adventure and a return to everyday life bearing a happiness that would spur co-workers to take them aside and ask, "Where did you find that?" And the answer would be "At Experience Travel." Ed Horrigan had signed his lease twenty-three years ago, long before things went south at Orchard Mall. He'd sensed a new start: Cinemas I and II and III had just been reupholstered and outfitted with cupholders at each seat, and First Bank had unveiled a second ATM for shoppers who needed funds before or after banking hours. The Dog House was adding exotic fish to its inventory. The meat-centered Flaming Pit had installed a sushi bar. Orchard back then was still truly Main Street Recreated. Everything you wanted in one place. Including a palm reader, something Ed Horrigan found fascinating. Almost as fascinating as, on this morning, a new face in the half-circle cutout. A new one, and one that looks so — what is that? Shock, or sickness? Some sort of out-of-it-ness. He's now seated in the readee's purple chair, and because this woman is making no sign of realizing he's there two feet in front of her, is reaching for the string of the bell and is startling the woman with one quick, soft ring.

Rosie's eyes are big and teary. No, she doesn't look well. Ed introduces himself and asks is she OK? Can he get her something? Water? Name it. Rosie wants to name it, to speak what she needs right now, but that is impossible. She is unable to put one word out. She shakes her head and somehow makes her right hand work to reach for the pad of Kleenex. Ed feels he must offer to get Bunny from across the way, and he tells her this: "Do you want me to get Bunny from across the way?" even though he is not sure this woman knows who — or what — Bunny is. Bunny is a woman. She and Irene are best friends. Ed's reasoning is that maybe this woman, whatever she's experiencing, needs the understanding of another woman. Sometimes that will happen, he knows — a woman will be comfortable only around another woman. Some women are fine with men, can interact with them like they have no differences in gender or uneven place in the world. Others are not. Maybe she is one of those. Ed would try to help, but, apart from dealing with his customers, has no social skills. A real, genuine little woman had told him so, had put it that way six and three quarters years back, a quarter of a year after Ed had made clear his feelings. "No skills," she had said in response to Ed's profession of love. "No skills," like they were in trade school and he was flunking woodworking. But Ed was in a little foreign country when this happened, this little foreign woman's little foreign country — you had to forgive her, maybe she was meaning something else by using those particular words. Maybe she was attempting to say something perhaps kinder, an assessment that didn't make him sound as awkward as he knew he was. "I can learn" had been Ed's reply. But she'd only pointed to the foreign little door of her foreign little flat in her foreign little country, which Ed that very afternoon had to make abrupt plans to depart, even though, as a travel agent, he still had four free days of touring left on his itinerary. Skill-less or not, he had never felt so in love, and so heartbroken.

He flashes to the present, to the here and now, where he himself is pointing in the direction of up the hall and Bunny's Card Nook. He scratches at his orangish mop — should he get Bunny to help? For her part, Rosie is answering no. She's capable of that one word now. "No." So Ed sits. Waits to see what he might be able to do for this person.

Late Monday morning is when Ed comes around for his weekly reading. Ambles over from Experience Travel and shoots the shit, to use his term, with Irene. Recounts any trips made over the weekend courtesy of tour companies or hotels or destinations that will exchange a free experience for the chance to get a travel agent enthused enough to pass along recommendations to clients. Those stories always flow into Irene taking his hand and telling him, "Ed, there is hope," before offering a vague but beautifully worded clue as to how his life might progress. Ed doesn't know this woman in Irene's chair, but he detects that she isn't up to the task of a reading right now.

"I can come back," Ed says. "I work here. The travel place. I'll be over there — or I can stay. If you want. Dervla's in the office today — uh, that's my sister — I can stay if you like. Or until Irene gets here."

Rosie puts up her hand to stop him. She hadn't wanted company, but now that Ed's here, she is glad for someone's presence. Almost like it is not her idea, she holds out her hand, motions for his. Ed knows the routine, shrugs. He's had his palm read only by Irene, so this will be something different. And it is. Rather than the hope promise, this woman gives a request. "Make a wish," she says almost inaudibly. Then, after a space, she considers what – if anything — to add, as she had with that very first woman who'd come to the window. As it had occurred to her with that very first woman coming to her window, as she had been at the bank, at this new window she will be a teller, too. A teller of fortunes. Everyone at Rosie's last window had wanted money. Paper money, coins, certificates of deposit. Here, the currency given back will be very different. She's not sure exactly what it might amount to, but she knows it won't be cash. So "But not for money" is what she repeats this time, too. And that's OK, because money is not what Ed Horrigan wants, anyhow. It would be nice, sure, but he really wants something else. He squints tightly like a little kid might at the conjuring of something he hopes will be magical, and in that fuzzy darkness he pictures his dream, the same thing each week for the six and a quarter years. In all that time, Ed's wish has never varied, except for the week his mother had her angioplasty and, of course, he had to direct any and all promise her way. But all the other weeks of all those years, over and over, he has squinted and envisioned himself back in the little foreign country and in the little foreign house and in the little foreign bed of the little foreign woman, Ed's feeling being that if you just keep sending out the same request, it's eventually going to come true. Like how he began all his long-ago Christmas lists with "brother" and, eventually, Harold arrived. Begging. Persistence had worked for him once, with the brother, so, even at the age of fifty-nine, he holds some level of optimism.

When Ed Horrigan draws open his lids, this new woman comes into focus. Not Irene, not the usual pleasant countenance looking up from his palm to say, "Well, Ed, first off, there is hope." She is saying something Irene-like, noting that the left hand is the one of inheritance, what you came to the planet with — it's all on there. The right holds what you will do while you are here. Irene would bring that up often enough as they got started — and Ed knows that from his visits, and Rosie does, too, from hers. Which is why she used it on that first woman. To have something at all to say. And she repeats it all again for Ed, but right now as she looks into Ed's rectangular right palm, she's seeing something Irene never spotted there. Like a mosaic is the picture of the nervous little foreign woman who, since last Tuesday, over and over again, has been dialing Ed's number, then hanging up just after the country code for the US and the 1-800-EXP-TRAV is punched by redial, and the scratchy transatlantic connection is made, and just before the ringing of Ed's phone begins.

4

This is Dennis's favorite part of the job.

The best part of working.

Yes, sure, there is payday, and there is his traditional stop at the Pit Pub every Friday at 5:01 p.m., but as far as the actual high point of his days at Orchard Mall goes, nothing tops putting up the new message every Monday morning.

He loved it instantly, the moment he was instructed in the task forty years ago, before the mall was even open, wouldn't welcome customers for another two months from the day he was brought to meet a big lineup of boxes stacked along the far wall of the garage next to the rear of Cinema II and was shown the several sets of twenty-six letters, plus an assortment of pauses, full stops, dashes, asterisks, colons, quotation marks, ampersands and those most exciting exclamation points.

"Dennis," Mall Manager Lawrence Block announced, "you are going to inform the world."

He said this with drama, no sarcasm, it was simply a fact. Lawrence Block was skating on adrenaline and taking everything extremely seriously. Had been since he arrived here from somewhere in Tennessee three months earlier to take the position of his dreams. Only forty-one years of age and the manager of this region's first fully enclosed shopping center. Of a whole entire shopping mall. "Wunderkind" read the newspaper headline upon his arrival, sending Dennis to the dictionary. The parent corporation down in Baltimore loved his six years of savvy, energetic and (most importantly) moneymaking work to date at two consecutive shiny and new East Coast malls, and had faith that he would make this place a great success, too. For his part, Lawrence Block was determined to prove his bosses right, dreaming that Orchard Mall one day would be entered into marketing textbooks. "And then there is the grand example of the groundbreaking success that was and is Orchard Mall," the fittingly thick chapter would begin. "Need we say more than just its name?"

Perhaps the stunning history would be accompanied by a photo of the ribbon cutting, which, sixty-one days from the one on which he showed Dennis the letters, would have Lawrence standing to the left of the mayor and to the right of Miss Congeniality, who managed to smile for the camera at the same time as she was hissing, "Get your hand off my ass," aiming that incorrectly at Lawrence, who had both hands innocently on his pair of scissors, rather than at the mayor, who had only his right hand visible, and his long left arm around and past Lawrence and on the backside of the beauty queen. But that day in the storage garage, any history, good or bad, had yet to be written, and those sixty-one days remained until the grand opening, which was the exact message Lawrence was instructing Dennis to spell out on the sign that had just been assembled by a pair of traffic-stopping cranes camped for a week up the parking-lot slope and next to Berkshire Road.

"Today we put 61," Lawrence said, snail-like, as if giving a complicated trigonometry lesson. "Then, tomorrow, we put 60. The next day we put 59. Got it?"

"Think so," Dennis said, and he tried hard not to sound annoyed. He needed the job. He was twenty-one. This would be his first full-time post. With benefits, too, including paid vacations — money for doing nothing. A new concept for him.

There would be no more cobbling together whatever part-time work he'd been able to find since age sixteen. Waxing bowling alleys in the morning, mowing lawns in the afternoon, vacuuming office complexes at night. Delivering papers, delivering pizza, picking up trash, picking up returnables. Sorting laundry, sorting newspaper inserts, sorting his options, that last action never complicated or lengthy. But now, this position of maintenance man, and full-time, amazingly was his, was 7:30 a.m. to 3:30 p.m., half an hour for lunch, and the last half hour of the day overlapping with the 3:00 to 11:00 p.m. person, who had yet to be hired but who would take his instructions — instructions determined by Dennis himself — as to what needed to be done by the time the mall closed for the night. And, if things worked out, Dennis could be back home in time for a nap before the office-vacuuming gig, which he'd yet to give up, nervous that Orchard was too good to be true.

There were twenty years between Dennis and Lawrence, and Dennis made about twenty percent of what Lawrence was paid. Dennis wore a navy jumpsuit with a graphic designer's costly version of a swirly colonial-lettering OM screened onto its back and his first name embroidered above the left front pocket as he walked around OM in a new pair of steel-toed, ankle-high boots mandated by the office. Lawrence sported designer suits with just enough odd details to make them trendy — extra length to the jacket, an unexpected color for the vest — along with tasseled Italian loafers. Dennis arrived at the mall via Pioneer Valley Transit Authority bus. Lawrence floated up in some sort of shiny, low, silver car that could fit only two people, and he parked it on an angle, using a pair of spaces so as to spare his doors the possibility of being nicked. Sometimes Dennis would look at Lawrence and he could hear Lawrence talking, but overtaking that was Dennis's father's cluck, out of nowhere — well, from the grave, actually — cutting in to say,

"Now here's a boy who had the sense to complete four years of high school."

"They're light," Lawrence was saying as he held up and admired an L he could already see hanging on the wall of his new condo, located in a snazzily renovated mill on the river in Indian Orchard.

"You're dumb" is what Dennis heard, and as he began to shrink and feel like nothing, worthless and even beyond having absolutely no value, if such a thing were possible, he also knew it wasn't Lawrence's voice in his ears. So he had to ask, "What?" and Lawrence repeated how the letters were lightweight and asked had Dennis noticed how they were imbedded with shining chips of something that would make them appear to move when headlights hit them on the sign up the hill?

Up the hill. That's where Dennis has headed every Monday for forty years, driving an Orchard Mall golf cart to which he attaches a trailer filled with the alphabet soup that allows him to write out the week's message left in his box at the management office. Dennis Edwards is still employed by the once-famous and groundbreaking Orchard Mall, a place Lawrence Block left three years after its opening, at the height of a publicity whirlwind that included mention in a *Newsweek* feature on how malls were becoming America's new downtown. There in four colors, in the big-deal magazine sold coast to coast and probably beyond, was a photo of Dennis's sign —

PARKING
LOT
FULL

— painted both neatly and on the spur of the moment the day the undreamable actually happened — all thirty-five hundred spaces filled and people taking to using the emergency lanes of Berkshire Road. Lawrence Block accepted the offer from a new mall opening on Chicago's Magnificent Mile and gave a two-week notice that allowed time for even more press — young management wunderkind genius makes the leap to the big city but says he'll miss this little one, and Orchard Mall. "I predict even bigger and better times at Orchard," he told the *Daily News* reporter who caught a final interview as Lawrence walked to his car parked on a slant for a final time. "Mark my words!"

These days, a waitress at the Pit who has a cousin in New York's retailing world places Lawrence in management at Trump Towers and says he was the brain behind the stories-high wall of water that cascades next to the escalators and down to the lightfilled café where the waitress's cousin reports Lawrence sometimes dines simply to eavesdrop and learn what visitors are saying about the place, and to cook up possibilities for making it even better.

"Orchard wouldn't be what it is without you," Lawrence Block had said with sincerity when he toasted Dennis at the Pit Pub a couple nights before leaving for Chicago.

"He's lying," Dennis's father said convincingly, overlaying his message on the great compliment.

"What?" Dennis asked.

And Lawrence Block, spearing another meatball from his happy-hour plate, said, "I've told them, down at headquarters, I've told them about you." He motioned with the meatball to accent each syllable of "I've said, 'This man is from another era. When people weren't afraid of hard work.' That is what I've told them time and again. You'll be seeing it in your paycheck, if you haven't already."

Dennis hadn't yet, but Lawrence Block was true to his word and, five weeks later, like a promised postcard that arrives from another continent long after you've given up hope of the traveler ever remembering he'd said he'd write, a breath-stealing twenty-five extra dollars began surfacing in Dennis's gross each Thursday.

"Don't question it, just be thankful," said Laurie Vanasse in the mall office as she handed Dennis his paycheck from the top left-hand drawer of her desk.

"Accounting fuck-up," his father sniped simultaneously, so Dennis had to ask Laurie, "What?"

Up the hill, at the base of the hulking Orchard Mall sign, stands the box for which only Dennis has the key, the one that allows him to open the little door accessing the hand crank that brings down the metal ladder that is his ticket to the world above.

Most of Dennis's efforts are unseen or generally unnoticed. You go to a mall — even a dead one — and you of course expect floors to be swept, trash receptacles to be emptied, windows to be washed, plastic palm fronds to be dust free. You'd like light fixtures to have working bulbs, you'd hope for toilet paper in the stalls. Those are among the thankless, anonymous tasks making up most of Dennis's week. They, and the extra things not required but done anyhow, like always assisting shoppers with directions to this store or that one, carrying bags to cars, leading lost children to the management office where Laurie will cut into the Muzak and announce the find. He does the extra things without expecting thanks, having been raised by an ingrate. Lawrence Block had been right: Dennis is of an ancient mindset that says it is not beneath him to do what others do not want to do, to be the lowest figure on the mall's totem pole yet not really care, as he is not defined by the eight hours he is someone else's possession. The job has changed things for him. Put him in a whole other orbit. It got him an apartment, not just a room, eventually a decent house. Money for clothes nobody'd worn before. Finally, money for a car, an economical hatchback from Japan that had his father spitting epithets through Dennis's head so often during the bargaining process that Dennis had to ask for three breaks before the final price was negotiated. The job meant money to go out and do things, to frequent clubs and concerts where there were other people, nice people, including people who were women, and it meant money to take them out to still other places, to take one, especially, out, and to buy her a ring. Money to get her some of the things she most wanted, which was not much, just a little bigger house with a second bathroom in which she could do her dog grooming. That was what she wanted, dog-grooming space, and, more importantly, she wanted Dennis, who did not wear a price tag, who remained simply happy to be human and alive and doing something, fitting in, belonging to a woman and to the regular world. And also to the community that Orchard has become.

From the sign he looks down at the space Orchard Mall takes up, sixty-seven point six acres all told, including building, parking lot and ring of ornamental flowering trees. He knows every square foot of it, and from up there he surveys, breathing new air, admiring the view. Most Mondays he can see the gentle rounded backs of the mountains to the west, the row of the pointier ones to the north. To his right, cars zoom up and down Berkshire Road, slowing and stopping only if instructed by the stoplight that had been installed after the mall opened and police on extremely costly overtime were needed to untangle the snarls. Closer, below him, the parking lot is free of cars and still neat from its largely unneeded weekend visit by the vacuum truck. The night's snow has melted under a big sun that makes doubtful the forecast of another couple inches later in the day. The damp asphalt stretches like a big grey sea. The parking space lines are orderly whitecaps, and it is perfect that the birds resting there are gulls. The miniature trees that dot the lot — Dennis sees these as islands — are just starting to get that subtle first wash of pale green that means leaves are due any second. Things are happening. And, up there on the sign, he is spreading the word.

S

P

R

I

N

G

Years ago, the scene would have been much different. The mall was new, Dennis was young, seeing the day's parade beginning, the first hundred of the thousands of cars that in a single day would make the turn into the lot. On a Monday morning it would be the efficient elderly, who'd scanned the Sunday circulars and clipped the ads and coupons and headed in to grab their share of the bargains limited in number. In the days before the abolition of the Blue Laws opened the Commonwealth's stores every Sunday, each Monday morning they'd claim the prime spots right in front of the best entrances, would use the handicapped spots if their plates allowed, and would be standing by the mall's main doors as they were unlocked by Lawrence Block, who enjoyed performing that job himself, taking the time to shake the hand of anyone who'd accept his warm clasp, welcoming them personally to Orchard, which would be nowhere without customers, something he made note of in most of his hellos. Also arriving early were young mothers who'd just seen their kids off to school and were coming by to collect whatever their households required. Then there were the women in some fuzzy existence that required them to neither be seeing anyone off nor welcoming them home, who had their days to themselves and who came to shop away the morning and then head to the Flaming Pit for a glass of Chablis and a stroll along the salad bar. Dennis saw them all, these shoppers, and their dramas, too. Kids begging parents for money, couples arguing over how much to spend on a washer/dryer, teens skipping school. The aimless hunched boys who blasted out obscenities if they said anything at all to one another while they walked to the mall to spend the day in the arcade were followed by cars bearing girls who'd skipped as well, loud and bubbling and applying face paint in the rearview.

There sometimes were rendezvous, one car awaiting another, an occupant leaving his or hers to get into the next, and that one would drive away, maybe in an effort at carpooling, but more like up to no good, Dennis thought as he'd turn his attention to the old guy who came by to feed the gulls, drive-up service, never exiting his car, just rolling down the window and tossing out handfuls of shredded Dreikorn's. Some other old men rode their three-wheeled bikes slowly around the lot's huge perimeter, many times. Few realized Dennis was up there. When he did get noticed, shoppers might make their children guess what letter he would be adding next, have them spell out what he was assembling. People sometimes asked if they could climb up, too. Or how they could get such a job; — that had to be fun, had to be. And Dennis would answer yeah, it is.

Over the years, he informed the world of a sweeping progression of excitement to feel, from the first "61 MORE DAYS!" down to "1 MORE DAY!" down to "GALA GRAND OPENING TODAY!" and then he heralded the great events for which Orchard Mall became known. Contests with big-money prizes: "SATURDAY WIN A GRAND EVERY HOUR!" Charitable efforts: "SHELTER SATURDAY: ADOPT A PET!" And celebrities, the appearances of actual stars who graced the Fountain Court, taking a seat in the gazebo as hoards lined up for autographs and pictures and general speechless gawking. "TODAY!" Dennis would remind, "BOB HOPE!" or "SEN TED KENNEDY!" "DINAH SHORE!" or "TONY ORLANDO AND DAWN!" or "CARL YASTRZEMSKI!" or, the best ever, "NUMBER 4 BOBBY ORR!!!" In a small blue vinyl-bound notepad he'd bought at Waldenbooks, the word "Autographs" scrolled in gold embossing on the front, Dennis preserved the signatures of each visitor. Photos were stuck in there, too. Of the star and Dennis. In the same actual picture. Touching, even. Telly Savalas's arm around Dennis's shoulders. The guy who played the chauffeur on TV's *Hart to Hart* shaking Dennis's hand like they were making an agreement. Two Hee-Haw Honeys in their checkered little get-ups, one hugging him from either of his sides. And the photograph he made an extra print of just to carry around and show off: Charo planting a kiss on his left cheek.

"JANUARY WHITE SALE!" "EASTER BUNNY BO-NANZA!" "MOTHER'S DAY MADNESS!" "FATHER'S DAY FUN!" "BACK TO SCHOOL BARGAINS!" "GREAT PUMPKIN WEEKEND!" "STRUT WITH TOM TURKEY!" And, of course, "SANTA ARRIVES!" Each with the requisite exclamation point. To remind everyone in every car that ever passed that things were never so exciting as they were when you found yourself on Main Street Recreated.

But now is now, Dennis is four years from retirement, the glory days of the '70s stunningly happened in a bygone century, and the autograph book remains in his locker in the garage space next to Cinema III, having last seen the light of day in 1988, when Suzanne Somers swung through on a tour to promote her Abdominizer. In the late '70s, a fast-growing infection of malls encroached, deflating Orchard's oft-used "Your ON-LY mall!" tagline, popping up in factories that had been empty for decades, in sweeping cornfields backdropped by the other side of the mountains Dennis could see from his perch on the sign up the hill. Each challenger was more eye-popping and wallet grabbing than the next; each lured more of Orchard's loyal customers, who came to prefer the newcomers' basics of modern décor, expanded theaters, full-size attached restaurants, licensed babysitting facilities, covered parking. Orchard management took out ads touting the mall's original status, its longevity. The much-heralded "WM First and Best" promotion in 1980 included costly TV commercials and even skywriting over the Eastern States Exposition fair across the river in West Springfield. Energetically run tenant meetings brainstormed ways to zing up shoppers' enthusiasm. Dennis did his part, headed out to the sign on Monday mornings to remind passersby they could come in from the cold — "IT'S WARM AT ORCHARD!" — or the heat — "WE'RE THE COOLEST!" The coffin nail of a fall day on which the Mountainside Mall in Holyoke opened, he ignored the office's assignment of "AUTUMN LEAVES — AND PRICES! — ARE FALLING" and instead hung a punctuation-free "WE'RE STILL HERE."

Dennis didn't have to worry when changing an executive decision. He was as much a part of the mall as any staffer in the office or any tenant in a shop. And also part of the intricate bartering system that store owners began when the mall opened, and relied on more and more as it went downhill. They exchanged goods and services, necessities. The Affordable Attorney defended the Music Man after he fell asleep at the wheel while returning home from a gig. In return, he taught her the electric piano, then sold her one at a nice discount. He played the twenty-fifth anniversary party of the Tax Man's brother and his wife in return for a year's filing by the Tax Man, and the Tax Man regularly did the accounting for the barber, for trims and clips. The barber cut the hair of the optometrist, who checked his eyes and kept in stock the line of disposable contacts he

favored. The optometrist gave new eyeglass frames to the photo-shop owner in return for a set of aluminum frames for the
enlargements he'd had made of the towering cup plants that
grew in his backyard. The photo-shop owner processed prints
in exchange for movie tickets, and the movie-theater manager
gave other tickets to the Pit manager in exchange for a seat at
king crab night. The manager of the Pit offered the same, plus a
full surf 'n' turf dinner, to Mom of Mom and Sis's Craft Shoppe
when the Board of Health halted smoking in the town's restaurants and he needed five nicely painted signs announcing that
fact. Bunny at the Card Nook put in brown bags beginning
readers and spelling workbooks from her kids' shelves and
brought them over to the Russian girl at the Orange Julius, who
was an actual Russian girl from Russia and who came into the
Card Nook so many times to admire the stock and then eventually confessed to Bunny that she could make out barely a
word of written English. For her part, she regularly delivered
cups of Orange Juliuses just to rack up points until there was
something she needed, and, each week when she did that, Irene
offered a reading, fifteen minutes full of hope and good words
that buoyed the Russian girl and made her proud of the little
finger that rose well above the top joint of the next, making
her, according to Irene, the pure Mercurian type, meaning she
was someone likely to be endowed with quicksilver intelligence,
sharp business sense and a charismatic personality.

Dennis's contribution was to do more of whatever someone else did not want to do. Non-mall tasks that over the years
he had more and more spare time to fit into his day. For a time
three decades ago, he filed for the Affordable Attorney all the
important documents a lawyer creates: folders and papers she
placed in a wire bin that awaited him whenever he had the time
for the task. In return, she helped Dennis's wife incorporate
when Dennis's wife opened her grooming business, and even-

tually helped Dennis's wife and Dennis through the simplest of divorces when all Dennis's wife could hear in her head was the jangling windup of her biological clock, and all Dennis could hear in his was his father saying who needs another idiot like Dennis in this world. For the Music Man, who let Dennis have any promotional T-shirts, stickers, key chains and geegaws manufacturers sent, he occasionally dusted the store, including the many accordions on display. He saw all the movies he wanted in exchange for minding the ticket booth while the movie-theater manager went to pick up his daughter from school each day at 1:50 p.m. For the Tax Man, who advised Dennis on the weekly twenty-five-dollar investment he'd made each week of the year since the blessing of full-time and the bonus from Lawrence Block, Dennis ran to the post office and to the mega office supply store that had opened across the street at the turn of the century. For Irene, Queen of the Unseen, he brought her car to the touchless automatic wash down the street, vacuumed her gray industrial rug, collected any foam peanuts being tossed out by the retailers so she and her Tuesday night clay class participants could safely transport home their finished work. In return, every Monday after he got back from his time up at the sign, she opened his square hand, the type that belongs to a person who is practical and rational, who can be relied upon to do exactly what he has promised to do, and on time, is persistent and sometimes successful and no touch of a scandal will ever come near him. Irene, Queen of the Unseen, would touch each of Dennis's spatulate fingertips, which she always noted are the ideal, showing both enthusiasm and confidence, and she would tell him what she'd been telling him for years. And even if all these years it had yet to happen, he liked hearing it, liked how she put it as she looked into the riverbed of his fate line and said she saw communication, change and hope. Always hope.

On this first morning of spring, Dennis Edwards is driving back from the sign, his little OM golf cart making an occasional muffled whirr as it passes over a bit of mushy snow. To underscore the importance of this week's one word, he affixed an exclamation point below the *G*. And to the right of the word he has made a circle with the asterisks he sometimes uses to represent snowflakes. Arranged in a circle, they also can be daisies, which is what he hopes they will be seen as today, by anybody who bothers to look up, as he was hoping maybe that one woman would, the one woman whose one car was one of maybe six in the parking lot first thing this morning when he drove out to the sign, whom he had watched rushing back to that car with determined steps, careful of the remaining snow but also smushing right through it at the same time as she hurried to her sedan and drove steadily to the main exit and took the last few safe seconds of the yellow light to make a rattling left onto Berkshire Road, in the direction of the city and the highway that runs all the way from here to the bottom of Florida, with many places to stop in between, one of them being Pennsylvania, where Margaret in the green-sided house is waiting already.

"I had a feeling you would come" is what that Margaret will say in seven hours, when the car pulls up and this woman, her sister, gets out and looks at the green-sided house — her refuge, her new home.

As we all do, that woman has her new destination today, and Dennis has his old one. His treasured Monday appointment with Irene. Every Monday upon his riding back down the hill to the Mall and visiting the locker room to wash his hands and check his hair, Dennis goes for a reading from Irene.

Today he notices from the sixteen paces away that ahead, there in the half-circle cutout, another woman is sitting in Irene's place. First, for nearly two full weeks, there has been no Irene. No lights, gate down and locked. And no one knowing her whereabouts, but Bunny assuring the tenants that Irene was fine and safe and they were not to worry. "She is just away," she'd said with a smile, sounding like the front of one of her best-selling sympathy cards, the kind that make it sound like the deceased person is at a resort rather than in a box.

Two weeks were the normal length of a normal vacation, and Dennis had figured that was the "just away." He'd felt a bit injured that Irene hadn't ever mentioned any plans — she was normally effusive about anything on her calendar, and why wouldn't she mention what probably was another trip to the Cape, her favorite destination? Irene had seemed preoccupied lately, but in a good way. Daydreamy was the best way he could put it. Maybe she just forgot she was going somewhere?

This woman in Irene's place in the half-circle cutout looks peaked, even though Dennis has never seen her before to compare her skin tone with any other she might ever wear. In turn, his own face registers worry, but Rosie doesn't see this. She's lost back at the green-sided house from the first reading, and at the bedside phone the little foreign woman keeps hanging up somewhere overseas. Twice in the same day, with that woman and with that Ed, Rosie knew — actually knew — that she saw something, and that something was and is the truth. Her feet have gone cold, even though on the first day of spring she has the space heater blasting next to them on number eight of its ten levels of power. She hears Dennis more than sees him, the soft shuffle he uses to get around, a habit developed when he had to sneak past his father and one that always wears the soles of his boots down first on their inner heels. Ed Horrigan has just left Rosie's window, said he would come back to check on her in a while — maybe, he said, Irene would be there by then, and Rosie had nodded, maybe she would, though

Rosie knows that will never be so ever again. Now before her in the half-circle cutout is another man, average height, curly dark hair, eyes big like he's just been surprised. He's dressed like he's there to fix something. Her head, maybe? She thinks she needs a doctor. Is there a doctor's office in this mall? She tries to remember. She knows an eye doctor is nearby, but how about one for the mind? She needs to call the young therapist in the zip-off pant legs. She leans to retrieve her bag as she hears, "Hello, I'm looking for Irene."

Rosie nods. Swallows. Has nothing to swallow. Sits up and reached for the nearby bottle of Poland Spring with the nipple-like sports cap she is embarrassed to drink from in public. She holds up a finger to ask for time, takes a sip and then a breath and then says weakly, "I'm filling in. She's not here."

"Sick?"

"Me? No. It's just —"

"No, Irene, is she sick?" He leans toward Rosie as he asks.

"No. Eloped." Rosie's voice is coming back to her. All she'd been able to say to that Ed guy was the letter *E* that began his name. But to this man, she's pronounced the whole word.

People say some pieces of news can be like a kick in the gut. You think that is all exaggeration until you hear something that not only kicks you but almost kills you. They are maybe too polite to add that the kick lands a little farther below the belt — at least that's where this information hits Dennis, who can't help but feel his head drop forward, nauseated, dizzy.

"You all right?"

He nods. Shakes his head. Then nods again. Shrugs. Shakes again. Winces. Looks up slowly. Whispers, "When?"

"Ten days ago, something like that. I'm her friend. Rosie. From clay class. I made this." That last sentence is one of those that just comes out when you're nervous. What does this man care what she has made? But there she is, pulling into the half-circle cutout the shiny slab-built business-card holder that had been her present to Irene the previous Christmas. Black with intricate little golden stars Rosie had painted freehand, without stencil or stamp, something she was proud of and that Irene had made a fuss about. It is stacked with Irene's cards, a wallet-sized version of her newspaper ad, "Queen of the Unseen" arcing over the word IRENE, which is where this man's eyes have fallen. Eyes that, if you looked closely, you would notice are getting teary.

"Who?" he asks.

"Who what?"

"Who, you know — elope?"

"A man."

Dennis's expression is asking for more.

Rosie has to think. "Oh, a man from Canada."

Canada. The breakfast of Special K and banana inside Dennis threatens to move skyward. North. To Canada. Irene. Canada. And that other word this woman has said. Elope. Marriage. Taken. Gone. He puts a hand on his midsection.

"You OK?" Rosie again. This man — has to be the "Dennis" that is stitched onto his shirt — is looking how she herself feels. Maybe there is something with the air in this place. A Legionnaire's type of illness breeding in the air ducts. Maybe Irene has gotten out just in time. If they'd been enemies, she might think Irene had done this on purpose — had given her the keys and made the offer in the hopes she'd get some fatal mall virus. But she and Irene got along fine. They weren't the kind of friends who were on the phone every single day, but they'd been faithful Tuesday night buddies, pretty good at constructing with coils, flops at the wheel, glazing, firing, starting all over again. Talking, laughing, drinking those drinks. Now she'd given Rosie this entire business. Something to do when that's what

Rosie needed. No, Irene wouldn't have deliberately done anything bad, wouldn't have put her in harm's way.

Rosie is wading through those thoughts, almost forgetting
the workman who at some point in this has taken the seat in
front of her. He is on his own planet as well. Now its only citizen. Something about his sadness makes her want to reach a
hand through the half-circle cutout to touch his shoulder.

She asks again, "You OK?"

The man answers, "Yes, I'm fine," and puts his hand up like
he is taking an oath. And that's when she sees something playing there, as she had with the others — a small movie that
catches Rosie's eye as sharply as if it had little claws coming at
her. Her head jerks back, and as he moves to rise from the purple chair, she does reach for him, gets part of the side seam of
his blue OM shirt cuff, catches a waft of some man cologne
that reminds her of warm fall leaves. He stops. "Give me your
hand," Rosie says quietly, and he does, sitting back down, turning up the palm of his left hand, the one that holds all the
things that might happen, the one packed with all that possibility Irene always had said was there. Rosie looks, too, at Dennis's muscled Mound of Venus, the dramatic plunge from Jupiter to Mercury that hints at one or more over-dominant parents
and a feeling of inadequacy, his calm, nearly lineless Plain of
Mars, the little star down near his wrist that Irene had always
told him would light the way. Both his Jupiter and Mercury are
set low, indicating the need for affection, something Dennis
does not show but that courses through him almost more than
his own blood. Rosie opens her mouth to start a story for
which she has no beginning. Nothing emerges. Just the picture
before her eyes. Like on a broken TV or one of those movies
from her parents' youth, soundless. There it is: Dennis and his
sad past, a small young little Dennis and his big old huge father
with his large and looming meanness, the chickeny voice spit-

ting out disapproval, this past as real and solid and unquestionably true as that first woman's future had been, as were the worries of the foreign little woman with the telephone. His story, playing there on his palm.

Rosie concentrates on the sharp lines that fall from above the lifeline, signaling a sudden loss or shift of circumstances in this man's early years. And there she sees past those early years, now to 1970. She knows as well as her Social Security number that she is watching Irene's moving-in day. Irene coming through the door of that first rental space, Irene carrying the big purple chair, Irene wearing clothing she'd long forgotten ever owning. Illegally wide bell-bottoms embroidered with rainbows and peace signs. Filmy white gauze top from the Goodwill. Hair poked with a pair of chopsticks that were souvenirs from her first trip to a Japanese restaurant. Dr. Scholl's that clapped against her soles as she entered, drums to the cymbals of the pair of clanging brass bracelets she wore every day during that era in her life. Walking forward as if toward a camera lens. But Rosie knows that Irene was walking toward Dennis. Rosie is seeing through his eyes. Seeing Irene forty years ago as she stopped to look around the former space of the peanut brittle man and wonder just what might happen as she became the newest tenant at Orchard Mall. The reel plays on. Irene was still, and Dennis wasn't looking away. Over Rosie washes the very same sense of captivation Dennis felt at that moment. About Irene. Something that tells her it still is there, in Dennis, bigger with each year — an astounding forty by now. And right then Rosie realizes the cause of his reaction to the news about Irene, and how Rosie has hurt him, simply by being there. By not being Irene.

"What do you see?" Dennis asks, his voice coming through to Rosie like bad reception on a radio. She gives him the truth, as she will for everyone who sits before her: "I see her."

5

The sun is serious by the time Mom pulls into the parking lot.

Full-on, no-nonsense blazing, not even bothering with a scenic preliminary show of emerging from behind big, fluffy, movie-style clouds. Pure, raging, beaming down. The sky turning it up on this big day of change.

Making the left off Berkshire Road, she glances at the Orchard Mall sign, at the "SPRING!" message above the melting snow. She shakes her head.

"Fucking idiot."

Mom is referring to Dennis. Mom hates Dennis. Dennis knows this. But he doesn't take it personally. One, he has been raised being hated. Two, Mom hates everybody.

And everything. That's just the kind of person she is. Nasty. Crabby. Not a kind word for anybody. Throwing no breaks, offering no crumbs of consideration. Nothing anyone does is good, everything they say is stupid. The whole world is rotten, and the only happy people are the ones who are dead. All this is the life view of a woman who makes her living selling hand-painted plaques bearing bright affirmations like "Love Happens!"

Mom is the Mom of Mom and Sis's Craft Shoppe, which first opened when the mall opened. The shop offers local craftspeople the chance to display and sell their old-fashioned country-style New Englandy wares in a modern, bustling setting. Pay a monthly fee to Mom and you can rent your own set of bookshelves on which to show off your specialty. You stock it, Mom sells it — and takes a handsome cut, of course. Dolls, wreaths, soaps, Christmas decorations, handknits, wooden toys, and an endless variety of sappy legends brushed onto roof slates and T-shirts are among the flotsam packed into the space that, before the closing of the major shops and the consolidation of the remaining ones, housed Spencer Gifts and its teen must-haves of blacklight posters, lava lamps, skull rings and rubber vomit. Despite the name she goes by, Mom is nobody's mother — carries on her birth certificate the given name of Daniela — but thinks that in the interest of her business it is much more homey to sound maternal. In her late sixties, and without an ounce of man-luring charm, she has little chance of becoming anybody's biological mother via traditional processes, but doesn't care. To Mom, babies look like big-headed aliens, kids irk her with their running free and their volume and their neediness and their breaking things, teens are nothing but disasters waiting to happen, and adulthood, well, what is so great about years of increasing misery? Though an enormous conservative, Mom thinks the pill should be stocked in gumball machines, rained from the sky. There are too many people already. Create somebody just to have him or her endure this miserable world? You gotta be kidding.

She fumes over the state of things in general — the money-sucking poor, the free-loving liberals, the world-twisting homosexuals, the widespread use of Spanish. Churns over all this while she sits at her desk to the left of her shop door, wearing a lace-frilled blue-checkered apron over her all-black petite separates, drinking cans of store-brand diet cola from a cooler of them she carries in each day and sips from while carefully painting heart-wringing messages of kindness and forgiveness.

This she does alone. The Sis of Mom and Sis, an unrelated, easygoing, moon-eyed woman who'd met Mom at a Start Your Own Business extension course forty-one years ago and gotten pushed into a hasty partnership, escaped about two years into the arrangement, way back when the shop was in its original location on the mall's side avenue, just past the corner-anchoring Waldenbooks and the cotton candy man. To be specific, Sis didn't so much leave as she just never came to work one Monday, and to prevent having to deal with Mom in person one more time, an action she said was an order from a certified mental health counselor, she mailed her letter of resignation and her request for half her investment. The sign reading "Mom and Sis" had been painted and screwed into the wall above the front door, the business cards and receipts and crafters' shelf lease agreements were printed with the two names. Because of her cheapness, Mom kept the name as it was. Figured, too, that in this world, things being the way they are, when a thief came through, he — and it would be a he because, after all, men make up most of those who are thieves and other horrid types — he would be less likely to want to hold up a business with two names on it, thinking there would be more than one person in the store. She figures a crook would pass her right by in favor of confronting only half the staff at a place bearing a sign that fairly blared how it was occupied by just one: Village Barber, for instance. Or the Music Man. Or Bunny's Card Nook. Or Irene, the Queen of the Unseen.

Irene getting robbed. And maybe closing down. Now that would be just perfect.

Mom hates Irene, too, of course. Just because Irene is somebody other than Mom. And because she is somebody most people seemed to like. But Mom also hates what Irene did for a living. As had Rosie's nuns, Mom sees palm reading as one of Satan's pastimes. Predicting things. Knowing the future is something only to be done by God, not some quiet little woman sitting by herself at a half circle cut into a wall. Who did Irene think she was? Mom had asked herself that countless times over the years, starting with the Monday afternoon on which Irene had moved her things into the mall. Mom and Sis themselves were new enough — they'd only unlocked and raised their gate for the first time a month earlier — when Irene came by, lugging a big purple velvet-upholstered chair, and announced brightly, "I guess we're going to be mall-mates!" Sis loped over enthusiastically, said, "Put that down for a minute," and then shook Irene's hand with the jarring motion called for when jacking up a car. Sis asked, "What are you selling?" and Irene said, "Readings," and Sis asked, "Books?" and Irene answered, "Palms," and Sis asked, "Plants?" and Irene answered, "Palm readings," and held up her hand to illustrate that here, this is what I read. "Cool!" said Sis, to whom a palm reading sounded like fun, because she was a rather happy type to whom lots of things sounded like fun, including starting a brand-new business in a brand-new mall, as she also was doing at that bright and revving time. She gestured for Mom to come over, and Sis said, "Irene, this is Mom. Not my mom, I don't have my original mom, really, but a stepmom, though she is just as good as an original one, I've always said, but this Mom of the business here, she's Mom by name and you can call her that, she asks that everybody call her that, that's just how it is. Mom! Come on, Mom!"

Mom did not come forward. Just stayed behind a display of thickly knotted macramé plant hangers in deepening shades of orange polyester twine. She nodded a silent hello and then spoke, but only to Sis, saying, "Sis, I need help over here, right now," though she really did not. She just wanted Sis away from this woman who certainly had to be nuts. So after Sis said, "Well, good-bye for now, come and visit anytime," and then returned to Mom's side and asked, "What would you like me to do?" Mom answered, "I'd like you to stay the hell away from her."

If you looked in Irene's palm-reading book, you would learn that palmistry has been hated by people like nuns and Mom for ages, having been practiced in China and India as far back as three thousand years ago. If you asked Irene, she'd tell you she'd received her share of disparaging comments over the years — people poking their heads into her doorway to call her a witch. A charlatan. A sham. A joke. Now and then she'd get a few letters — unsigned, of course — from those who wanted to pray for her soul despite, they noted, its already being eternally damned. But they were once-in-a-while bumps that lessened in occurrence considerably once the mall began its slide and fewer shoppers took note of Irene's presence in the world. Mom's dislike of Irene, however, was ongoing. Daily. Began with and finished up each year, then started all over again, an unbroken thread of disapproval. The tiniest issue that had anything to do with Irene instantly escalated into a problem Mom dragged to mall management with the hopes of having Irene evicted. Back in the era of a crowded Orchard Mall, teenagers hung outside the palm reader on weekends, daring one another to go in for a try. Mom was worrying about shoplifting, as if any of those kids would have had interest in her miles of silk flower garlands or crocheted doilies starched to the strength of a steel beam. If she saw someone enter Irene's with an Orange Julius cup in hand, Mom would ring the office to alert the manager of the offense — a tenant allowing food and/or drink in a shop. Hers were piddly complaints that usually brought no response, especially not in the ten-month reign of the eighth mall manager, Louie Seligson, who became addicted to readings after his first one brought the great news that those two corresponding creases arcing around his Mount of Venus were a double lifeline, a second chance, marks representing a physical guiding power, a constant guardian capable of protecting him against the type of horrible medical calamities and accidents that might level anyone else. After learning this, and after becoming nearly unable to stop staring at this insurance policy literally etched into his right hand, Louie visited Irene every other day, excited, enthused, bearing first a pen and paper for writing down her pronouncements, then investing in a small tape recorder and setting up the stand for a microphone to capture every bit of her insight, and also to free his hands for additional examination. Since it was the mall manager angering Mom those times, there was nobody to call when she wanted to complain about preferential treatment given the tenant across the way by means of patronage. So she phoned all the way down to the main office in Baltimore, which acknowledged receipt of her complaints but, as she'd put it, "the world being the way it is," never did a thing to rectify the situation. Louie Seligson was gone in ten months, but because of a promotion stemming from his success in organizing events (in back-to-back weeks he'd managed to snag appearances by one of the Iran hostages and two of The Four Tops), not because of his visiting Irene. Even so, Mom afterwards stood in Bunny's doorway and boasted of connections with the management in Baltimore that she could use any time she pleased. To get rid of anyone. Any time at all. So you just watch out. And she looked over her shoulder to see if Irene in her half-circle cutout window down the hall was listening.

The minor chords of the theme from *The Godfather* are wobbling from the ceiling as Mom, still bundled in her little black woolen coat, is setting down her cooler of cola and un-locking the metal gate to her shop. It is already past lunchtime and she is only just opening. Next to her stands the newest mall manager, an optimistic, trout-shaped woman named Hannah Pomfret, fourteenth in the dynasty that had begun with some-one named Lawrence Block. Hannah appears to be of grade-school age, at the most had to have graduated from business school maybe yesterday, had taken over six months earlier and probably will be there for the remainder of the mall's life. And in what has to be an unknown bow to Lawrence Block, she bears a prim enthusiasm and dress code, attiring for success despite the failure moldering all around her, coming in early each day wearing a fine-quality-yet-on-her-helplessly-ill-fitting business suit and matching shiny high heels that clack with a sound close to painful as she makes her many fact-finding, idea-generating rounds throughout the mall. Hannah Pomfret is nodding and focusing intently as Mom is saying loudly, the vol-ume with which she always speaks, "Emergency. Car. It was so bad I had to rent one. Rent one! Mine will be in the shop for who knows how long, and what it'll cost me, I can't begin to imagine. Certainly ten times what I take in from this dead-end business. All I know is you can't fine me for opening late. I had no choice. I almost didn't get here at all. You're lucky I didn't get killed risking my life to get here in the snow. And for what? Who comes here anyhow?"

The mall has its policy. Each business is to be open 10:00 a.m. to 6:00 p.m. Monday through Saturday, Sunday optional in the decade since things really started to sink and closing time was switched from 10:00 p.m. There is a fine, $100 per offense. The goal is to keep all shops open consistently so customers can be confident their mall is ready and waiting for them at the posted hours. Since Orchard's press-released decision eighteen years ago to consolidate the locations of the thirteen remaining businesses from their scattered spaces in the mall's three streets to the mall's main thoroughfare, any penalties for late opening, or not opening at all, have not been strictly enforced. Management simply is grateful someone is paying rent and arriving at some point to turn on the lights.

"Don't worry, Mom," Hannah Pomfret says, using the tact necessary when addressing the occupant of a ledge. "I'm not here to fine you. I just saw you there and wanted to say hello."

"'Cause if you're going to fine me, I'm going straight over to the Affordable Attorney. I'll have a solid case in court. I'll go for harassment damages to a woman small business owner who had to pay to rent a car just to get to work at this ghost town of a hellhole. Really, I'm lucky I didn't kill myself trying to get here to keep your rules. If I had, just imagine — imagine how you'd feel."

"I have no problem with this, Mom," Hannah says, still calm despite Mom's starting her trip down the road to hysterics. "Just glad to see you, just wanted to say hey."

Hannah continues her walk. Mom being Mom, doesn't know when to quit. "Well, if you're thinking about fining me, don't — that's all I'm saying." She calls this out, and as she says the word "don't," she puts up her left hand as if to push the fine away. Moves it up just as Rosie, still sitting in a daze behind the half-circle cutout, focuses across the hall and catches sight of the hand. Of the palm. The palm in which she suddenly sees the image of a closet door. And then the door opening. And the dark floor. And high black rubber winter boots and low black winter loafers, then, behind them, a short row of black summer shoes neatly lined up, and, in back of those, a couple of empty plastic flowerpots, nested, and a sack of potting mix next to them, once opened and now closed with a metal twist tie colored the dusty green of lavender leaves. And, in back of that, in the far right-hand corner of the closet, she sees the last thing stored on that floor: a light-blue vase with a vine of soft pink flowers swirling up the side. And then the mall mezzanine zips back into view, nearly the exact place where Rosie is standing, only it is another day being shown, and a man is holding that same light-blue vase. He wears a maroon blazer with a small tag on the pocket, the name Durham written on it. He has the vase in his hands now as he looks from side to side and then at Mom, to whom he whispers, "I really think you have something here. And I can tell you this much: it's worth a whole lot of money."

6

"Who are you? What are you doing here?"

Rosie doesn't know the answer to either. Or even how she's gotten across the hall to this shop door, to this woman and her palm with the vase on it.

"Get away from me or I'll yell for help!"

Mom is warning this. To Rosie, meaning that Mom will have Hannah come and escort Irene back to her half-circle cutout. But Hannah is dozens of yards away, having clacked into the Music Man's shop and is busy there in another conversation as he plays "Black Magic Woman" softly on the piano organ, drowning out the church-organ version of "Annie's Song" drippingly filling up his senses from the overhead speakers. The mall's music still originates in Orchard's original eight-track system, a reality that keeps selections time-capsule dated and all too familiar to the tenants, who've had them drilled into their brains for decades. Instrumentals of hits by Bread, the Carpenters, the Kingston Trio, Englebert Humperdink and The Beatles play behind their daydreams. A violin version of the theme song from *Here Come the Brides* or *Family Affair* or *All in the Family* or *The Man From U.N.C.L.E.* An up-tempo version of Barry Manilow's "Weekend in New England" that wavers painfully from a particularly worn tape.

The wanderer's anthem "King of the Road" lurches into the cheery Coke ad "I'd Like to Teach the World to Sing" as Rosie lets the vision of the vase evaporate. She finds herself stalled a foot away from Mom, staring at Mom's palm, where she's seen the closet and the shoes and the vase and then the man, and has heard what he's said as clearly as if he were standing here now. The only feature that registers on the hand in front of her is what is known as a "waisted" thumb, skinny around the middle, the type belonging to someone who never fails to search for ulterior motives.

Rosie looks into Mom's face, pasty and, ironically, the shape of the boxes they put chocolates into each loving Valentine's Day. Mom uses no makeup except to draw a thin line in black above her top and below her bottom lashes, and continues that out from the far corners of her marbly little green eyes just enough to give the illusion they are larger and lifted. At least that is supposed to be the effect, according to the woman at the makeup counter at Steiger's department store back when there was still a Steiger's department store at the mall to put a makeup counter in. Mom has used the same brand of eyeliner all these many years, probably a fifteen or sixteen, one swipe and then another, both applied just after washing her face with grocery-store soap.

Unable to recall exactly how to walk, Rosie nonetheless focuses down the hall, makes her legs move and manages to get past the end of Mom's shop and escape through the next open door she can find, the same one Dennis uses to get to the big white letters in the storage garage behind Cinema III. She shoves it forward and makes the long walk past the pay phones that, in the days before every other person on earth had a cell phone, kids monopolized to call other kids or to arrange for rides home or to relay lies to sleepy parents who just might be groggy enough to not fight the request for another few hours at the mall when they'd really be spent at a party in the basement of some classmate whose parents were out of town. She moves past the shining fire extinguisher and the woven fire hose folded so neatly in its glass box, and the big hammer that you would use to break the glass to access that hose only in case of emergency. Past the bulletin board empty except for the poster prematurely announcing a strawberry shortcake special at the Tax Man's church three months later, and, on Hannah Pomfret/Orchard Mall stationery, a letter to all tenants reminding them that in the hope of creating a "buzz" (she used that word and gave it boldface), flea markets now will be held every single Saturday, not just once a month. And this weekend's flea market will have a new feature:

SATURDAY!
APPRAISAL DAY!
APPRAISALS OF ANTIQUES
BY GENUINE LICENSED APPRAISERS.

$5 FOR FIRST ITEM APPRAISED,
$1 FOR EACH CONSECUTIVE ONE!

YOU NEVER KNOW WHAT YOU HAVE HIDDEN IN YOUR CLOSET!

That last statement is true. You don't know. Even if you are Mom and have an exact written inventory of your neatly organized closet. You still don't, really. You don't know that something in there will be worth a whole lot of money. Don't know it will help you right out of the financial jam nobody but you knows you currently are in. Would have no idea. Ever, maybe. Might go to your grave not knowing.

Unless somebody with the power to know the future tells you.

On this first day of spring, on this first day of whatever is going on, Rosie somehow has become someone with this power. She had determined where to send Sheila — Sheila, that was the name Rosie heard coming from the woman at the green-sided house — first thing this morning, it had started with Sheila needing to go to Margaret, and then had continued with Ed Horrigan and the foreign little woman who was starting to turn the gears of getting back in touch, then it had happened again, with the guy — what was his name? The maintenance-type guy on whose palm Rosie saw reality she knew to be absolutely, wholly, totally and unmistakably real, both about the pain of his past and the huge hurt of today's news that Irene has gotten married. All these things are fact to her now. She knows them just as she knows the contents of some stranger's closet. Just as she does the thoughts of the woman awaiting Sheila, the one phoning Ed, the man striking Dennis — that is his name — the Irene that Dennis loves more than anything, Rosie knows these are facts. Doesn't know how she knows them, but she knows they are true. Just doesn't know what to do with them. Or, on that first day of spring, with herself.

7

At one point in the late 1980s, the eleventh manager of Orchard Mall came up with the idea to turn one of the mall's vacant "streets" into an arts community.

This man, Gerry Donnelly, had an interest in all things creative. Painted many of the mall's announcement signs himself rather than relying on computer printers. Was an enthusiastic amateur wood-carver in his leisure hours, filled the inside pocket of his Harris-tweed blazers with plain little surfboard-shaped letter openers he fashioned from a light-stained wood that showed off the grain, and he handed them out good-naturedly to business associates and tenants and shoppers he often stopped for input on how Orchard could better recreate Main Street.

Gerry asked that question despite knowing full well that at this point in the history of American retailing, malls had pretty much decimated Main Streets nationwide, so why would anyone wish to copy them in that state? He knew the effect personally from his trips every morning from his home in Ludlow, over the bridge and past the little town common that marked the official entrance to downtown Indian Orchard, once Main Street edged with pharmacy, bank, greengrocer, butcher, baker, clothing store, cobbler, stationer, pet store, barber, dentist, doctor, most of the people and services and stores that Orchard had sucked out of existence. Most of the storefronts had been vacant for decades. A state representative had taken over the greengrocer's as his local headquarters, and kept that up pretty nicely with flower boxes at the window and both American and POW flags waving. A few empty storefronts down, a Tae Kwan Do studio's window — formerly that of the stationer — was decorated by a poorly toupee-ed mannequin dressed in white pants and belted top, and sunken to one knee as if executing some move. A few blank buildings down from that, a pizza place located in the former local branch of First Bank specialized in the deal of a slice and a can for just $1.50, handed to you via one of the windows through which, back when you were in college, you might have received your first bankbook from a teller. From the small space in which the cobbler long ago reattached the loose tongue in your dress shoes, the tiny Indian Orchard Chamber of Commerce opened only for the monthly meeting of the four or so members, but kept continuously lit its sign painted with the slogan "Picture Your Business in Indian Orchard," something really no one could or wanted to do.

Within the victors' category, the malls that thrived were those offering an indoor world somehow all the more fantastic than the outside one. Zoos, pony rings, skating rinks, wave pools, roller-coasters, paddleboat canals, paintball mazes. Just plain being indoors once had been the draw at Orchard. With its parent company preferring to invest in construction of new malls rather than renovations — including of this historic one — ingenuity was called for. And that's how the Art Lane came to be.

A promotion grant was sought from the state's arts commission, a quarter of it won, publicity spread with affordable rents stressed and advertised to artists who turned up to tour the cavernous spaces on the mall's Pleasant Street, just past the other side of the cinemas. They walked by the empty bins in the former Strawberries Records, through the wordless aisles of

Waldenbooks-competitor B. Dalton, around the now-dark hexagonal glass display case that had been the bejeweled centerpiece of Kay Jewelers. Minus the rustic crates for their Levi's and the bust-only mannequins for their nursing bras and their clear plastic feet no longer wearing Italian sandals, the featureless all-white heads that once wore wash-and-dry shags, and the metal cages empty of purebred Schnauzers, the Lodge, Great Expectations, Pappagallo, Ava Gabor Wigs, The Puppy Pen all easily could become studios, classrooms. Galleries even. The main mall access doors to gargantuan Sears, it was noted, could be unlocked for those who needed virtually unlimited space to create enormous murals.

Many of the creative types who came to scope out the stores admitted they were averse to the idea of being in a mall, a place so commercial and modern and screaming suburbia, far on the other side of the invisible tofu curtain that separated the hardscrabble blue-collar Indian Orchard area from the hip college towns to the north. But none of the creative types could argue that the price wasn't right, and a modest but greatly appreciated group of five artists and craftspeople soon signed leases that had them moved in and their latest projects well underway by the night of the Art Lane open house — by invitation only — for the city's elite. The politicians. The prominent businesspeople. The all-important bankers. And, of course, TV and radio celebrities. Orchard's time-weary tenants mixed cynically with these big names, standing next to them as they selected their smoked cheese cubes from the buffet, or ordered their Dewar's at the cash bar, or, as was an awestruck Bunny's experience, watched them simply crank an extra sheet of paper towels in the restroom, as did Channel 23's Kiki Cutler after she looked into the mirror to re-apply lipstick to a face that Bunny previously had seen only on the twelve-inch screen of her bedroom Quasar.

The Art Lane is where Rosie ends up that first day, the vision on Mom's palm sending her shooting down the hall and then back out again to consider returning to the half-circle cutout, but then taking the left at the Town Common. She finds the farthest one of what used to be called husband benches, due to their providing seating while wives shopped, back when wives shopped here and husbands had to wait. She sits between two plastic palms and stares at her reflection in the windows of the space that once housed Lane Bryant and its large supply of clothing for large women and that now is the studio of Bethany Colrain, Weaver of Wearable Art. That's what her sign reads. Not unlike Irene, Queen of the Unseen. A name, an occupation. A pronouncement. A fact. Rosie stares at the cones of red yarn stacked artfully into a pyramid on the other side of the glass and wonders what words might come after her name after this day is through. She focuses on her reflection. She doesn't think she looks any different than she had when she found the keys on her porch that morning — had that been just this morning? — but something has changed for sure.

Back on Main Street, Mom is at her desk, eyes on the three customers walking down her aisle one. She is watching their hands as they pick up items, put them down. She is making sure the mugs or refrigerator magnets or booties are not being slipped into coat pockets or purses. She stands and cranes her neck and yells, "That's them," just as there come big laughs from the three women who have found what they'd asked for — the newest addition to Mom and Sis's inventory, spookily real one-sided toddler-sized dolls meant to be stood facing into a corner, where they appear to be counting for hide-and-seek or punished for some infraction. A month ago, Mom first displayed a few of the dolls in the window, and, in the week since the college student who sewed them delivered an eerie trio of three siblings, they'd sold fast.

Satisfied that the women are not shoplifters, Mom sits back and picks up her brush to apply more white highlights to all the O's in the legend "REMEMBER THAT GOD LOVES YOU NO MATTER WHAT TERRIBLE THINGS YOU DO." It is far from poetic, but it sells each time she hangs one up.

"Whaddaya want — I don't have all fucking day," she snarls at half volume when she looks up and sees Rosie standing in the doorway, Rosie having managed to uproot herself from the husband bench and find her way back to Pleasant Street and to Mom and Sis's, where she will say what she feels needs to be known.

"Whaddaya want? And whaddaya doing in there?" Mom nods across the hall, where the half-circle cutout is lit, its curtain pulled aside, but the half-circle cutout is vacant. "Where is she? That Eye-rene. They finally lock her up? Staying closed nine days now without permission. That's an offense here, you know. I'm counting. And I have connections. A big fine will be coming her way."

Rosie nods. Shakes her head to erase that. Clears her throat. Clasps her hands. "I didn't know. I'm just a friend of Irene's. I'm Rosie Pilch. I'm filling in for her. I don't mean to bother you, but . . ."

Mom snorts as, in three little swipes of the paintbrush, she creates the dove of the all-knowing, all-compassionate Holy Spirit flying above the reassurance of unconditional love from the heavens.

"Filling in. Ha. Like there's any business to handle."

"I won't take your time. I just, well . . . "

"Well?"

What can she do? Rosie jumps in, says it fast: "You have a vase. It's in your closet."

Mom continues to paint. Rosie increases the pace of her information. "In the closet that when you open it first are your black winter boots and next to them the loafers." Mom looks up at this point, eyes narrowing. "The low-heeled ones, they're black, too. And in back of that is a row of shoes you only wear in the summer." Mom now puts down the brush and slowly rises, her hands balling into fists at her sides. Rosie continues, "And behind the shoes there are three, maybe four, but probably three, there are three pots all one inside the other. Next to that a black bag of potting soil that you've opened but closed back up with a green wire thing. And behind that, behind that is the vase. A blue vase. Light blue . . . " The words are ticker-taping from Rosie as she adds how a vine of pink flowers crawls up one side of the vase, then she asks if Mom knows what she is talking about. Does she?

"What I know is I'm going to have you arrested, you little shit — breaking into my home and then coming here to brag about it?" Mom asks in a voice like a metal trash can being dragged to the curb. She reaches for the phone, which sits cutely in a phone-shaped bird's nest of woven twigs.

"Listen to me." Rosie is whispering now, and she takes a step closer to Mom's desk. "I've been nowhere near your house. I don't even know you, never mind where you live. I'm not here to upset you. I just know this — about the vase. Don't ask me how I know, because I don't know how I do, but I know it. About the vase. And I'm telling you to take that vase and bring it here on appraisal day. Coming up. There's a sign in the hall. You won't be sorry. I just wanted to say that. To tell you to bring the vase in for that."

"That is, that was, my great-aunt's vase . . . " Mom is angrier, yet speaking more slowly now.

"Bring it in," Rosie tells her. "To the mall. Saturday. Appraisal Day. Show it to the man named Durham."

The three shoppers are at the register now, two of them holding one doll apiece, the third clutching a pair of pink-skirted twins.

"There's no discount if you buy two, ya know," Mom warns without turning to them. She is still locking eyes with Rosie, who sees safety in numbers and takes the opportunity to turn and walk out Mom's door, across the hall and through Irene's door, where she grabs her bag and coat and shuts the curtain and the light, closes the door, quickly pulls down the gate, fumbles, turns the key and closes Irene's shop and, too bad about the rules, goes home very early.

8

This is home: a little brick cottage on a quiet side street in Ludlow, built forty-two years ago from plans ordered when the man and woman who would become the original owners noticed a sketch in the Sunday paper and aaahhhed at the sweet details of the front door with a storybook rounded top, over that the little peak with the tiny window, the brick arch that linked the one-car garage to the house, and, though this wasn't on the sketch because, on the sketch, the little brick cottage at that point existed hanging in white space with only a few foundation plantings to anchor it to the planet, a municipal golf course for a backyard, all that open space and green and quiet, even the little electric cars that drove across it softly humming as they delivered many neatly dressed men and a handful of pastelish clutches of women from manicured tee to manicured tee.

On this first day of spring, despite the snow yet to fully melt, there are many such people behind her house enjoying the day in this manner. Rosie does not play golf, so she holds no envy as she parks her car in the little brick garage and zombies herself into the little brick cottage, eyes straight ahead, not wanting to see anything else unexpected. Maybe it hadn't been such a good idea to drive herself home — she can't recall a minute of the fifteen-minute trip — but it is done. All Rosie knows is that she is back some place familiar, and that she has to find out what is wrong with her. There definitely has to be something off, some illness to explain the things she is seeing and knowing. It would be far easier to accept a physical problem than the scary reality that she could actually know people's many secret privacies, including those that have happened long ago. And those that have yet to occur.

She locks the door and crosses the kitchen, and in the small front room goes to the shelf next to the fireplace and gets out the huge fat medical book that she'd bought after her dear same-birth-month-and-year cousin Al went just like that in 1990. This was how everybody was putting it at the time — "Did you hear about Al? He went just like that." Just like that. Rosie had heard this in the background like a sad-truth litany murmured in the emergency room, in the funeral home, in her own home afterwards, just like that, just like that, isn't it something, isn't it scary, that you can be young and healthy and in your prime and you can go, just like that? Rosie had wondered what the "that" was. She had asked this of the doctor in the emergency room, the doctor who was the first person to say the "just like that," only he also used some Latin words, something about the heart, that being fitting, as Al had held within his chest a fine and golden one. But deeds and demeanor end up being nothing when you stack them against heredity. The medical book had cost her $38.95, and she'd only flipped through it a few times after Al had gone. The unpronounceable terms and dissected views overwhelmed her, and she had shut it hard, finally realizing what was done was done, just like that, and there was no need any more to look up what might have caused the loss of Al, because Al was gone for good and that was that.

But on this afternoon, Rosie thanks herself for never having tossed the book in the pile she assembles for the library book sale each May. She grasps a thickness of alphabetized pages and jumps ahead to look under *H*. For hallucinations.

Which are what she suspects she's been having, causing her to suddenly be able to see into one woman's future, one man's past, another man's present, and another woman's closet.

"An apparent perception of an external object when no such object is present. Typically associated with psychiatric disorders." After only a single encounter, Rosie knows Mom would agree with that definition. "Causes also may include but not be limited to neurological damage, seizure and sleep disorders, drug reactions, substance abuse, grief, stress, as well as metabolic, endocrine and infectious diseases."

Rosie has experienced some of those things over time. Who hasn't? Grief, stress, sleep disorders, those are as inescapable in modern-day everyday life as phone calls from telemarketers. She reads on. About how deaf people can have musical hallucinations, of all things. How those in sensory deprivation, like explorers and hostages, can have visions. And how, in states of mourning and stress, voices "heard" can provide calm and assurance.

Well, there's no doubt Rosie has been stressed. Specifically, for the past eight months, since rumors began bubbling and First Bank bigwigs were visiting from Boston with a scary frequency. Their coming around never was good news. The contingent of four to six normally made bi-monthly trips out to Springfield, and over the years returned home to make a string of atrocious decisions, including the early-nineties uniforms with striped ascots that gave a dated flight-attendant look to the staff. When they started poking around last fall, it was with a trio of accountants. Then, four weeks ago, came the word. And the six free sessions with the therapist who ordered Rosie to make that list that had helped her, and who also had directed her to get out of the house, the results of which aren't looking good only one day into that exercise.

She hears him again the next day, the second day of spring, as she sits locked up in the house once again. More confused than she's ever been. She hears him, and she forces herself to get up and go outside. Gets no farther than the garage. Gets into the car. Shivers there for maybe ten minutes. Doesn't know where to go. Scot is on his third day of a business retreat in the Adirondacks, wearing a harness attached to overhead ropes while walking blindfolded along a skinny little steel cable fifteen feet off the ground while co-workers fifteen feet below call out encouragement, the whole exercise meant to illustrate how we are all walking along skinny little steel cables every day of our lives, not knowing what is ahead or whether we can make it another step, and very much in need of good words from those who are there to catch us should we fall. For purposes of immersion in the power of the retreat, he will be unreachable during this five-day period, except for notification of dire emergencies. Rosie has the emergency number somewhere in a general e-mail containing Scot's itinerary. But she doesn't know how to name what is going on, so how would she phrase it over a phone line? She'd had the same problem when she thought to call Irene's cell phone the night before. But she'd barreled through that simply because she thought that if anyone could help, it would be Irene. Rosie dialed, only to have Irene's phone ring and ring. Rosie knew nothing about Canada, or phone use there. Did cell phones work once you went over the border of a whole other country? Going online via the same iBook G4 Scot had been using the night they met, passed down to her after he recently met a savings goal that allowed the long-awaited purchase of a paper-thin MacBook Air. Rosie called up an e-mail form and wrote Irene a single line of congratulations on her marriage ("Congratulations on your marriage!"), followed by "Please call me ASAP!!!!!" and a reminder of her phone number. Rosie checked incessantly for a reply, including through the night, which was easy to do because she hardly slept. No reply. Around dawn the thought occurred as to how much Rosie might expect to be online during her own honeymoon, and at night. She scrolled through lists of friends, family, found no one in whom she'd feel comfortable confiding the events of the past day. Most of her friends are from the bank. They are unemployed now, too, but the "too" no longer applies to Rosie, as, thanks to Irene, she has a job now — if she wants it. So how could she call any of these people and complain? However strange it is, she has a job, and they do not. Irene would have been the one she'd have run to. With no luck there yet, she looks out her garage door and thinks — maybe one of the neighbors?

She gazes at her neighborhood. To the right stands the white-sided Cape occupied by the Cormiers, a couple seen only twice a day — first at 9:15 a.m., when Mr. Cormier helps Mrs. Cormier onto the Senior Services van that collects her for her ride to elder day care, and second when Mr. Cormier is back out there at 3:15, a parent at a bus stop waiting for his wife's return and the *beep beep beep beep* of the van as it backs into the drive. The Cormiers' extreme hearing loss makes even the simplest back-and-forth about the weather a great challenge. Without typing out the details of the previous day, how could she relay to them what is happening to her? She x-es them off her list. Considers those living in the house to the left of Rosie's front yard. There, Maggie Yee is testing out her second week of life as the mother of twins. Sure, the doctors had told her way ahead of time, and she'd certainly seen the four huge feet on the ultrasounds, heard a pair of rapid don't-bother-me-I'm-very-busy-in-here heartbeats on the monitor, had grown to a size far larger than any of her friends had ever come close to while expecting, yet Maggie still was pretty speechless to find two babies in her arms. From the driveway of that suddenly full house, Grant Yee exits each morning at 5:10, immediately and secretly grateful for the oasis his hated insurance-adjuster job now is. And, just as he leaves, his delighted mother-in-law slides into his spot on the driveway, backseat full of casseroles and folded laundry and an overnight case, on the great chance her help is needed for more than just the daytime hours. Maggie Yee is normally a good ear, but right now is in her own world of shock.

Across the street from Rosie's stands a silent home. Big realty for-sale sign on the lawn. Not one of those skinny metal deals, this is a signpost for which a deep hole had been dug, and it has been set deep into the ground, a wooden arm extending from it, and from that, on wrought-ironish-looking chains, sways the sign that invites you to call Julie Dias for a personal showing of the two-bedroom, one-and-a-half-bath brick bungalow that has been empty since the previous fall, all dark and unadorned throughout Christmas even, all because the Rileys just for the heck of it last summer had taken a tour of one of the aircraft-carrier-sized homes on one of the newly created roads scarring the hill leading to Three Rivers, and even though they could not really afford it, they bought it and moved in before unloading this place on Rosie's street, and now they somehow are carrying two mortgages, and can you imagine the stress of that as they are not rich people. The for-sale sign doesn't tell you that, gives only the number of rooms (six) and baths (one and a half) and the phone digits for the smiling, curly-haired woman who awaits your call.

There's a rabble of life to the left of that house, across the street on an angle from Rosie's cottage. From that little ranch come and go the Mintyks — quiet longtime widower father Rudy and the collection of three very noisy teens who have recently acquired a fleet of rusting autos with plastic tarps for most of the windows and female silhouettes stuck to the back bumpers, and have turned their late mother's once-showplace of a yard into a grassless rutted parking lot. For the span of a few months after Al went just like that, Rosie would come home to find Rudy Mintyk already home from his day mixing veal loaf at Blue Seal, and clipping her hedges or cutting her grass, things he'd never done in his own yard, and she'd approach him to thank him and say it wasn't necessary, but he'd shake his head and, over any whirring or motor roar, would shout, "I know how you feel," but would not look at Rosie as he announced that, and he'd keep going with his gift of yard work. Rosie always had the feeling that if she gave Rudy Mintyk more than half a smile, he would give her his whole life. And, though he was very handy, a crowded, instant family with someone to whom she was not interested in giving more than half a smile was not a life she wanted. So, on the morning of the second day of spring, she keeps away from Rudy and from the rest of her neighbors, and once in the car for good, keeps her hands tight on the steering wheel until she removes the right one, the one that holds all the possibility, and uses it to put the key into the ignition.

9

The Affordable Attorney hasn't always been that.

At one point she was The High-Priced Attorney, though her sign didn't say that. Back in that life, the sign for her firm chanted a whopping seven names of varying lengths and ethnic origins, none of them hers. But on the Yellow Pages ad and on the business cards and the letterhead, there she was, alphabetical order making her eleventh of the twelve other lawyers in the firm. Maria Nunes, attorney-at-law.

Her specialty was commercial bankruptcy. Her clients were the many small and large businesses that found themselves in much trouble, who required her help in extricating themselves from commitments that often resulted in one of those familiar newspaper ads that shouted, "OUR FINAL DAYS — EVERYTHING MUST GO." To meet with her, the ill-fated clients had to go to the mall. Which was where Maria's firm was located, its management having been captivated by the modern concept of everything you need being under one roof. "It's the way of the future," the senior partners enthused at the employee meeting in 1970 that announced the move from the Main Street in Indian Orchard to a newly created fake indoor one on the edge of the suburbs.

The firm relocated to a modest-sized storefront next to Thom McAn and then angled around to an enormous space that was spicy-aired Hickory Farms. So you were fixed when it came to shoes for either gender, and all you could eat from the bottomless sample dishes of dried banana chips or long trays of constantly restocked salami triangles speared with toothpicks. For a larger meal, you had a greater selection of eateries than you ever had within walking distance in downtown Indian Orchard: the Food Court and its dozen selections of tempura, Greek salads, eggplant parm, tacos and, of course, all-American fare, was just on the other side of the fountains. And you also had nature — the firm was close enough to the Fountain Court that the ever-splashing waters could be heard at the firm's doorway, where a pair of park benches were situated for relaxing, and the employees-only entrance at the back of the space opened to a thick stretch of woods that separated the rear section of Orchard's parking lot from a quiet neighborhood. And do we even have to mention that those employees who never had time for shopping now just needed to step out the door for anything they needed?

All this was touted at length by the senior partners on the first day of operation at Orchard. There was applause in which Maria did not join. She kept her arms folded across her chest. She hadn't battled her way through law school to end up in a shopping center. She saw it as demeaning and, after several rounds of the champagne toast, finally said so.

Her superiors only smiled. Told her to never mind, this was the start of something great. She — they'd — all see. Malls were the future. The firm was ahead of its time!

First to leave in the long succession that started when the mall's popularity ended was the specialist in criminal trials and driving while intoxicated. Then went the firm's man for personal injury. Followed by the one who took his knowledge of wills, trusts and estates. Then the woman who was the expert in health care and elder law. And the guy whose catchall title had been point man for "counseling on most legal matters, but specializing in auto accidents, motorcycle accidents, pedestrian accidents, bus accidents, slip and falls, liquor liability, dog and animal attacks, workers' compensation, defective products and amusement park injuries."

New hires did not happen, so with each departure the workload for the remaining attorneys increased, as did their shares of the rent. Sitting at the Orchard Mall Fountain Court one day eighteen years ago, just before the water began the little programmed dance it did exactly on the half hour, Maria started considering a way out — starting a new practice, one that would assist regular people, especially regular female people, especially regular female people who had been on the bad end of things.

"Women do the majority of shopping for their families, so I'm here among many of the people I want to help," she told the *Western Massachusetts Bar Review* when a reporter came to do a story on why she'd remained, the one person who was the only evidence a law firm had ever called the mall home. Maria said she liked the open-door setting in which to concentrate on her new areas of concentration: the family-centered issues of abuse prevention, adoptions, alimony, custody, shared custody, paternity, restraining orders, support enforcement, guardianship, divorce, and the increasingly alternate resolution of mediation. And, though she'd never have predicted it (if you wanted a psychic, you'd have to go down the hall), she feels at home after all these years, here on the little avenue containing a barber, an optometrist, and, yes, a palm reader. They've become her friends and sometimes her clients. The tenants and the management like having a lawyer in the mall, someone who lends prestige and a sense of professionalism to the gathering of shops. And, according to Irene, Queen of the Unseen, the lawyer has a heart line that begins high on Jupiter; she is someone who should be looked up to. But Irene knew that even before she opened Maria's palm.

Like many of the tenants, Maria comes for a reading once a month. Her day is the last Thursday, just before she pays herself and plans her weekend by opening the *Daily News* to the Weekend section and making a list of the most interesting events — plays, concerts, book readings, cooking classes, a Halloween-season tour of the old graveyard you drive past a billion times without knowing any of the fascinating stories literally lying there.

Irene, Queen of the Unseen, saw that enthusiasm and general life interest in her, though anybody would have been able to spot it easily.

When Rosie settles into the chair at the half-circle cutout that second day at the mall, what she sees is different. Sure, the Maria who floats toward her in a flowing linen wrap she'd picked up in Springfield last fall at the annual Mattoon Street Arts Festival seems energetic as she introduces herself, tells Rosie how much she loves Irene and hopes she'll return soon, then breathlessly asks Rosie if she's ever heard a throat singer — a group of them all the way from Tibet are to play at UMass tonight, and Maria has an extra ticket. She proffers the ticket between thumb and first finger, palm facing Rosie, who for first time sees another Maria, the one who sits at her desk and stares at the piles of paperwork for foreclosures and bankruptcies. The same clients who years ago had come for her assistance in the legal side of buying a house or starting a business are now unable to pay their bills. Yes, this is a lawyer's day, but there are so many of these kinds of clients lately, and no sign of things turning. Rosie sees that it is painful for Maria to drive to work past so many of the for-sale signs on homes, some of them homes of her clients, and then, as she rolls past the little town common that marks the official entrance to downtown Indian Orchard, all the for-rent signs on a street once edged with pharmacy, bank, greengrocer, butcher, baker, clothing store, cobbler, stationer, pet store, barber, dentist, doctor, most of the people and services and stores that Orchard had long ago sucked out of existence. Rosie sees in Maria's palm how her hand had lifted to wave at the state representative as that morning he hung his American and POW flags outside his storefront, the signal that he was in and ready to for any visits by constituents who might come in to register their concerns and avail themselves of the free coffee he was about to brew. The Tae Kwon Do studio was dim, as was the pizza place, but the Chamber's window was optimistically lit, as it always was day and night, for member morale. Rosie sees Maria trying to keep her eyes on the road and her mind off how different this drive once was. How not long ago, it seems, she'd raised her hand to wave to the greengrocer arranging his wares into an edible mosaic, to the stationer setting out the sandwich board that announced the addition of a color copier to her printing options, to the long-ago co-workers she'd park next to, then walk with to the Main Street office that still might be in business if it weren't for Orchard Mall.

Maria now goes to the big office supply store — or sends Dennis there — if she needs a color copy of something. The vegetables in her refrigerator come from the big food outlet — actually called that — Food Outlet — next to the big office supply store. And as she drives down the real Main Street, she can't even glance next to the former pet store, to the granite-fronted vacant storefront that had housed the law firm that had thought it was such a great idea to move to the mall.

"I see you going back from where you came."

Rosie's voice jars Maria back to the here and now. She's still holding the ticket to the throat singers. She's yet to learn the name of this woman seated in Irene's window. She takes a fast breath when she considers what this woman just said. Maria had been only three weeks old when her parents had brought her to America. How could this woman know she was from somewhere else and not, like so many in the area, a generation or two removed? How could this woman know how much Maria yearns to go back to Portugal, but there always is work to keep her here. Always work. Maybe after all this craziness with all the sad clients. Maybe after that calms down.

"How do you know?" she asks Rosie, who answers, "I just know."

10

For any of the tenants who need them, Bunny's cards are free, chits she accumulates to spend when the time comes. Irene had done the same with her readings, but when it came to looking at Bunny's palm, she did so with nothing expected in return. Bunny was Irene's closest friend at Orchard, though not her oldest. They didn't have the shared bond of holding leases dating back to when Nixon was bombing Hanoi and those auditioning to play Santa didn't require a CORI check. They hadn't shared the thrilling early years, the customer complaints about the lack of parking, the grumblings from those waiting in long lines, meeting the many new staffers hired throughout the mall to prevent the great exhaustion at the end of the day from nothing but work, rather than from uninterrupted boredom. Bunny had signed her lease in leaner times, as recently as when Bill Clinton was indignantly repeating that he did not have sexual relations with that woman. Bunny was to the dead mall what a seminarian is to the Roman Catholic Church. A quizzical presence. New blood. New energy. New hope. Plus, in a retail setting, new merchandise. Hence, a new source of customers. The possibility that a couple more shoppers might walk through the doors next to the Flaming Pit because they found themselves in need of a sympathy card or they wanted to tell somebody they were "Just thinking of you!"

"I don't know, I've always wanted a card store, and with the kids out of the house, and with the low price of rents here, when I started looking around for space, I really couldn't pass it up." Bunny had explained this to each tenant when she came around on her moving-in day bearing free samples of last year's model of outdated three-for-a-dollar greeting cards that would be her bread and butter.

"I don't know, always wanted a card store," she repeated to Irene after she'd made the sixteen steps to the half-circle cutout window and offered her a selection of birthday cards that contained a spinner to make them suitable for anyone, age one to sixteen. "But you probably already knew that." Bunny added this and gave a goofy eye-rolling look, like how silly was it to be telling information to someone who, after all, was the Queen of the Unseen.

"I don't know, always wanted a card store," she repeats to Rosie that second day Rosie comes to the mall and Bunny rings the bell, re-introducing herself and explaining herself and then finally asking where has Irene gone. But she does so with a wink and a grin that tells Rosie she already knows, Bunny being among the safest of places to store any of your information. Sharing a secret with her is like driving it into a secure parking garage that has one of those rows of forks built into the tar that will rip into its tires should it try to leave.

Often when Rosie stopped in to say hi to Irene, Bunny was coming in or going out, and Rosie would greet her and then would wonder who'd name an infant Bunny, then would figure the name had to have been something else to start with. Bunella? Bunnina? Irene never used any other name, only Bunny, when she mentioned to Rosie that she and Bunny were going to the Cape for the weekend or that while Irene was going to her brother's for Christmas, Bunny had volunteered to come by Irene's house each night and morning to pull closed and then pull open Irene's blinds for the illusion of a living soul inside.

"It's good that you have the store you always wanted," Rosie says to Bunny, hoping to make a start toward the topic most on her mind. "I didn't grow up wanting to do this, of course."

Another half smile. "Irene thought you'd be great as a palm reader. She told me she couldn't think of a better person to leave this to." On the word "this," Bunny sweeps her arm in an arc, like the five hundred square feet were some kind of game-show prize.

Rosie leans in. Thinks about how to say it. Then, in a whisper, simply does: "Do you think she left me anything else?"

Bunny tilts her head. "I don't think so. You mean like inventory?"

"Well, not exactly . . . "

"Because, you know, she doesn't really sell anything here. She'd thought about that once, maybe notepads in which you could jot the reading she'd just told you, but then she worried that people might come back and wave the pages in her face when the things didn't happen. Because you know they weren't going to happen." Here she smiles again. "The rest of us, we're just hoping to get rid of our stock over the next nine months and make a clean break. I know I'm not placing another order. Which is a sad thing. But, hey, it's reality. This certainly isn't the Mall of America."

"I'm not thinking stuff so much," Rosie says while brushing non-existent dust from the counter beneath the half-circle cut-out. "Not like merchandise. But maybe she left me what I'd need to know to do this kind of work."

"Hey, it's no big secret," Bunny says, even though she is lowering her voice like it indeed might be. "That's why she didn't do the notepads. We all know Irene couldn't predict what was for lunch even when she'd packed it herself. You really don't need to know anything to do this. You know how she put it — be nice to them, send them away hoping for something better. Isn't that what we all want? From anybody?"

Bunny has a point, but this isn't the time to get into philosophy. Rosie just answers, "But do you think she knew what she was doing — do you, do you think sitting here gave her any, any, you know, powers?"

"Right." Bunny follows that with a little "Ha" noise.

"I'm not kidding. Do you — do you think that could be possible?"

"This is just for fun, Rosie. You know that." Bunny says this with the gentle voice you'd use when telling a child that a fairy tale is only that. "Because Irene did — she had fun with it. Enjoyed it, and people enjoyed coming here. She would have stayed the last six months, to the bitter end, if it wasn't for love. You know how that goes, right? She told me you're engaged. Or practically." Bunny glances at Rosie's vacant left ring finger. "Don't worry about what to do here. You'll be fine. You don't need to have any special, what would you call them (here she moves her hands in a wiggly, spell-casting effect) powers." And she makes the sound again. "Ha."

Rosie takes and holds the kind of deep breath requested annually by her mammographer. Then she lets it out and says, "But, well, the thing is, I think I do. Have, you know, powers."

11

Scot is not around. This kind woman Bunny is. Is right in front of her. Correction — she is next to her now. No longer at the half-circle cutout, but behind it, next to Rosie, pouring tea from a pot, chamomile made with the actual teeny little chamomile flowers, a dried store-bought brand labeled Slumberland sold in a tin cylinder with a label in the shape of a puffy-topped bed, served in a green pot with a thicket of lilies of the valley growing up its sides.

Bunny doesn't want to knock Rosie out, simply to calm her, and this is the only non-caffeinated tea in the collection Irene kept on the lower shelf of the lamp stand. She wants to calm Rosie, whose story she is believing, because stranger things certainly have happened — not to anyone Bunny personally knows, but Bunny has the enormous blessing of an open mind, and doesn't even the Bible say something about everyone having different gifts, including prophecy? That gift could be Rosie's. Why not? So when Rosie says, "I'm seeing things," Bunny lets her go on. Doesn't know what she is talking about at first, but lets her continue. "I saw this woman's sister. In her hand. Like it was a little movie. Can you understand what I'm saying?" Rosie stares into Bunny's eyes right then with such intensity Bunny rolls her chair back a few inches. "And the woman who wants to phone Ed. The one that Ed guy down the hall is mooning over. Like Dennis for I —" Rosie stops at the first letter of Irene's name, hangs her head. She is holding people's private information. Private. "Maybe I shouldn't have said that." Bunny doesn't respond except to roll her chair forward, then back into place, and to pour more tea. She hadn't known Rosie's first customer, so the things Rosie says about her mean nothing, really. But Bunny knows Ed, and because Bunny is the keeper of so many of the tenants' secrets, this is when she begins to believe. How many times has Ed wandered in, supposedly to pick up a birthday card, and leaned against the sympathy rack for the better part of an hour while telling her how impossible it is to forget the little foreign woman in the little foreign house in the little foreign country? Dennis is the kicker. Bunny flashes to the Flaming Pit six years ago, the after-work drinks celebrating her birthday. Everyone there. Including Dennis, who orbited Bunny's part of the lounge for a good hour before she was free of chatters and well-wishers, which was when he sat down. Dennis looked over to the fireplace, where Irene was trying to interpret a Dylan lyric for the Music Man, and whispered into Bunny's right ear with the economy of a telegram, "I am in love with Irene. I have been since the first time I saw her. In 1970 — thirty-four years ago now. Please don't tell her."

Bunny said, of course, "What?" but Dennis, finally emptied of the need to tell somebody — and trustworthy Bunny was the perfect somebody — had returned his gaze to the fireplace. Finished the last two slugs of his beer. Got up and walked past Irene and out the door. Six years Bunny has kept that secret. Has honored the request. She knows Irene had been very fond of Dennis, but she never had given a hint of any additional interest. And now it is forty years and Irene is gone and married. Rosie is continuing — "And that Mom" — she gestures across the hall — "I could see into her closet, Bunny. Her closet." Here Bunny shakes her head just because the idea of seeing into anyone's closet, never mind Mom's, is just weird, and, really, who cares about Mom? But Ed. And Dennis. Rosie has seen some things that for certain are real and true. Which is good enough for Bunny. Yes, it frightens her a bit, and she clasps her hands together almost by instinct, in case Rosie happens to glance at them and perhaps catch sight of a palm and another truth, but she doesn't make an excuse to leave. She just asks, "And what did you say to, to these people about what you saw?"

"I told the first, the woman — yesterday — she was the first person to come in and I just sort of, I was speaking without knowing I was. I told her to go to the woman I saw in her hand. I even knew her name. Don't ask me how. It's Margaret. I mumbled something about that little foreign woman to Ed. And I told Mom about the vase, and now I think she'd like to have me arrested." She ends it there. No need to restate Dennis's name or complete Irene's name, as it is not Bunny's business.

"Well, you know you have to tell them, that's what I think," Bunny says as she nudges into a neater pile the already neat stack of horoscopes in the box to the right of the half-circle cutout. "You actually could be helping somebody."

Helping. There is that idea again. What Rosie always had felt she'd been doing at her bank window. Is she supposed to be doing it at this one, too?

"You know that I'm being serious," she says to Bunny as more of a grateful statement than a plea.

And Bunny says back in all seriousness, "I know you're being serious."

12

"You can't be serious."

This is Scot's response to Rosie's story of what has been happening in the two days she's been at the half-circle cutout. Then he laughs, "Come on," and continues tossing muddy socks into her washer. Then, without any laughing, "Are you all right?"

Rosie answers, at very low volume, "I don't know."

Like many of those in the survey tacked to the inside of the half-circle-cutout wall, as a kid Scot had Ouijaed, rolled a Magic Eight Ball, pulled predictions from fortune cookies, avoided walking beneath ladders, took note of the black cat ahead, minded his step around sidewalk cracks. But he stopped at the actual belief in things like seeing into somebody's life as if it were a movie you'd Netflixed and popped into your player. How could somebody know what she'd never been told? And, if she did, shouldn't she be living on a mountaintop in Tibet? Or back in the Bible times? You don't find those kinds of people living in a little brick cottage at the edge of a municipal golf course in Western Massachusetts.

But one of those kinds of people does live there. And on the night of Rosie's second day at the mall Scot returns from his retreat and begins to learn all that has occurred since she spotted the keys on the porch and the first truths — they had to be truths — in people's palms. But she has to find him first. Upon returning home from the mall that second day to the truly breathtaking presence of Scot's car in her driveway, she searched the few rooms of the house until she located him and his woodsmoke smell downstairs, in the laundry room. Something pointy stuck into Rosie's neck as she shrink-wrapped around him, and it was the only reason she finally disentangled herself to find a twig hanging on a string tied around Scot's neck. And the twig was all he could talk about. For maybe twenty minutes, that's all that happened, Scot talking about the trip, but mostly about the twig.

"Yes, I know, I thought the retreat sounded stupid, but really, Rosie, you can't imagine what it feels like to have that kind of support. I had no intention of walking along a cable that high in the air — fifteen feet is a lot, you'll have to try it some time. But they got me through. Other people from Accounting, yes, but also the second vice president and the head of Game Development, even! They were cheering me on, saying, 'You can do it, Scot!' And they were chanting my name." Here he loudly demonstrated — "Scot! Scot! Scot! Scot!" — on the chance she couldn't imagine. "And they awarded me this!" His voice was that of a high-school senior who'd just learned of a full boat to Harvard. He held out the twig bound by the twine around his filthy neck. "It's a reminder that I walked from that one tree to the other one — a reminder that I can do anything! I'm going to wear it forever. But I'll have to be very careful with it — it's just a little stick. Think about that — it's fragile. It needs to be looked out for. That's the other message it carries, other than the amazing thing I did. It reminds me that we're all fragile, we all need care." He dropped the lid of the washer and pushed the start button. "Don't you agree?"

Rosie nodded. Pushed the stop button. Said, "I have to tell you what happened to me."

For most of the next twenty minutes there in the laundry room, she did tell him, pausing only to respond to Scot's sharp, "You're kidding." "What?" "Like exactly how?" and "You can't be serious," or to drop her head and wonder why he couldn't just softly say, as he typically did when Rosie was up against something big, as he had when she lost her job, "Wow," and "Tell me more," and "We'll figure this out, you and me. Don't worry, you're not alone."

Scot is there on this new night she needs him, but his reaction is as pointy as the end of the twig that right now fails to remind him that Rosie, like everybody else on this earth, is fragile. That she needs care.

"I don't know — I have no idea why this is happening, but I can't just drop it," she says as Scot exhales lengthily and keeps rolling and unrolling a sheet of fabric softener. "When it's not frightening me, there's some small feeling that it's right. That I'm in the right place for now. Like how I felt at the bank. My favorite part was talking to everybody. Maybe it sounds silly, but that's what I miss most is that, the interaction. Thing is, however it's happening, now I really have something to say."

"So if you looked into my hand," Scot says as he puts down the dryer sheet and opens his palm, and Rosie grabs his hands with a big "Don't!"

"Tell me what you see." He is smiling now, playing. But Rosie isn't.

"I don't want to."

He tries to wrestle free. Rosie turns her back. She feels hands on her shoulders. She leans back into what she hopes will be understanding. But Scot's voice in her ear is asking, again, "Tell me."

You might think the first thing Rosie would have done upon realizing she could see and know things in life would be to stare at her own palms. But you are not Rosie, therefore you have not had this happen to you, so you cannot truly comprehend how the idea of knowing exactly what your palm holds is way too frightening. It's kind of like how physicians are not allowed to treat their relatives. According to what you see on medical programs on The Discovery Channel, these people can crack open chests while wearing little hats with smiley faces printed on them and their favorite J. Geils is playing in the background. The troubles of strangers can be sad, but they belong to strangers. The physicians' own stuff, or that of their loved ones, is another matter. Too close, too many emotions held. So the doctors stay away from their own children's tonsils, and Rosie has kept away from her own palms. In the two days she has looked away as she washed, assumed her hands are clean from the extra scrubbing she has been doing, has yet to look down as she holds them in her lap. Now she turns and folds Scot's into one another.

Scot shakes his head. He'd braided his hair for the return trip, an exact plait that held every strand in place even after all the challenges of the retreat. He moves the tail of it through his fingers as he says heavily, "I don't know what to think. It's all too strange."

"Well, imagine how I feel."

"I can't," he says. "I'd like to, but right now, I can't. Maybe that's the problem."

13

Though the answer probably is tucked somewhere in the heel of her hand, just how big the problem will become will remain a mystery. By not wanting to know the secrets of the past or what might happen next, Rosie is in the minority. Lots of people are craving such information. Needing to know. Dying to know.

"I'll die if I don't find out why I never was hired."

"I'll die if I never know what her final thought was."

"I'll die if I can't find out what she knows."

That is what lots of people tell those who purport to know more than the rest of us — those like Rosie, who the next morning is back at the half-circle cutout, back at the job it is clear Scot doesn't understand or support. He'd stayed over, but on the couch, where, after he and Rosie finally emerged from the laundry room, he moped for the remainder of the night, playing with the twig and waiting for Rosie to change her mind and give him proof that she indeed could do the crazy things she was alleging. He finally slumped into a sleep, and when Rosie, still awake, went to cover him, she was glad to find him with hands under a throw pillow.

The next morning he is not there to disappoint her further or to roll his eyes as she heads out the door, then to the driveway, then to the mall, where she unlocks and raises the gate, unlocks the door in the wall, turns on the light, sets her lunch and bag and coat on the chair just past the half-circle cutout, then sits at the curtain and waits. The jaunty horns of "Tijuana Brass" play from the sound system as Rosie leafs through the box of newspaper horoscopes. She reads, "It can be hard to be patient as you wait for what you want, but you will not have to wait much longer." Then "Keep the lines of communication open. It's important that you hear the advice of others." And "Be yourself. Know that your personality will get you through." Finally, "Your partner will be enthusiastic about your new situation. Sit back and enjoy the encouragement."

Just about everyone is waiting for something they want, is the recipient of some advice, can forget to be themselves. But not everyone has a partner, so this clipping doesn't fall into the one-size-fits-all bit of half-circle cutout wisdom. And because Rosie has a partner, one who is not enthusiastic about her new situation, and there is no encouragement to celebrate, she rips it into a series of smaller and smaller squares.

The bell, and then a "Hello?"

Rosie halts the ripping. Slowly pushes aside the curtain. In the purple chair before the half-circle cutout sits Dervla of Experience Travel. Rosie knows this only because that is the name and business printed in white on the red airplane-shaped badge on the lapel of her blue jacket. She's heard that name recently, but where? Then Dervla says, "I'm Ed Horrigan's sister, Dervla," and Rosie remembers.

"This isn't the day of my reading — I'm here the second Tuesday, you might see it on the calendar if she — Irene — has one back there. I love Irene, and I'll miss her, but I'm so happy for her. Aren't you?"

Rosie nods. Gets the thud of a reminder that, in dealing with Scot last night, she'd forgotten to check her e-mail. She knows there was not yet a phone call from Irene.

"I never brought her coffee because she likes tea — well, you have to know that — but I don't know what you like, and I was just going for coffee and saw you were open — I wanted to introduce myself and see if I could get you a cup. Unless you like tea?"

Dervla cocks her head at the half-question, causing the fringy bangs of her auburn bob to fall into eyes that look permanently surprised — big, round, with the eyeballs floating like some huge news has just been received. Set into her face as white as primed sheetrock, they are a dusty blue that you don't see too often, and Rosie stares into the color as Dervla offers to return with a few slices of her homemade raisin bread, and gestures with her hand as she estimates the height of the stack of slices she's eaten over the weekend because she's bought one of those bread machines — remember when everybody had a bread machine? Without meaning to, Rosie shifts her eyes from Dervla's eyes to the palm of her left hand. Then she sees the travel books for Spain arranged on Dervla's daughter's yellow polyester quilted bedspread, and the passport application, and the disappointment (yes, Rosie can actually see feelings, too) from Dervla, who is just plain jealous. Dervla's excuse for not allowing the daughter to go on this trip is concern for her safety out in the big and scary world. But Rosie knows it really is because as a kid Dervla had never gotten to travel, which is why she pushed her brother to start the agency with her, though she's still never made the time to travel beyond the Eastern seaboard, and Rosie says immediately, "Let her go. She's saved for it, waited for it. She's old enough. Nobody says you can't have a trip to Europe as well," and Dervla's mouth drops open and she says, "Huh?" then, as if somebody has hit a button controlling the tear ducts in her giant eyes, she begins to bawl.

Rosie pushes into view one of the individual packs of Kleenex Irene had stored just past the box of horoscopes. She doesn't know what else to do as Dervla softly sobs with hands covering face. Through the fingers, she manages to get out, "I never got to do anything like that at her age, or ever," which Rosie, of course, already knows, just as she knows, and says, "The suitcase your daughter will borrow from her grandmother will be stolen from the baggage carousel at Heathrow on the return trip stopover, so your daughter should put all her souvenirs and valuables and prescription medicines in a safe carry-on." She speaks this smoothly, clearly, as if narrating a film on the realities of travel problems. She hears herself and wonders who is talking.

Dervla seems to ignore the details. She is busy choking out: "I never went anywhere. I never went anywhere."

Right now, Rosie is just hoping Dervla will go somewhere — namely away from the window. Rosie hasn't slept well, had stayed awake hoping that every creak of the house was Scot coming into her room to apologize, to hold her tightly, to say he understood even if he didn't, because she didn't, so how could anyone else? Her head is starting to tighten. She needs the bottle of Motrin Irene stored next to the tea. Dervla empties the personal packet of Kleenex and pauses in her mopping to look over the wad with a mixture of awe and concern and say, "Jesus you're good. I mean I, like, what Irene tells me, it's always nice enough, but, wow. How do you know these things?" Rosie shrugs. Dervla stands. Finally goes somewhere. This one morning it is only as far as back to the travel agency, but there she dials her daughter, the one person who causes many, many more to arrive at Rosie's door.

14

Dervla tells Rosie's words to the daughter, whose name is Delilah, and who's always laughed at her mother's having her palm read over all these years. That was something crazy people did. Surely. But now that the palm reader has gotten her the OK for Spain, a proposal that only two people had known about before this, and she has done so complete with giving the color of the bedspread, Delilah is converted. She comes to the mall after class the very next day and stands in awe as she puts out her hand to introduce herself and to thank Irene for the words about the trip and to find out would she maybe meet somebody when she went away, because all the guys in those Spanish travel books on her bed, and even her Spanish textbooks in school, they are so incredibly hot, let's hope they're not all gay. And in her hand Rosie sees there another hand — the crawling one of Delilah's driving instructor.

"Mr. Kiley" is the greeting Rosie gives. "Stay away from him."

Delilah tells her friend what that Rosie has told her, because Delilah's friend has Mr. Kiley for driving class, too, and the friend goes off to the mall to see Rosie and brings her sister along for support because she is scared of Rosie, but she wants to go see her because she is more scared of Mr. Kiley, who makes sure she always is the only student scheduled to be in the car on the days her road class is held, and who too often makes her pull over so he can move her hands to the proper ten and two positions, but will keep his over hers way too long.

"Your next road class will end up stalled on Chilton Road," Rosie tells her. "The engine of Mr. Kiley's car will suddenly seize and Mr. Kiley will say he'll call for help and he will dial his phone but he will be faking it so no one will arrive." Delilah's friend stays home from that class, but Delilah attends hers, and she becomes the one who ends up stalled on Chilton Road, and having to use the legs that had gotten her All-Western-Mass. Honors in the 880 to get away from him, and to the nearest house.

The girls tell everyone they know. About Mr. Kiley and the car. About Rosie in the half-circle cutout. Word spreads throughout school. Everyone wants to go see that woman at Irene Queen of the Unseen, and to learn how totally awesome are her abilities.

Delilah and her friend are among the newest believers. And not every kid in school, because on the whole only half the population of the United States would consider going to a palm reader, but at least half of them repeat the story to their families. And not everyone in all those families, but maybe half of them, retell somebody what they've learned. The news is amazing enough to begin with — both that Mr. Kiley, with a peppy young wife featured on the driving school television commercials, pointing to a blackboard drawn with traffic signs, even though she never really teaches at the school, and with their two lovely little boys who are always dressed identically even though there is a three-and-a-half-year difference between them, and with the scholarships the driving school donates to a deserving high-school senior each June, would try this — and that some woman in a mall would know everything about it. But, as happens in life, at least half the retellings make the attempted assault worse, the girl not only one but one in a dozen that in the fictionalized version now include a couple of boys on whom Mr. Kiley has leapt. The new versions also make Rosie lots more all-knowing than she already is. Therefore, beginning the second week of her new job at Orchard Mall, making her someone you have to visit before another second goes by.

During the Irene era, many who took a seat in the purple chair at the half-circle cutout window wanted their palms read as a lark, simply had spotted her sign and shrugged and asked themselves, "Why not?" Or they went in on a dare, the price being your friend's or date's ten-dollar bill, the condition being that the hand extended was your brave one rather than their cowardly one. But because of the word spread after the Kiley incidents, the majority of those who come to Rosie are some degree of serious. Bearing wishes, hopes. Wanting to know the whys or wheres or whens of their lives, most of those questions being directed to the future, the past being done and gone and known, but what is to come still a big huge mystery that just has to be revealed ahead of time, if possible. Whys, wheres, whens — and don't forget the all-important who.

Love is the most popular topic, would be at the head of the list if Rosie ever were asked to line up people's concerns. Second would be money. They launch right into this, even before Rosie has the chance to open their hands. Can you tell if I'll ever be rich? Will I ever be out of debt? Will I ever pay off my credit cards? My loans? My mother?

Money money money.

I want to win the lottery. I want to win at the track. At Foxwoods. At Mohegan Sun. At Atlantic City. I want the winner-take-all at bingo. I want the top prize at the church raffle. I want to win. I want to win a lot. I want to make a lot of money. I want to inherit a bunch of money. Money money money. Sometimes they are more specific. I wish my old neighbor would just die and leave me all that money I just know he has socked somewhere. Or specific and mean. I wish my father would drop dead. Oh, and if he has any money, I wish he'd leave it to me. Money money money.

Rosie does not often see tall stacks of paper money awaiting those who sit in the half-circle cutout. Actually, she never does. Maybe a few scratch tickets that are worth a few hundred, and she does see the neat rolls of big bills the old neighbor hid (in the pockets of the suit coats hung farthest from the closet door) — but she does not see him exiting this life anytime soon, actually sees the headline for the newspaper story that a few decades hence will have him second in line for the honors of eldest person in the Commonwealth, the record-holder then being 114.

What she usually sees aren't things you could take to the bank. Just to heart.

The workplace party being planned for the woman who thinks no one there appreciates her.

The chocolate bar on the kitchen counter and the laundry folded without request and the little side garden finally planted and the other tiny gestures being made by the husband whose wife is complaining that he does not care.

The silence at the dinner table of the two who just have no future. The snap of the fire burning behind them, the sounds of cutlery on dinnerware, her offer of "More?" and his response, one word: "No."

The shame draped on the first-grader who, twenty-one years later, can still hear the teacher snapping, "You are bad, you are bad," when she chose a girl for dance time. "You are bad, you are bad." Biting tone, stoning tone. Rosie reaches up to cover an ear with a free hand. "You are sick, you are sick," the mother says twenty-one years later when this woman brings her private life into the open by signing her new legal surname on Christmas cards. Then, "You are loved," says the woman who now is her life. But it is Dennis's childhood all over when this woman who's come today to the half-circle cutout carries with her only the words of the teacher and the mother, only the bad, which is the habit of too many, to ignore the good and push it aside and heft onto their backs the negative, lugging it with them through life. This woman carries with her the words of only the teacher and the mother. Rosie sees the wife's wife leaving.

For another, she sees a dog living just three houses down the street. The boy who answered the door and said he'd not seen the missing dog — he'd lied. Check the back bedroom, his, the dog is there.

Rosie sees letters on a wall. Initials in a heart dated 1877, sees CH and DH living there still, even though the sitting room of the house they built more than a century ago is now a computer room, and they are fascinated by the machine, which is the reason for all the extra files you find on it. That is CH and DH, playing.

Rosie sees welfare as the only answer right now and interjects that this session is free, by the way, and she sees you by the end of the year working in the hospitality industry, in Phoenix, yet, even though you've never thought once about leaving the area. She sees you in a burgundy suit, golden nameplate, making reservations, the recommendations of where to eat, tour, shop, the thirty-percent discount offered throughout the chain to employees, and that, one day before the end of the year, will mean you.

"You should not bring up the subject of his sister and he in turn will not bring up the subject of your sister," she tells one woman. "And the roast beef will burn on Sunday," she adds as the woman, stunned because all she came to the window to ask was directions to the ladies' room, scurries the sixteen steps to the door.

Rosie sees the charred hunk of meat through the window of the door of the Westinghouse clearly as she sees the image in the next palm, the near-death experience that probably would have happened regardless of who'd adopted the boy forty-four years earlier, because the poles that hold up power lines are pretty much everywhere, as are kids who one day get the idea it might be fun to climb to the top of one. Then she sees the boy as a man with a side career as a motivational speaker, driving around southern California promoting the self-published book that fills twenty cartons piled in his garage. "You need to go online and order *Wireboy: The Story of My Childhood Electrocution and Then My Return to a Normal Life I Wrote About*," she tells the woman at the half-circle cutout, who says, "Huh?" and then, sensing Rosie's seriousness, reaches with her free hand for a pen as she is given the Web address that will connect her with that garage storehouse and the author son the woman had given up when he was two.

Except for the theme from *Bonanza* playing on the sound system, the space is quiet in that woman's wake. Rosie shakes her head to push aside the image of Wireboy plummeting to the fortunately placed grass tree belt. One month into her days at the half-circle cutout, she's created a file in her head where she shoves similarly disturbing images collected from the hands placed before her. She stuffs the falling Wireboy on top of the last sight that has kept her from sleeping: the stiff circle of white fleece that is the sheep that hasn't been seen since last May, that has not, as the owner who'd come in the previous day had hoped, simply wandered off to another farm. And that's when Bunny appears at the half-circle cutout and shoves forward her cell phone. And that's when Rosie hears, "So — what's happening?"

Irene's voice.

All the way from near the Arctic Circle.

15

"It's me! I've been trying to reach you off and on, but there's not much reception up here. We're somewhere up near Russia, I think, or thereabouts. Sticks is scouting a left-winger up here. Not your typical honeymoon, but I'll take it!" Irene might as well be phoning from a beach in Tahiti, that carefree and relaxed and happy is the vibe coming through Bunny's iPhone. "I was able to get through on Bunny's number, so I thought I'd see how you're doing. What you ended up doing. I hope you didn't mind my leaving you the keys and all. It's just that I thought you'd be perfect."

The volume is loud enough that Bunny can hear Irene's every word. She smiles and waves to Rosie and heads back to her shop. Rosie closes the curtains, rolls her chair to the side and says slowly and carefully, "Irene, I really need to ask you things."

"Oh, Sticks is just the greatest husband in the world," she starts, and Rosie drops right over her words with "Irene, sure, I'm so happy, but, yeah, um, well, yes, you'll have to tell me about him, sure, but, Irene, well, I'm seeing things."

"Sorry?"

"I'm sorry. I'm sure Sticks is wonderful, but I need to talk to you, I did try calling, I couldn't get you. I e-mailed . . . "

"E-mail's a joke here. I can't remember the last time I was able to get online." There is a space that Rosie prays isn't a disconnection. Then Irene continues, "What do you mean? What are you seeing? You mean behind the cutout? I've never had bugs or anything . . . "

"Not bugs, nothing's wrong with the space." Rosie stops. "In palms, Irene, I'm doing what you do — did — with people, I look at their palms. But I see things."

Irene can hear Rosie; the connection isn't at all bad considering the distance. But that doesn't mean she understands. She asks slowly, "What are you talking about?"

So Rosie tells her. About Sheila. About Ed Horrigan. About Maria. About Mom. About Dervla. She almost tells her about Dennis, just because he had been in that first day, but skips over all those others to tell her about the driving-school owner, the roast beef, about Wireboy and the birth mother of Wireboy.

"I'm sorry, Rosie, I don't know what to say. Or, really, what you're saying." Another pause. Irene is farther away now, but not in miles. "Maybe, are you sure?"

For the month since the start of spring and finding the keys on her porch, Rosie has been frightened, stymied, curious, amazed, grateful. For the first time, anger hits. And it is directed at the woman who'd thought the job would be a help. "This was your idea." Rosie gives each of the words a push toward the border. "You wanted me to do this."

"Maybe you're exhausted. It was tough for you to lose your job. I just wanted to help." Irene sounds bedside-ish. Like she is patting Rosie's head.

"I am not making this up."

"I didn't say that. I just, I don't know . . . "

"Well I don't know, either." Rosie snaps that, then says nothing. The line is silent except for a slight whistling Rosie guesses must be the wind that has to be cold wherever Irene is. "I thought you might have — that this might have happened to you once."

"Never. Really, Rosie, it was all made up. You know that. I just told them stories. I felt they got their money's worth. I never knew anything about them. Nothing. If I had any magical powers or whatever, I would have been counting the seconds until Sticks wandered into the mall. I would have seen who and what I have now. I'm sixty-one and it's all starting for me. Pretty unbelievable. I wish I'd known this was my future, but I didn't know anything. Anything at all. Never once."

"Well I do — I know lots," Rosie snaps. "And I don't know what to do with it." She wants an answer, wants some understanding, wants guidance, wants comfort. She gets only more of the whistling.

"I'm sorry, Rosie. Really. I don't know what to say." The connection wilts. Rosie finds it hard to hear. She holds the phone closer, curls it into her shoulder as Irene says, "I'm sorry – I should have asked you first if you wanted to do this. I was just so concerned about you, sitting there at home. Whatever you want is fine — you don't have to keep the place open." Then comes something indiscernible, and then, "Just lock up and give Hannah the keys. I'd like my chairs back, the table and lamp." Then a sound like something being dragged over stones. Then, "Maybe Dennis could take care of moving those to your house?" Irene says something else that gets run over by noise, but is clear again when she says quietly, but loudly enough to be heard over all these miles, "Just go home, Rosie. I don't want you to feel worse. I really don't want that. I thought this would help you. That's what I wanted to do. To help you."

"I know that. But I don't know what's happening here, and I thought you might have an idea."

"I wish" is the last of what Rosie hears before the line goes blank. After several hellos, she looks at the phone to find only Bunny's screensaver, a multi-colored peace sign that doesn't do much to prevent Rosie's urge to fling the device all the way onto Berkshire Road and in front of one of the many cars it right then is her wish to be inside of, moving away from this place very quickly, and for good.

16

Mom makes the right into the parking lot. Glances up at the sign. Dennis is up there, snapping the final ! into place for the message that reads:

FALL INTO SUMMERTIME!!!

"What the hell does that mean?" she asks no one. "It's summer, not goddamn fall. And why put up an invitation for stupid people to come here and get hurt?"

With the way everybody was suing everybody else these days, wasn't a message like that just asking for it? And of course if a shopper did fall, of course they'd do so right in front of her place. What a dumb thing for that shithead to be writing out. Didn't anybody think ahead the way she did? And why didn't they?

She is snarling this but also paying attention to the traffic. No sense in getting in an accident herself — especially with this car. This nice car. This far cry from her old piece of junk that had been on its last legs and cost her an entire day's car rental that one day in March. Just amazing, with its front and side air-bags and a readout of interior and exterior temperature and the latitude and longitude at which you are this exact second, and a call button that will get you a live person speaking to you to tell you how to get where you want to go or to send for help if you for some reason have gone off the road and are incapacitated.

With heated leather seats, and a console compartment for all sizes of coins, and with a key chain holding buttons that pop open your trunk and lock your doors and unlock your doors and also start your headlights blinking and your horn sounding if you determine you are in a panic situation, which of course is a likely possibility, the world being the way it is. A stereo that allows you your choice of the five discs you loaded into it when it isn't offering you access to the thousands of tunes on your iPod, if you have one. A net strung across the trunk to prevent your groceries from rolling around when you take a corner. Popping and blinking and music and net and a 24/7 voice asking, "May we help you, please?" Paid in full, all for the price of one dumb old light-blue vase that was the one and only dumb old thing her great aunt had left her, despite the great cost of the red-and-white carnation Christmas arrangement Mom had FTD-ed to her assisted living place in Pittsburgh each and every December first for the eleven and a half years the great aunt had been assisted in her living there before she no longer needed assistance because she was no longer living. The light-blue vase had seemed like one big insult when it arrived that day in the mail way back in the 1990s. Got shoved to the back of the closet, and she had forgotten about it all these years. But it has ended up paying for a beautiful car. Who could have predicted that?

Mom clutches the steering wheel with a palm that bears a head line interrupted by a circular shape, a portent of emotional disturbance that symbolizes a clogged dam of sorts, the flow of psychic energy having collided with a mental obstruction and forced to whirl in great circles, unable to either ignore or break through the interruption. All those, plus the line does not have the preferred gentle slant across the palm. And when there is no line, you can bet that sympathy and imagination will be lacking. But none of this is known to Mom. She thinks only of finding a safe and secure place to dock the car for the day. Up near the far entrance to the mall, she parks at an angle in the space-hogging my-car- shouldn't-be-anywhere-within-a-million-miles-of-your-piece-of-garbage-vehicle manner she remembers Lawrence Block using, a habit that at the time annoyed her greatly. She selects a trio of empty spaces over near Pearle Vision, a chain store in a freestanding building that has nothing to do with the mall, except for over the years siphoning Lens Is More's customers, and that now is benefiting from the strangely increasing traffic that daily heads to Orchard. Eight cars are at Pearle already, and it isn't even nine-thirty. Mom isn't complaining. She knows that before the day's end, she'll be in the back storeroom to replenish her shelves, lugging out more birdhouses and tea cozies and tooth-fairy pillows and sock monkeys and all the other big sellers being scooped up by all the customers who've been finding the mall since someone started the stupid rumor that the woman who's taken over for Irene the Queen of the Unseen back in March has started seeing very true things in any palm put before her.

LL

Should there be another? Do any words in the English language have three *L*'s in a row? Dennis doesn't think so, but, right now, as he looks at the word "FALL" there on his announcement of "SUMMER," three *L*'s are making sense. The letter always reminds him of Lawrence Block, how Lawrence had admired one of the big *L*'s that first day, had gone home that first day with one beneath his arm, not even hidden in a box or shrouded by a garbage bag, had made no effort to conceal the fact he was taking something that did not belong to him. But when Dennis had known him, Lawrence Block pretty

123

much got what he wanted. The big huge responsibility of Orchard Mall. And then, from nowhere, a more important posting. Where is he these days, Dennis wonders, as he often wonders. They'd had roughly the same starting time, and Lawrence Block was long gone off into the faraway world. Dennis is still at Orchard Mall. Doing the same things, going through the days of his life. Days that have gotten busier and fuller and weirder since the first day of spring.

Today's message is Mall Manager Hannah Pomfret's idea, not his. And it still looks funny to Dennis. But that happens often enough. Spell out a word, stand back, more often than not it will look wrong. Even simple words, like "THE" or "AND," three letters can have a way of appearing to the eye that they are lined up incorrectly. As did the six of his name. On one do-nothing Monday a few years back when the only assignment was to spell for the thousandth time "SEE WHAT'S IN STORE!" he took the *D* and the *E* and the *N* and the *N* and the *I* and the *S* and hung them up, then climbed down and drove the cart to the end of the parking lot just for a look. He had long daydreamed how "CONGRATULATIONS DENNIS AND IRENE" — or maybe, ladies first, "IRENE" should have been up front in that line — would look up there the day after they announced their engagement. He had seen this many times on the marquees of Holiday Inns and Best Westerns, the joy of people's formal pairings misspelled up high in sans serif for the world to see. Correct spelling or not, Dennis would love something like that. The sentimental appeals to him. When Signy had been his wife, he'd done a few romantic things, including venturing into Frederick's of Hollywood when Frederick's was still at Orchard and buying the shiny, red faux-silk women's underthings that the men's magazines at the Village Barber told him women love to prance around in, and, as it turned out to his good fortune, Signy actually did. And in advance of each of the ten Valentine's Days they'd shared as husband and wife, he'd sent a check to the *Daily News* to have his and her initials featured in a heart-shaped space in the special "For Lovers Only" section.

CONGRATULATIONS AND A HAPPY LIFE! he might have written one day, to himself and Irene. But today, this Monday, the first one of summer, there will be no long life with Irene to look forward to, so he sticks to what Hannah Pomfret has requested on the Orchard Mall work order.

Unlike the previous four managers, Hannah does things officially. Nobody since ninth Orchard Mall manager Tim Murphy in the early 1990s has bothered with forms, but even he hadn't filled in every box and line like it was a bill being put before Congress. Hannah probably had been one of those little girls who played office, made herself a desk from a carton in her attic and took calls — "Miss Pomfret speaking, may I help you?" — using a banana for a telephone. She is efficient and thorough, but thankfully no Napoleon, which had been the tenants' term for one of her predecessors, a snail of a man who, by himself with no order of help given to Dennis, dragged all the mall's ashtrays to the garage in a time long before smoke-free environments were law, and who once threatened tenants with a parochial-schoolish ACLU-daring dress code: skirts for women, ties for men, no jeans on either gender.

Hannah Pomfret is like a perky day-camp counselor. A different fresh idea blossoms from her daily. Even as the calendar marches toward the mall's eventual closing, she is trying to start a walking club of the type she's read about in industry magazines that run features about the flocks of oldsters and heart patients and back sufferers using malls' pleasant temperatures and flat terrain as their gym. One recent Monday, she had Dennis write

MALL WALKERS WELCOME!
WE ARE OPEN AT 8 A.M.!
JUST FOR YOU!

And she ink-jetted the same announcement onto the multi-colored placards she set throughout the mall on tall metal stands, and she came in earlier than required to unlock the place, and sat on a bench near the Pit to await the walkers who never arrived, who instead had headed across town, to Mountainside, to power-walk past lively, merchandise-filled stores brightly lit even when their security gates were still closed. The experience was uplifting: the aroma wafting from the pans being removed from the ovens by the early crew baking the Mrs. Fields, the enviable physique of the mannequin using the cross-trainer in the window of the fitness store, the tri-colored English setter pups tumbling in the shredded newspaper of the pet-store window, the cashmere sweater sets glowing with golden fall tones.

"It's so alive there," informed Hannah's landlady, who walked Mountainside three mornings a week, used her mall-walker discount card to get a free coffee with her breakfast at the food court, might stay to pick up a few things, then head back home, happy and anticipating her next visit. "Orchard?" she asked disgustedly, like Hannah Pomfret had no connection to it. "Who goes to Orchard any more?"

It is a challenge to keep cheery. But Hannah does the best she can. Focuses on the positive. Maybe the walking idea just needs time, might take a while to catch on as well, as the flea market one had, as the appraisal day had. She takes special pride in the fact that appraisal day back in April had been such a stellar event that it had attracted even Mom, who never showed up at anything, carrying a parcel to only one appraiser, then returning to her stand looking dumbstruck. Every other Saturday throughout the winter, flea-market space had opened in the cavernous old McCrory discount store. This had been Hannah's idea, and was a surprising success. Tables were a very affordable fifteen dollars for the day, and all sorts of people lugged their junk in first thing in the morning, and exited carrying other people's detritus as darkness fell. In the mezzanine, shoppers checked out the lineup of tables that comprised the Saturday sports-card show. Hannah had a connection in New Hampshire, who had a connection in Vermont, who had one back down in Northboro, and, as a result, one Monday just before Christmas Dennis climbed the ladder to replace the "HANUAKKAH!" he was certain he'd misspelled with:

THIS SATURDAY!
10 AM to 1 PM
BILL 'SPACEMAN' LEE!!!

That Saturday, wives and children and girlfriends and mothers accompanied husbands and boyfriends and sons. Browsed while their men admired the fading signatures of Gerry Cheevers and John Havlicek — or at least somebody's impressive forgeries. The women bought boxes of All-Occasion Assortments and this year's calendar, all at seventy-five percent off, from Bunny. They got their toddlers' hair cut at the Village Barber, who had a little plastic pony he placed on the big barber chair just for this purpose, having to drag it from the backroom and dust it off, as it had been a dog's age since he'd clipped the hair of anyone but a retiree. His typical customer was the old man who came in with the wife, or who was there for a matinee or an afternoon at the Pit Pub, using up another day without having to be shut up in his lonely house. But this was a different kind of day, one that also benefitted Mom, as on those busy Saturdays women flocked to one of the few places in the mall where they could purchase something that interested them.

Cars filled more of the parking lot than had known the feel of rubber for a good twenty years, and people crowded the doors and lined up for autographs and photos. For that one day of the week, it was almost like the mall's old times, if you didn't notice that the featured star was a longtime has-been, or that the big stock in trade was outdated memorabilia and old things, and, quite frankly, just plain junk. Unless, since she arrived at the start of spring, you went to that palm reader who has gotten more and more people talking.

Dennis hangs that final exclamation mark after "SUMMERTIME," then closes his eyes and stretches. The warm breeze reminds him of the one that had hit him when he and Signy had walked from the airport in Florida the first of the two times they'd vacationed there, leaving the airport over the line in Connecticut during a February freeze, and a few short hours later exiting through a sliding door and into a startling measure of the tropics. He opens his eyes and looks out to the full green hills and imagines the ceiling of leaves covering entire worlds that have nothing to do with humans. Insects going about their day, mice and snakes, frogs and birds. Foxes — or is it just fox? — Rabbits, bears, even. Or bear. Whatever the plural, they are out there, maybe sitting on their mountains looking over to the roof of Orchard Mall and wondering what world is being lived under there.

Had all those creatures mused that a couple months back, and then had they stopped on this morning to ask the same question, they would have noticed a distinct difference. Nothing that rightfully could be called historical, but, as recent Orchard Mall history goes, it would come pretty close. Which is what Dennis, too, has been observing from this place much closer to the mall, from the sign above the wide and slowly growing lake of cars in which normally floats only a handful of autos. Short lines of them, or a sprinkling farther away when the trees bore their leaves and shade was sought. Over the past couple months, something has been happening. Cars and pickups and family vans and enormous SUVs are entering the lot at a more and more regular pace. And staying. For more than just to pick up prints or take advantage of matinees or use the wide vacant expanse of tar for a teen's first driving lesson or a handy meeting place for carpooling or a safe place to attempt rollerblading. They are there to spend money, spend time. But, mainly, they are there to have their palms read.

"You will draw fulfillment from palmistry in direct measure to the frequency with which you practice it."

Irene's old book from Kenmore Square had promised that, and, fittingly, the prediction has come true. In the good early days, Irene had read an average of one palm per hour, a session taking maybe fifteen minutes — twenty if Irene were feeling generous. When things dipped and the slow years started, she might read two a day, not counting the freebies swapped for a movie pass or the occasional tenderloin, and she relied more on the typing she'd always taken in for extra cash. Had she been here these previous three months, she wouldn't have had time to use the bathroom.

"Initially, you will be amazed by the wide variety of lines on the palms placed before you," the book had warned Rosie when she first started bringing it home each night to cover another page or two, "and you might be overwhelmed by the signs that you must translate in your reading. But, as time passes, you will be at once humbled and fascinated that this process offers daily something new to learn and to share with those who place their hands in yours."

Overwhelmed is a good word. For three months, Rosie has been reading, and seeing, and being right. And doing a running commentary on the visuals she has been getting, like you might have to if you were watching a silent movie and happened to have a sightless friend along for the show.

Telling her clients — customers, patrons, she hasn't yet figured out what to call them — everything she was seeing, that had been a decision seconded by Bunny that second day, when Rosie had confided what had happened because she just had to tell somebody, and Scot was away, and this woman Bunny was there, suddenly not in front of but behind the half-circle cutout, pouring tea from a pot, chamomile made with actual flowers, a dried store-bought brand labeled Slumberland sold in a tin cylinder with a label in the shape of a puffy-topped bed, served in a pot bought from a flea-market vendor on whom Irene long ago had found upward hooks along the lifeline, an indicator of achievement. The hooks appeared following an indication of misfortune, hinting there had been an effort to struggle with difficulties. And when Irene told the teapot vendor woman this, the teapot vendor woman told her that struggle was her middle name. "Well," said Irene, wishing to just take her new/old green teapot and get back to the half-circle cutout window, "life is hard." The teapot vendor woman nodded and tapped her sternum and said solemnly and without one bit of sarcasm, "And nobody knows that better than I."

Bunny wanted to calm Rosie, whose story she was believing, because stranger things certainly have happened — not to anyone Bunny personally knew, but Bunny had the enormous blessing of an open mind, and she figured they could happen

— so why not to Rosie? So when Rosie said, "I'm seeing things," Bunny let her go on. Then encouraged her to say what she saw.

From that day on, Rosie began to do that. Didn't make a big huge announcement that she could now actually see things, just did her readings, focused as usual on the palm, but now offered more, describing the images actually playing there. On top of the lines she sees the information, rooted in past and present and future, of those who now, three months into her time at Orchard Mall, now are waiting in groups of twos and threes at the beginning of the gray industrial carpet sixteen steps away.

Rosie warns one to stay away from the fourth stair out his back door, it's about to give.

Explains to another that her mother has hidden her one good ring in the cap of the Black Flag ant spray under the kitchen sink, the can that had been otherwise empty, and when her father shook it and found it sounding empty, he tossed it in the basket, and it went to the dump many Saturdays ago.

Says to yet another that his cat will come back on Tuesday if canned food is left in the driveway, in that favorite yellow bowl.

Her information could be the cinematic lengthy kind, or nothing more than a stew of strange bits that make no sense to her, but hold enough long-awaited answers or directions or secret realities to widen eyes and jack up eyebrows, erect neck hairs and give a full view of bottom-teeth dental work when mouths fall open as she sees, and says:

"Go with the Delaney House for the retirement party, rather than the Lakeview, because in another week and two days the woman who owns the Lakeview and to whom you are giving the deposit will be closing the business, and leaving the country, and you will be funding her trip."

"You never really needed to repeat after rinsing. And while on that subject, test your well water again for lead and sodium, even though the test you just had done said you had little to no discernible levels."

"Try a hot-water bottle even though it is old-fashioned."

"Do you need to make this decision today — by tonight? Maybe take the summer to calm down and start going in the direction you want to."

"The boy, he is sorry, sorry sorry."

"She said she sent the check and she wrote it out, just never mailed it — but not on purpose."

"I don't see a lottery number to give you, but I do not see any approaching success to your current method of choosing your number by the calendar dates on which you sleep with your doctor boyfriend."

"Privatize your cafeteria and there will be bad press on the front page for two consecutive days, and the food will get worse than it already is, and the new staff will be headed by a man who might impress you at first, but who will lick the mayonnaise knife in between orders he'll make at the sandwich station out back."

"There is a picture of you being displayed in a small house you once lived in. You left this picture behind, on the high second shelf of the pantry, and the new people found it and they put it in a frame because it is a curiosity to them, who you are, and what your picture was doing in the house they bought. The house has a nine on the door and a sign that says, "BEWARE OF DOG," even though you did not have a dog back then; your mother bought the sign because a magazine article said that for this one-dollar investment you could perhaps ward off burglars and thus save thousands in property loss and heartache."

"Sorry, but you will be only the second-best-looking woman at your twenty-fifth reunion; the first will be Diane, who everybody will say again and again really hasn't changed since grammar school, never mind high school."

"You think he will need more amusement than this, but you will be very happy to know that he really is the kind of guy who will be content on a Saturday morning sitting on a couch and reading *The Eastern Guide to Medicinal Plants and Herbs* with a cup of tea balanced on his leg."

"At the first restaurant of your vacation you will get the waiter with the tin whistle in his back pocket. He will only be carrying it for someone else, does not use it himself, does not know how. Kind of like your sister with the cigarettes back in high school. At least that's the story she told your parents."

"The baby will sleep way longer than you will expect her to, and you will worry for no reason, but she will be that way all her life, and so will you."

"Hire him. He is old but is more than competent and needs the work to get out of the house because she is driving him nuts now that she is home all the time."

"That one needs space."

"She needs company."

"They don't like you."

"You don't like yourself."

"What?" They say, leaning in, "Repeat that?"

"Who told you?"

"What?"

"Huh?"

"How do you know?"

Rosie will repeat the information, but is truly unable to say how in the world she knows what she knows. Like that the black horse wants to run more than he's allowed to when you go riding, so repair the fence by the front road or he will go through it and be missing for three nights. Or that you cannot and will not cruise through calculus. Or that every time the doorbell rings it is not something wrong or some bad news, and you are not in trouble. You are not.

Rosie knows that your neighbor boy took your handmade cardboard bank from your room in 1966, when everybody else was outside for your eighth birthday party playing toss the water balloon, and he spent the money all on Mallo Cups just so he could collect the points, and after he did and got a stack of them cut out, he never bothered to send them in for redemption, so it was a waste for all concerned, except for the Mallo Cups company, of course.

She wants you to go ahead and just buy a sweater; knitting isn't worth the aggravation it's causing you, plus you think the yarn you're using is all wool and it's only part wool, read the label.

She informs you that yes, those black people, or Caribbean, or whatever they are, will buy the house next door, so start getting used to the idea now.

She suggests you sell the land and use the money to take yourself on a vacation every year like you want to now but can't afford to because all your money is tied up in that land, which you will never use.

She assures you that you do not look fat in the purple slacks.

And informs you that you're out of your no-salt butter, and the diamond he gave you — yes, it is real.

Rosie delivers all this good and bad truth with the reliability of the paperman who pushes the *Daily News* through her mail slot each morning, in the kinder seasons riding his bike and hefting a big shoulder bag like in the cinematic olden days.

"It's gotta be weird," Bunny says during one of her daily visits, usually to share a cup of early afternoon tea, most recently doing so behind the curtain hung with a "BACK IN 20 MIN" sign that recently became necessary to provide a break from genuine customers.

Rosie leans back in her chair and nods, agrees, yes, it is weird. "But you know what? I actually like doing this." How free she feels saying that to Bunny, but how awkward she feels each time she says the same thing to Scot, which is often enough, as often enough he asks her why isn't she looking elsewhere for employment. As she said yet again to him — was it just last night? — "People want answers, explanations. I don't know why I have them, but I do. It's just a lot to get used to. Both here and when I'm not at the mall. I have to be careful where I look. You don't realize, but hands are everywhere."

The toll taker on the turnpike extended one of his while he awaited Rosie's change that morning, and just before she placed the forty-five cents into the palm she didn't mean to look at, she saw how the toll taker had lied on his college application twenty-three years ago about all the extracurricular involvement he'd had with underprivileged kids while in high school. Rosie tried to get used to the scenes being part of her day, as much as she could take in stride the Hollywood-grandmotherly crossing guard signaling for her to stop at the intersection near the closed-down wallpaper store which was when Rosie spotted on the woman's white glove one of the Hollywood-grandmotherly type's '70s visits to Plato's Retreat. Or feeling the disappointment of the dramatic way a wife whipped around and yelled, "You will never ever change" — all that disappointment seen in the cupped hand of the older man outside the grocery store, shooing away a fly.

Rosie once had read of a doctor phoning the Miss America pageant office after spotting a definite melanoma on the back of a contestant in the swimsuit portion of the contest he'd viewed on television. He'd saved a life with that information. Rosie doesn't examine backs. Only palms. And on her TV screen, she saw an upcoming hospitalization for exhaustion in the hand of the perky starlet waving to the audience before she walked across David Letterman's stage to greet him with a kiss. Spied a new life path and altruistic repurposing in the palm of the local talk-show host back when she was still running ratings-geared segments like "Are you disfigured and sick of people staring at you?" And the imminent 2:00 a.m. call to the ministry in the hand of the game-show host as he swung his arms around the silicone twins bubbling on either side of him in the Jacuzzi that was the program's grand prize.

The pitchman with the portable kitchen blender that you could use even in a boiling pot of soup, holding up his hand to tell you it's never been so low in price — Rosie could see him as a little boy kneeling at his little-boy bed, praying that his knees, rather than those of his god-hero Mickey Mantle, would hurt on game day. On a commercial, a child showing her clean hands to her mother showed Rosie her lucrative future in organizing wedding shows held at civic centers and exhibition halls nationwide. A man being sworn in to give testimony on the Court Channel, Rosie knew he would lie about the attack being in self-defense. The program was recorded, the verdict long ago received. The hearing was all over, but Rosie knew this small-but-big part: the man had lied.

All this, and more, in just the three months since spring's first day. Rosie's head is filling. The neat slots of her gray metal cash box are, as well. She counts and recounts, but no, there is no mistake — her weekly take is nearing seventy-five percent of what she'd been making at the bank. Is enough to disqualify her from unemployment benefits. So, really, she is employed again.

"I'm on track again with my honeymoon contributions," she announces to Scot that first Friday night of summer as she serves a toss of pasta and vegetables, the single full meal his chart is allowing them daily, breakfast and lunch being a small bowl of Special K and one-percent milk and the sliced on-sale fruit of choice. A recent television commercial touted how, over two weeks, this practice could result in a five-pound weight loss, and that was what Scot felt they needed, since he'd unboxed his summer clothes and found the waistbands of his shorts too tight. Rosie's had been fine — looser, actually, probably due to a small loss of weight from all the changes over the winter — but she goes along with the meal plan, a small thing she can do to put a smile on his face during a time he seems to be scowling so much, as he has since returning from the retreat.

Though it aggravates and stresses the masses, planning meals and lots more calms Scot. He is rarely happier then when sitting before a calendar or spreadsheet, ready to create a path to a goal. He had nominated Hawaii as their honeymoon destination, and Rosie had enthusiastically seconded, then Ed Horrigan at Experience Travel had warned it was such an expensive place that a bottle of water might cost as much as eight dollars. So Scot worked out a weekly savings plan that would fund their airfare and hotel and a very modest purse of $110 a day for eating and recreation. On his computer he designed a payment booklet, and opened a joint account at his credit union, his name and Rosie's all official on the first page of the passbook, a page Rosie stared at with a mixture of wonder and nervousness, never having seen an official anything include both their names, and in such bold-faced proximity. This is the book into which, since shortly after the first day of spring, Rosie is once again making her share of the deposits.

To that announcement, Scot only answers an unconvincing "Great," and then, quickly, "Have you ever thought of a career in food service?"

Rosie is pouring the wine just then, the five daily ounces Scot has researched are positive for cardiac health rather than celebration. "Yeah, don't I pour nicely?" she jokes. "You can leave me a tip." And he runs over that with "Because there are a few jobs at work, in the cafeteria. You like dealing with people and all, it could be good for you. And we could carpool, save more."

"I already have a job."

Those words are lining up in her brain, but she does not use them. Ever since that night three months ago when Scot returned from that retreat and drove to the little brick cottage at the edge of the golf course wearing that twig and all sorts of renewed self- confidence, and the great insight that can rain on you while you're spending twenty-four hours on a lake island with only a plastic tarp and fishhook for supplies, and then greeted a slate-faced Rosie who was full of fear and wonder and mystification and whispering something about powers and knowing, and telling him to keep his hands from her view — ever since that night, Scot has been on a campaign to find his fiancée a new place to work.

"I just can't see it" is Scot's line, repeated hard whenever Rosie starts to report on her day.

"Thing is, I can," she'll say back, trying to sound even but knowing each time that her defense is coming across sharper. "I can see it all. What's wrong with that? It happened — it's happening. People want to know things, and I can tell them. It's happening to me. And if it's OK with me, why isn't it OK with you?"

Scot's answer will be a shake of his head and a plunge of his hands into his pockets. Then a walk to the paper to troll the classifieds like Rosie had back in the spring, reading them aloud while she grits her teeth.

"Knowledgeable and competent person needed to help with payroll." His tone is friendly and even, like he is a service you've dialed. "You are that — you could do that."

"Receptionist twelve hours per week, no weekends, computer and phone skills. You have those. Chain-saw worker to cut branches." Pause. "No, sorry. But, listen. Avon — we train. They train, I mean." He stresses that last thing as if it that's all that would be needed to make Rosie consider changing course.

And Rosie tries the considering. She tries because she loves Scot, and does not love how this thing that has happened to her, that still is happening to her, is creating some wall in which there is not even the smallest of cutouts, half-circle or other. She puts herself into the shoes of each position he reads. Pictures herself forwarding calls to an inner office, walking door to door — do people actually do that these days? — with a carton of the latest eye-shadow palettes. Even imagines hefting the chain saw in the direction of miles of offending branches. But the payroll position she can't conjure. She no longer is interested in dealing with money, as she reminds herself each time she moves aside the curtain at the half-circle cutout and greets her customer (Client? She still isn't sure the term to use) with "Make a wish but not for money," as on this next morning she says to the woman in the T-shirt, who tells Rosie she's been to Hollywood, but the one in Florida, rather than the one you'd think. And the woman who's been to that Hollywood in Florida is silent for a moment, then asks, "Well, what else is there?"

Rosie folds her hands in her lap and wants to answer that there is lots.

Lots.

Especially when it rains good onto you after a few miles of bad.

On this first week of summer, a whole season having started since Rosie last heard from Irene and got her direction to just shut the shop and go back home, Rosie is still at the half-circle cutout and feeling like it is where she was always meant to be. Really, there isn't much difference between the old job and this new one. People come to her window, most of them wanting change of one sort or another. They hand over their money, Rosie hands them back a validation. There she'd been a teller. Here, she tells. Here, as they'd been when she'd handed them a handful of money, they are grateful.

"Thank you," says the man on whose palm Rosie sees next week's long-awaited vacancy at the assisted-living facility, and his mother's the next name on the list for getting a bed.

"Thank you," whispers the girl who is warned that she's bought an inferior home pregnancy test and she should pick up another on the way home and get the true answer she needs.

"Thank you," says the man to whom Rosie confides he would have more success dating if only he trimmed his ear hair.

"You have helped me, you really have helped me," says another, and all she's told him is the simple thing that he's trying to plug the headphones into the jack for the power cord, and that's why no music can be heard. "You have helped me."

"You don't know how you have helped me."

Now Hannah Pomfret is the one saying this. Again.

Her first lengthy visit had been on Rosie's second full day at the mall, when she'd introduced herself and said she'd been looking forward to meeting Rosie, whose name had been in the letter Irene had sent to the mall office saying she was eloping, and, if it were OK with Hannah, a friend named Rosie Pilch would be taking over the space.

"It's so nice of you," Hannah had said that second day.

"You're probably used to busier places to do your readings."

"No problem," said Rosie, who'd not slept much that first night, had kept the TV on all night, fearful of silence and dark after her very weird day. On the Syfy Channel she found reruns of the guy who claims to communicate with your loved ones who have died. Or, as he put it, have passed. Like some test had been held and they'd known all the answers.

"Name starts with a *K*, a *T*, a *B*, a *D*, a *J* . . . "

He went through nearly the entire alphabet before a guy in the audience yelled out, "Wow! I had a brother Jack!"

A few channels up, she'd found that white-bearded psychic who, in his red cape with white fur lining and his diamond-shaped eye patch, looked like a cross between Santa and a pirate. For the first time, Rosie hadn't just flipped past. She sat up and watched as he took phone calls and, just on the first few words from a caller, knew all about an errant child or a philandering spouse or a debt that was sapping all resources. He spoke in monotone, as if bored, even as he invited you to call, call now, know the future, and added with redundancy, "in all and in its total entirety." The number was burned into the bottom of the screen, just below the red brocade tablecloth on which the Santa-pirate shuffled cards, laid them in various patterns, then gathered them to start over. A small crystal ball sat to his right, and a stick of incense burned next to that. A big electric full moon glowed behind him on the wall, where little pointy stars had been painted. Call now, call now, call now, we take all major credit cards. Rosie got the urge to grab the phone. Maybe this guy, fake as he seemed, knew what was happening to her. But who was she to proclaim anybody else fake-looking? Did she herself have the appearance of somebody who could know the storeroom inside another's mind?

Hannah, there that second day, answered that for her. "I can tell already that you will do fine. Like Irene, you aren't —

how shall I put it — scary. You're approachable. I never went to a palm reader before I started working here. But when I met Irene, I had no fear about it. I feel the same way with you already, if you don't mind me saying that. So — do you have a moment?"

Rosie was just lifting the gate after fumbling again with the key.

"Sure, sure. If you just give me a second to get settled here."

Reluctant to start everything all over again, having spent the morning sitting in her car in her driveway, Rosie took her time letting herself through the door and onto the other side of the half-circle cutout, switching on the lights slowly and putting down her lunch bag. Finally, she took her place in the office chair and drew the curtain to one side. Hannah was there, big smile, right hand extended.

Rosie took a breath.

Looked down.

And the magic thing started again.

She saw swirls of what she could only interpret as change. They just about spelled the word for her, then switched to form big heavy vehicles, the kind that need tractor-sized wheels to get themselves around. Money changing hands. Heard the ear-splitting metal *bang bang bang* of work being done.

"Your family in construction?"

"Nope. Far from it. My father is an academic — Guatemalan folktales. My mother works at Sturbridge Village. Dresses like she's back in 1840 and living on the farm there. Feeds the pigs and herds the chickens, or whatever, washes the sheep in the river. And she wouldn't let us have even a hamster when I was growing up. Do you see my folks constructing things?"

"Somebody is. Or did. Or will be. I can't exactly tell."

"Well, I want a house — I mean I'd wanted a house . . . I'd

hoped to stay here a while. I was looking at places on the weekends, had an agent taking me around to view property — but now I'll only be here as long as the mall. End of the year." Hannah's face deflated at bit at that last line.

"No question about that," said Rosie, "but something's going to be built somewhere."

"I was looking to build, then decided I didn't want the hassle."

"I see concrete."

"That makes sense. When I was eight, our house burned. My family has been living in brick or stone or stucco ever since. I was hoping for stone myself, you know, like something a craftsman would make. A stone house. I guess you'd need concrete to hold the stones together."

"I see stones, too, so that makes sense. And lots of money."

"You think I'll get a stone house someday?"

"Well you are there in all the commotion, and you are happy."

In the palm, Hannah stood in a gray pantsuit and hard hat and muddied work boots. Face beaming lighthouse-strong with pride.

"I like that! You're good!" Hannah's mood was up. Hope had happened again. Rosie had done what Irene had asked of her, without making anything up. "You seem to have a more refined view of, you know, the future, than Irene. But I'd imagine there are different schools of palm reading."

"I'd imagine," Rosie agreed, and she shrugged, then quickly turned that into a shoulder scratch she hoped disguised that she had no idea what she was doing.

Whether or not Hannah caught on, she becomes a regular customer, visiting Rosie for a reading once a week, rather than the usual monthly trips she'd made to Irene. She will extend her hand, and Rosie will see how very young Hannah had named all seventeen trees in the circular yard of the house that eventually would burn, had said hello to them each time she went out: "Hello John Glenn, Frank Lloyd Wright, Amelia Earhart," all those who, like the trees, at one time had shot skyward.

She will see the value Hannah's job holds for her, will find familiar the enjoyment she knows it gives, the enthusiasm she has for daily being among the public.

In turn, each time she comes for a reading, Hannah sees things.

Not things, really, but people.

Waiting to see Rosie.

Waiting, and then getting their palms read, and then, what the heck, I'm here, why don't I walk around, hey, look, I can pick up a card, get a haircut, check out prices to Florida, catch a matinee, visit the salad bar, buy a camera.

And they do.

Some of them even come back to do that, to have their palms read again and then do a bit of browsing, or shopping, or eating. Many of the visits are nostalgic and rather negative — "Look at how this place has gone downhill! Remember when it opened? You couldn't even get in the door." But, really, who cares what these people are saying? They are here. And that is the main thing:

Once again, people are coming to Orchard Mall.

17

The newspaper reporter arrives one early morning in mid-July after receiving the press release Hannah had e-mailed to announce that a reader of palms is bringing good fortune to Orchard Mall.

Hannah is proud of coming up with the wordplay. It makes her think about putting the letter in her portfolio, to show how she can turn a phrase. She hits the print icon on her computer and clacks off to space number sixty-three so, as she promised she would, she will stand that late July morning at Rosie's side as the moral support and as Orchard Mall's official representative.

"You'll be sure to put that this is just for fun, won't you?" Rosie asks the newspaper reporter, Mary Ellen Watson, who is scribbling away even before the first question, and who has the ability to take notes without looking at her pad.

"Yes, of course."

"Because it is."

"You don't guarantee anything."

"Right — but," Hannah throws in with pride, "you'd be amazed at what she knows."

"Well, why don't you show Dave and me?" asks Mary Ellen Watson, waving toward the mustachioed photographer who accompanies her with a chunky black Nikon to capture the scene.

"Go, go behind your window," Hannah urges with a big

smile.

It is 8:00 a.m., an hour before any shop opening, and, sixteen paces behind Hannah, a crowd already has gathered at the pulled-down security gate that minutes before had to be pulled up just to let in Rosie, Hannah and their guests. Despite Dennis's reminder outside

WE'RE

SO

COOL

(68 F)

this crowd isn't here to walk the mall. It is here to find out the future.

Rosie opens and closes the door to the wall, settles into her chair, waits for Hannah to slide the spare one next to her, moves the curtain to the side, then takes Mary Ellen Watson's hand, adorned with two silver bands on the thumb, a look Rosie found fascinating on enough of the hands offered to her, but after several experiments from her jewelry box, didn't feel was for her. She turns this particular hand palm up. "Make a wish but not for money," Rosie directs. Then she looks down at the palm. Then she goes white.

And in the photo that runs next to the story about the reporter's car flying through the rungs of the Indian Orchard bridge on the way back from the interview, Rosie, seated with the still-intact reporter before her, looks horrified.

Now, you don't want anybody dying just so you can get big huge publicity, and nobody's death happened, but it was close enough — Mary Ellen Watson having to be fished from her car by quick-thinking hydroelectric workers snacking on crullers on a nearby retaining wall, photographer Dave, in the car behind her, braking in time and then there to document the whole thing with shots that Rosie thirty-five minutes earlier had told him would win him the top award from the New England Associated Press News Executives Association at the convention up in Burlington the following spring. From her hospital bed the following day, the reporter requests a laptop and taps out the story that begins, "I am paid to be a skeptic," and goes on to tell how she was laughing to herself as she left Orchard Mall, saying this was a pretty stupid way for a sad and dying mall to get publicity. And the next thing she knew, just as that Rosie had told her, the reporter was drinking the Chicopee River.

"You look at your eyes in the rearview mirror too much when you drive," Rosie had started out that morning as she took Mary Ellen Watson's palm through the half-circle cutout. Hannah had grimaced — couldn't Rosie begin with something positive about the woman's cheery character, her unflappability on deadline, whether or not Rosie had any idea of those things? No, in this case, Rosie could not. Hannah could tell from her urgent pace as Rosie said, "I tell you this because looking at your eyes in the rearview mirror too much when you drive is soon going to bring you into great danger." And she went on to describe how a fast glance into the mirror on the bridge between Indian Orchard and Ludlow within the next twenty-four hours would be disastrous.

"Please do not take that bridge. If you do, please keep your eyes on the road."

The interview had barely started, and it didn't last much longer after that. The reporter was embarrassed because what Rosie had told her was indeed the truth. Her eyes, King Tut-wide and the color of freshly-minted gold, were her best feature, and since college she'd splurged on a range of L'Oréal shadows and liners and nutrifying mascaras, all because she held a slight pouty resemblance to the line's slightly pouty

147

spokesmodel, Isabella Rossellini. The reporter assigned ten minutes of her morning routine to shading, lining, blending and brushing in front of a bulb-encircled makeup mirror she'd owned since high school thirty years ago, obtained by her mother through the saving of S&H Green Stamps. Often throughout her day, Mary Ellen Watson would enjoy catching sight of her eyes in a shop window or restroom mirror, and, way too often, would glance into the rearview to see the only thing on her she felt approached perfection.

She'd had her share of near misses due to this habit, but always struck out at the other guy — you idiot, you asshole, do you want to kill somebody, look where you're going! After much horn- honking and swerving and swearing, she'd continue down the road, shaking, sweating, lesson learned; she knew to keep her eyes on the road and her hands upon the wheel. But the lure of her own beauty always caused her to quickly forget.

This, Mary Ellen Watson writes from her hospital bed. A catharsis. A confession. A very good story that will take second place in the features category at the same convention at which photographer Dave will win first the following April, and a significant way in which the word about Rosie, Queen of the Unseen, washes across local consciousness.

Television follows.

Without having to be phoned and pitched, radiant and blonde Kiki Cutler, the Katie Couric of local TV, and a bearded perspiring videographer she fails to introduce, show up at the mall office one afternoon the next week and ask Hannah for permission to stand outside Rosie's space and interview some of the people in the line now snaking all the way down Main Street, as far back as the Orange Julius.

Hannah is only too delighted, and escorts Kiki and the cameraman to space sixty-three, where the young woman next in line is only too thrilled to give her story.

"I love this kinda shit," she says, and her pack of friends nod. Yes, yes, they loved this kinda shit, too, they assure Kiki. "It's all freaky and cool and maybe you find something out, ya know? Like I wanna get married but I wanna have fun first for a lotta years, but I don't wanna wait so long that I'll be too old to have kids, even though now you can have 'em when you're like eighty. I don't wanna wait that long and be some old-baggy-ass mother. But I do wanna have my fun. Maybe she knows when I'm gonna meet the guy I'm gonna marry. How many years will I have to have fun?"

Behind them is a more subdued client. She tells Kiki, "My sister died. I want to know if she's OK. I mean I know she's dead, but is she, you know, OK?"

"Is it mine?" asks the man who requests that only his hands be shown during his interview. They are clasped nervously, the thumbs fumbling with the tail of his shirt as he croaks out, "She told me it is, but, I mean, she's lied to me before. I really need to know if the child is mine."

"I don't believe in this sort of thing and am collecting data to make a case on Beacon Hill that this type of activity should not be allowed in the Commonwealth," says a college student whose case will not go anywhere, but in the process of talking with legislators, he will meet the man of his dreams.

Kiki's videographer films Hannah at her desk, busy with the phone calls and correspondence that result from increased interest in a place nobody has cared about for a couple of decades. Which is what Kiki points out in her brief interview.

"Nobody's really paid attention to Orchard since, what, since Mountainside came along?"

"You're right," Hannah says, then holds up an optimistic finger and adds, "But whatever's happening now, that's changing things."

In a montage of images underlining those changes, the Affordable Attorney waves as she closes the door to a meeting with yet another new client. Dervla, wearing a telephone headset, opens a directory of cruises and quotes prices to a caller. The Music Man tilts his head rapturously as a student delivers "City of New Orleans" on her mandolin. The Village Stylist quickly sweeps a small mountain of hair from the floor beneath the third of her three chairs — the only one vacant — and calls, "Next?" to the six people occupying her waiting room's six chairs. The Russian girl asks, "With everything?" to the three men ordering a couple of hot dogs after emerging from Cinema I and a viewing of M*A*S*H*, the latest in its special series of films popular forty years ago, when the mall was born and enjoyed its first big boom.

Then Kiki, all serious, like narrating the path of a crime, adds, "But not all who run businesses at Orchard Mall are as delighted."

"There should be a moral code here," rasps Mom, as she rings up yet another sale to someone who's just come from or who is just about to get in line for Rosie. "It's as good as stealing, what she's doing, taking money and giving nothing in return. The rest of us here for years doing honest labor, she comes along — from nowhere. Claims to be doing this witchy voodoo stuff or whatever. She should be arrested."

"I'm just doing this as a favor for a friend," Rosie says stiffly when she is filmed through the half-circle cutout. She looks washed-out, tired, which she is, and frazzled to be on television, which she is, both frazzled and on TV, where viewers that night at 4:00, 5:30 and 6:00, then again at 11:00, watch her say, "Irene Cervelli. She was here since the mall opened, practically. She left the area to get married. I'd lost my job. She asked me to do this. I'm only doing a favor by taking over."

"But you must know what you're doing," Kiki counters

while she protectively holds one tight fist around the microphone and the other behind her back. "You must know something."

Rosie shrugs. She has no reply but that she knows what she knows, but also knows that it makes sense to only the bearer of the palm on which she sees:

The phone message that awaits on the answering machine of the nice old lady who for fourteen years has come to the half-circle cutout the first Monday of each month at the stroke of 3:30 after buying a few cards from Bunny while her husband has the sparse remainder of his hairs clipped, and after a browse through that nice Mom's shop maybe to pick up a little small something for the neighbor child, and after then strolling past the waterwheel to arrive in time for the 4:30 early-bird special at the Flaming Pit — Rosie knows not only the contents of the phone message but actually hears the voice that will tell the woman there is no easy way to say that this nice old lady's Bichon Frisé has expired while at the groomer's.

That job as volunteer advisor to the college radio staff, this next woman in line will take it, but when she makes her first visit to the station she will find the components at the station old and unrepairable, and the college will have no funds to update them, so this next woman in line will not be needed. But she will not tell her family, who will by then be raving to everyone in the world that she has become a college professor.

"Baskets," Rosie whispers to the woman holding the dozing baby, the woman who has come in specifically because of the baby, the birth of which has cost her the job at the recycled plastic pellet factory, and now she is wondering, just like so many have, which course of employment to take, and "baskets" is what Rosie sees in her hand. Baskets far fancier than the ninety-nine-cent ones she dumps potato chips into when guests stop over. This woman will be selling these baskets at home parties to the enthusiastic pockets of people who covet them the way Rosie's mother once had salivated over Hummels. Some company down south will make the baskets, and the baskets will make the woman a surprisingly fine living. "Baskets," Rosie says, and the woman answers, "Huh?"

She does tell Kiki Cutler that, time and again, "Make a wish but not for money" is ignored, is responded to with "What will be tonight's winning number?"

"If I don't see it in your palm, I can't give it to you," Rosie will say, because that is the truth. People are always asking for lottery winners, saying that if Rosie were truly, really a palm reader, she could be giving the winning quick pick. She does try from time to time, especially when taking the palm of someone who looks particularly needy, but usually sees nothing but pain and loss, the writing of bad checks, the line in the pawn shop, the sneaking into the secret places at home where bills and coins are squirreled away by a mother or girlfriend or teenage son. On the Tax Man, who had been in line after the basket woman, Rosie spots the fate line, and then the distinct image of the available and leggy and man-seeking woman staring at the selection of canned vegetables in the canned vegetable aisle down which this man never bothers to venture because who needs vegetables?

"Aisle six," she says to him, and the man leans in, not understanding, because who would understand what that meant, so Rosie repeats the information, because this would be a perfect fit if ever there were one, she knows. She can see their shared interest in the late Dale Earnhardt, the identical style of mourning-black #3 stickers that decorate the respective rear windows of their trucks, their matching unfulfilled wishes to visit Florida and the site of Dale's final race, and their unspoken dreams that they might one day name a son (or daughter — though they've yet to meet, each independently feels the name is handily unisex) after him. "This time," Rosie adds, "you have to listen to me. Go to the Grand Z. You know — the grocery. Right down the road. Right now. Go there. Aisle six. Now!"

From the hallway, Bobby Vinton's "Melody of Love" is on the Muzak. Dennis is at the entrance to Rosie's space. He places himself behind the man with the Pekingese in his tote bag, the dog who goes everywhere including Mass each morning, and Rosie will be able to tell this man that it annoys the dog when the man makes him stay in the pew when he goes off to receive communion. Dennis holds a picture of Bobby Vinton, of himself and Bobby chatting, a photograph made back in 1974, when that song was on the radio fifty times a day. Louise Pomainville, mall manager number eight and the first woman with that title at Orchard Mall, had snapped her Instamatic just as Dennis had asked Bobby, "Is that a perm?" not to be smart, but because Dennis had the same kind of hair, only his was blackest black rather than Bobby's blond, and even though Dennis's has been curly since birth, people often ask him that very question, though much less so now that men aren't getting perms like they used to in the '70s, when Dennis got that question most frequently. He is thinking of this while the song is playing and as Rosie is holding the hand of the woman who could be the age of Dennis's own mother, had he ever really met her to know how long she'd been on the earth. The woman wears a silky tracksuit, shiny white material with stripes of peacockish purply swirly things on the pants. Rosie is speaking softly to her, is not looking into the woman's face, just addressing the palm. Dennis can't hear this, but she is telling the woman that the boy indeed had heard her, the little boy so long ago, he did hear her telling him to get better. But he just hadn't been able to.

When the woman vacates the purple chair and walks the sixteen steps to the door and then the twenty or so more to the

husband bench where she has to sit and let sink in the stagger-
ing and long-hoped-for fact that the boy indeed had heard,
Dennis stands at the half-circle cutout and says, "Look what I
found."

Dennis is lying, because he hasn't found the picture, it has
been in his autograph book back in his locker. But he wants to
show Rosie the picture because she'd mentioned her mother is
Polish, and bringing in a photo of this also-Polish person is one
way he can once again enter Irene's space and sit in Irene's purple chair at Irene's window.

"Look," he says as he takes a seat. "Bobby Vinton."

Rosie reaches for the photo. Then for a swig from the aluminum water bottle that had been the last First Bank giveaway
of her life there. She looks at the young Bobby, then the young
Dennis. Shoulder to shoulder, formal, Bobby smiling warmly,
Dennis wide-eyed.

"My parents still love him," Rosie says. "They got all his
music that was re-released on CD. They even went to Branson
— in Missouri — you can see him there. In person. He has his
own theater."

"You need your own theater." Dennis turns to the line behind him. Then realizes he is holding things up. But doesn't
want to go anywhere. Just wants to be there. The place where
for so long Irene had been. "I just wanted to say hi, and to
show you this so you could tell your mother."

And as Rosie hands the photo back, she catches sight of
Dennis's palm. Something swirling.

She hears Irene on the phone: "Did I know anything while
I was sitting there? You gotta be kidding. The only thing I
knew for certain was that I would die alone and miserable. And
look at me now."

Irene hadn't known — didn't know. Held no clue as to all
the enormous feelings Dennis carries for her. He'd never said

anything, she never picked up on anything, nothing ever happened, then something happened — for her, and with someone else — and here is the only result that Rosie sees right now, as she sees during his reading once a week: a man lost, defeated, shuffling. Right now pushing the purple chair away from the window.

"You look tired," Rosie tells him.

"Hannah wants me to change the sign twice a week now," Dennis says, coming up with that because he has nothing else to use as an excuse. Would Rosie understand how much sleep can be lost to the act of regret? The things he should have said to and done with Irene, had he the confidence she would not laugh. He touches the wood below the half-circle cutout, like there might be some molecules of her left. That was all he wanted, only that much of her, that small a thing. Why hadn't he said anything to her, ever, why hadn't he?

"Twice a week?"

"Excuse me?"

"The sign. You were saying?"

"Oh. Yeah. Hannah thinks people should always see something different up there every time they look at it. Though, really, you'd have to change it every hour in that case — what if somebody just went out for an errand and in fifteen minutes came back on the same road — they'd want to see something new, too. Anyhow, Hannah says we should take advantage of, of, of whatever it is that's happening here now."

"What exactly is happening here now?" Rosie asks him, the "is" as large as it would be on Dennis's sign.

"Only you would know," he says quietly, then quickly adds, "I'm not joking — I'm not disrespecting what you do. Because I think it's something. I mean I don't understand it, but look what you're doing. For these people. For the rest of the place."

Rosie ignores the line for another few moments. "Thank

you," which she says without meaning to. Of course, the response is "For what?" and Rosie says, "I don't know," though she certainly does. Here is a man who appreciates whatever it is she is doing in this half-circle cutout. Whatever it is that is happening in her life. She repeats, "Thank you." And she looks again at Dennis, at his dark eyes with roof overhangs of bushy eyebrows, at the graying national park of hair, takes in his soft manner, politeness. Even his sadness is appealing in a way. He needs to be needed. And Rosie knows who he needs, and how impossible that is, now that Irene never will be his.

In that silence, Dennis holds out his hand. In that silence, Rosie takes it in hers. He can't voice any wish. Leaves it unspoken. But Rosie knows it. Dennis still wants Irene. Has since that very first morning forty years ago. She knows he'd just finished vacuuming the gray industrial rug in the space she'd be leasing, when Irene came through the door carrying that big chair, and she stopped just at the threshold and looked to the ceiling, at the lights, and was seeing something right then, and Dennis didn't want to interrupt, because he'd been told what type of business would be conducted on these four hundred and fifty square feet, and, if this was the woman who was going to be doing all the spooky reading, well she looked already in some sort of trance. And other than that, she looked a lot different than Dennis figured she would. Younger by a generation, and a beauty queen compared to what the other tenants had been expecting — certainly no haggish Halloween-mask material, like Earle who back then worked the night shift had been betting she'd be. Like most people, Dennis only knew psychics from movies and TV, so he was surprised, too. By Irene's wartlessness. And by the way he couldn't stop staring at her.

"Think she'd ever look at you?" cracked the voice in his head.

"Think this'll look good here?" asked the woman with the

chair that she was setting into the far corner of the shop. And Dennis had no choice but to mumble a confused "Huh?" as his first words to the woman he would from then on love.

So he hears Rosie ask for his wish, that it be anything other than money, and in his mind he casts it: that Irene would know this truly, and truly not mind the fact that he loves her still, and maybe even truly love him back. He knows that is technically more than one wish — three, really — but as they are placed in a row, with commas rather than periods, he is hoping it will meet the qualifications of Rosie's direction. More than money, more than anything, that is what he wants. From that first day, and even through meeting Signy and marrying Signy and living with Signy day in and day out, and more than ever after being left by Signy. But in the ten years since that leaving, nothing really had happened between Dennis and Irene. Not like that, and you must put the "that" in quotes. Sure, they'd gotten much closer over the years. She hugged him before and after either of them began or returned from vacation periods, and at major holidays. And a few times just for his doing little things — scraping the ice off her car at the end of a rotten-weather day, once a year without fail painting the wall that holds the half-circle cutout.

He shuts his eyes. Slowly the lids descend, a little jerkily and reluctantly, like a curtain ending a grammar-school play. You expect to hear applause when they close fully, Rosie descending with them as they float down. There is a peace to the moment that feels like an hour, and he wishes it would last longer. Dennis bows his head a bit, making a prayer of what he wants — a most powerful moment, when he might have everything he wants. Everything. And Dennis Edwards wants only one thing — one person. Rosie has known that from her first day at the mall. In that way, there are no secrets between him and this woman who really is a stranger.

His eyes open. Fast.

"You know my wish," he tells Rosie in a microscopic voice that quivers at the edges. "And you know it's no good anymore."

Rosie nods once. She is reminded of the sacrament of confession — everything put into the open for the other person to know. Yes, the priests said, back when she learned all that in third grade, you were confessing to God — they were only the intermediaries — but Rosie knew that she still was telling her third-grade sins to a human with ears and a brain. Someone was taking them in. As she is with what Dennis's palm has revealed, and what his words — "You know" — make clear. She is taking in the deepest secret of this man, this man who really is a stranger, and he truly believes she knows what is in his heart. Rosie needs to peer so closely his skin becomes a blur, but that is necessary in order to make sure she is seeing correctly the truth in his hand. So she can say with all certainty, "Maybe so. And I know that's a horrible fact for you. But listen, and I am not making this up: someone is waiting. Just for you."

18

Your daughter is majoring in photography and that is why she joined the school newspaper, but she will end up writing poetry instead. Not anything close to professional and nothing that will come close to the rhyming kind that you prefer, but it will be fulfilling enough for her and will actually do some bit of good in the world.

Your father has kidney problems, and though you normally wouldn't give him the time of day, you are going to end up giving him one of yours — the left one. He will never come up to you and hug you and say, "Gee, thanks for doing this." But you know that fact even at this moment, and you will do it anyhow.

Even though you right now think you could never give your heart to another dog, you will go to petfinder.com. There is a big confused Saint Bernard/Great Pyrenees puppy rescued after having been chained to a bench for four months in Allentown, Pennsylvania, and you will fall in love all over again when you first see its face there.

You want to call the baby Myles, but if you do, everybody is going to want to spell it Miles, and he will go through life having to repeat the five letters over and over, but really it will not be an issue because, despite what the ultrasound technician told you, you are carrying a girl.

Your grandfather wants you to come to Florida and live with him for the rest of your high-school years, only because he knows you will be happier there. Unlike your parents, he doesn't care that you smoke and got yourself a tramp stamp and that little earring stuck into your right eyebrow. He just wants to give you a break.

Move the magnolia tree you just planted. There is too much shade in that spot. It will grow, but not as it should, and over the years you will look at it and wonder, "Why isn't it getting any taller?" If you do this now, you will not have to be always asking yourself that. And you will have a taller tree.

Go confidently in the direction of your dreams! Live the life you've imagined.

OK, so maybe that last bit is stolen from Thoreau, specifically from a refrigerator magnet Rosie's mother sent her over the winter, when it was clear that Rosie was going to have to go somewhere other than her kitchen table each morning, but it is late in the day in late July and her eyes are tired. In the palm before her, she sees a woman's sadness over feeling stuck and like her life is not the one meant for her — though the woman can't really say that she has an idea of which one she is indeed supposed to be living — and Rosie knows encouragement is needed. She also sees this woman walking along the edge of a pond as she does her thinking, and so she feels a nature quote would be appropriate. It hits the target, Rosie can tell, because the woman chants "Thoreau, I love Thoreau!" then reaches through the half-circle cutout and hugs her. "It's like you're speaking for him, to me." Rosie shrugs and says, "I don't know about that . . . " But the woman knows. "Oh, yes, that is what happened. It's like you were speaking for him. That is what I need — to follow my dreams! Now, can you tell me what my dreams should be?"

Rosie can't, because they aren't in the palm right then. "If I can't see it, I can't say it." She often says that, and she often thinks to have Mom paint that up on a piece of slate to be hung next to the half-circle cutout, but doesn't really care to talk to

Mom, and, more, doesn't want to come off as trite even if the truth is as simple as that. She can't tell you what she does not know, and she does not know it if she does not see it. So she has no idea of that woman's dreams, since they aren't there on her hand, but lots of scenes regarding other things are on other people's palms. Including, for a month now, that presence waiting on Dennis's right hand.

He comes back later during that day. It is evening at that point, and he keeps adjusting his place in line so he'll be last. His workday is over by this point, so he could spend the entire night shuffling like this if he wanted. It would be a small price to pay to finally make it to the half-circle cutout and have all the time in the world to make sure Rosie has seen what she did. That she wasn't just being nice. Because he can see her being that. He sees how much time she spends with customers — or clients, what does she call them? — and how she often leans through the half-circle cutout to hug someone at the end of a reading or, if someone appears really shaken, she'll come out through the door and stand there with them, her arms around them, joining them in their sorrow or their wonder, whatever is the result of even their being told something like, "Give her a guitar rather than the bicycle even though she really wants a bicycle. The birthday he got his first guitar, Elvis really had wanted a bicycle, but his mother was too worried he'd be run over on it, so she bought him a guitar instead. Also, to her credit, Elvis's mother knew he had a musical gift, just as you know your daughter has a gift. Look how famous Elvis got because of what his mother did."

Dennis moves back in line again, giving up his space to the guy who is told that in the YMCA locker room he will eventually see naked, and in this order, the district attorney, the man from the radio finance show, and the auxiliary bishop.

And he moves again, this time for the man who learns that

his company will want him to take a taxi from the airport to the hotel, but he should take the van shuttle because they are running a contest and he will not be the grand prizewinner, but his ticket number will get him one of the other prizes, and he will end up with a free dinner for two, including complimentary drinks.

Each customer gives Dennis more time to study the oddity that is this new face in the place where Irene's had been for so long. Not that Rosie's face is odd in any way. Dennis has no artistic experience, but to him she looks like someone who's just been sketched. Her movements are fast and impermanent lines, like the birds he watches from up on the signs. Her eyes are as bright and sharp as she looks into palm after palm and, from sixteen paces away, her voice is imperceptible, but he can tell it is even and steady and gentle, whatever it needs to be as she informs her clients or customers or whatever she calls them that they'd been overcharged when they'd picked up their prints down the hall. "But it was just an oversight and not the fault of the technician, who is new and who is very nervous about running the cash register, and she charged you for four-by-sixes rather than three-by-fives, but the difference is only a dollar and a half, so when you discover this you might want to just not make a big deal. She needs the confidence. She sees words backwards. Numbers as well. She's trying. Don't mess up her day, because I know that you are the type that would drive fifty miles back to the store if they overcharged you a quarter — no offense, I hope."

From sixteen paces away, Dennis watches Rosie's mouth moving. She is telling the next person, the woman he just now let go in front of him, "The next time you send one of those jokes on the office e-mail it is going to end up offending the guy in the corner whose nationality you cannot guess just from looking at him," but Dennis only sees the dance of her lips. Just as it is his turn, he nods to allow a latecomer before him, and watches them again as Rosie directs the woman, "Stop eating off those commemorative plates with Jackie Onassis's face on them, there is a warning on the back not to and you never read that and it will make you sick, not because of anything about Jackie, but because the paint on them is not something you should put food on. You should just hang them on the dining-room wall like you were going to in the first place when you saw them in *Parade* magazine on that Sunday the party you were supposed to attend, though you didn't really want to, got cancelled due to snow, and you got to look at every single page in the big papers, something you rarely give yourself the time to do." Dennis hears none of this, but is glad that whatever Rosie is relaying is taking a while.

Her "Next?" startles him, and he is disappointed to look behind him and find the hall empty for the night. A glance at his watch — ten minutes short of closing — answers why.

He walks the sixteen steps and takes a seat in the purple chair. Its soft back is appreciated after the long stretch of standing in the hall. But Dennis would have waited another hour in order to have Rosie's open-ended time for more of what she'd told him last time. This time starts with a smile as she says, "I saw you doing crowd control, very nice of you."

"Maybe, but it was self-serving."

"Dennis, are you studying what I'm doing? First you have to have somebody leave you the business." It is a joke. Not really funny, but a try. Rosie realizes he is the wrong person for Irene references and hurries to say, "I could leave it to you. And you could try it."

"I'd be the wrong person. I don't know anything. That's why I'm here." And for the second time that day, Dennis extends his hand to Rosie. "You said you saw somebody. You know — here."

163

He moves his hand closer. Rosie keeps her eyes focuses on his face. She's seen Irene on his palm before, and she's seen the figure. The figure is the only being she'd mentioned. As it is the only thing she sees now when she lowers her eyes to the open hand before her, taking it into hers and looking closely. She hears water. She sees a shape. Feels its anticipation. Knows the anticipation is for Dennis. She looks up.

"Nothing's changed from this morning," Rosie tells him. "Somebody's still there. Waiting."

"Who?"

Rosie shakes her head. "All I know — it's there, it's loving. Hey — that's good news, right? But I can't say it's her. You realize that, right? It's not who you want it to be. But someone is waiting."

He nods. Because he believes her. And he has to accept that it could not be Irene. He had no idea how important it would be to hear this. He doesn't mean to, but the assurance of Rosie's message makes him helpless but to close his hand around hers.

19

Whenever there is someone waiting at the little brick cottage at the edge of the municipal golf course at the end of Rosie's day, it isn't anything like the loving, mysterious presence that waits at the edge of Dennis's palm. The being who waits there more resembles an employment counselor.

"Across from my parking lot, there's a dance studio."

"And you want to take some lessons?" Rosie tries to sound light. She doesn't want to start anything. Scot's temper has been getting shorter the longer she has been working at the mall. "Well, might be a good idea to know how to dance for the wedding."

"No. You. You should give lessons. There's a sign: 'Instructor Wanted.'"

Two days before, he'd seen a sign somewhere for a dog groomer. The previous week, a big newspaper ad inviting all to take the real-estate license exam, even though nobody these days is buying houses. And a day before that, he'd announced that a guy in his office had a brother at Home Depot who was looking for help in the millwork department.

What is a millwork department? Or millwork, for that matter?

Rosie is flat on the couch pondering this. It is only Wednesday, but she is exhausted. Today she'd had to all but dial the phone so a woman could talk one more time to her mother in New Mexico a few minutes before the mother's heart was ready to go just like that. "Now!" Rosie was shouting at the woman as she fished for her cell phone. "Now!"

Right now, she wants to just talk about that with Scot. To wonder aloud at all she has seen on this day. But the stories would only give him more ammunition that she shouldn't be doing what she is doing. Which is what he believes. What she should be doing is what he would like her to be doing.

"Now you want me to teach dancing."

"It might be fun."

"Funny would be more like it — you've seen me dance, Scot. Plus, I don't want another job right now. I want this one. I really do."

"You're graceful." It is like he hasn't even heard her. "I bet you could pick it up in no time. I could maybe get some people from work to go over, as exercise. They say dance is great exercise."

Rosie cuts in, "Scot, why can't you support me on what I'm doing now?"

Now there is no reply, no sound except for the soft *chush chush* of the little checks Scot is making in pencil next to the list of errands and activities he's accomplished since rising, a list that begins, as it does daily:

Up
Shower
Pray

So, in case he gets nothing else done, he will have those easy ones checked off. But today he'd also filled his gas tank, checked the oil and topped it, dropped the entire audiotaped Stephen Covey collection back at the library and on time, had his teeth cleaned, inserted "Affordable Hawaii" into Google and surfed for the thirty minutes he allots himself daily on the

Internet, and had yet another game idea rejected by the creative team.

"This board game has a bit more going on than your previous suggestions, yet we find 'Whose Turn to Be Intern' to be tasteless, not to mention dated," read the Post-it stuck to the top of the box Scot had shaped and painted in the image of the White House.

Tasteless. Dated.

The bastards.

In two years, Scot will be forty-eight. By that age, according to plan, he was supposed to have created a game on the level of nothing less than Monopoly, Scrabble, Battleship and Trivial Pursuit. And also was supposed to have written a book about the path he'd taken to this pinnacle of success. Today's note will be saved in a file. It hurts now, but will make a brilliant illustration in his best-seller. Not to mention a nice method of revenge. As he thinks further, Scot pictures the book packed in a box, as if it were a game itself. And maybe the main characters — he, Rosie the loving spouse, Arnold J., the shortsighted head of the creative team — could be cast in pewter and included. Maybe his entire experience of trying to sell a game idea could be a game itself. Throw the dice and advance to the space that tells you your idea is tasteless, not to mention dated. Lose a turn. Next throw, land on big success, a launch in the fall just in time to make this the most sought-after Christmas gift — harried parents standing in thick lines as they had in the days of the Cabbage Patch Kids, a hit-of-the-season game invented by Scot being sold for big bids on eBay, or scalped for hundreds of dollars through vague newspaper classifieds that hold only the title, phone number and words "CALL NOW."

Scribble scribble scribble scribble, Scot adds all that to his grand plan.

At a time like this, Rosie is very tempted to look at Scot's

167

palms. Just in the way you might look at the hands of anyone you love, she'd done so for three years before Irene left, but can't remember one thing about them, other than they are cold very often and needed rubbing to help the circulation. But since Irene left and everything started, the palms, and hands, and the rest of Scot, have stayed pretty much away from Rosie. And his general temperature is pretty evident even from across the room.

"I really didn't mind it that much at first, you were happy there," he says without looking up from his list or acknowledging that he indeed had minded from the start. "It was giving you something to do, so I felt what's the harm? But now. This. Taking it seriously. And everybody knowing about it!"

His hands. Rosie bets to herself that Scot has the spatulate thumbs of someone with manual dexterity, that his Mercury finger, the one of communication, leans away from the others, signifying a deep need to be alone. She ventures that his Mercury and Apollo lie close to one another, meaning there is difficulty in personal relationships. Maybe his middle fingers lean outward, toward the ulna, which would signify that repressions are very deep. His Mercury that certainly has to be hiding behind Saturn translates to an unwillingness to communicate, whether due to shyness or lack of confidence.

Scot now stands in the kitchen of the little brick cottage on the edge of the municipal golf course. He redoes his ponytail. Parts the tail into two sections of hair and yanks them sideways to pull the hair-protecting coated rubber band farther up. He does this angrily and ends up hurting himself. Which angers him more. Rosie has seen him angry about the things that make anybody angry, but not angry like this.

"You don't seem to give a care about how this looks," he says, his voice loud enough to startle.

"Well, how it looks to who?"

168

"To people," he shoots. "In six more months, we're scheduled to have our photograph and engagement announcement in the Sunday paper. What will you put down as your employment? Think about it. How does a job like this sound?"

Right now, even though Rosie is just barely home, it sounds like something she wants to run to.

"They get like this, ya know."

Tina from ceramics and from First Bank's Graphics Department knows and shares. She's been engaged three times, married twice; she's seen this. Commitment shaking an otherwise unshakable man.

Tina from ceramics and First Bank's Graphics Department is saying this through the half-circle cutout. She'd been going to Irene for years, and wasn't she surprised when she stopped by in early August and found Rosie instead? So was this why she wasn't in class any longer? And was this what she was doing now? Tina thought it was funny that somebody would just take over a palm reader, like anyone could have the powers or whatever. She didn't think it was so funny when Rosie took her hand and saw the neighbor guy rooting around and taking stuff — including a brand new perennial garden soaker hose — from Tina's garage when she left for the day. Tina has been back every other Friday since that first reading — twice as often as she'd visited Irene.

"Jimmy?" she asks. "You remember the ashtray I made last year? Shaped like a *J*? It was for Jimmy. Well Jimmy was big into the wedding thing. Almost more than I was some days. But I think all of a sudden it hit him. That whole tied-down thing. Days of freedom over with, all that. He started acting weird. Scot, he's freaking about the wedding, not this. He'll get over it."

"Jimmy got over it?"

Tina from ceramics and First Bank's Graphics Department scowls. "No. He was the one between Raoul and Dave. I have Dave now — legally!" She waves a ring, but rather than admire its sparkle, Rosie is stuck on the "have," which sounds like how you might "have" a cat or "have" an illness. Tina smiles widely behind the solitaire and band. "He's the one that got over it, over freaking out. And then he was fine. He's working on his brother now to get married. Says it's the best thing. Though the brother just says misery loves company. But I think I believe Dave. That he's OK with commitment." She shoves her hand forward now. "Should I? Believe him? That he's OK?"

Rosie moves from being stuck on more words — "working on" — and looks into the palm of Tina from ceramics. Sees Dave from her marriage in an upholstered rocker, staring ahead with intensity, but there is no one there to look at, no television playing. Yeah, Dave is being quiet. And, Rosie knows, miserable. Something encircles him like the rings of Saturn. There is nothing like regret. She sees that around Dennis, and when you catch the sight of it for the first time, there's no mistaking it for anything else. What she sees is not a moment of sadness, or the leftovers from a bad day, or a moment of contemplation. Regret is big and wide and orbits around and around, ever reminding you of what you missed, what you could have had, what you could have been. Dave is smoking his corner-store generics, and, really, he cannot breathe. But that isn't due to the cigarettes. Has not been able to for some time. Ever since the night a week or so before the wedding when Tina had accused him of not really loving her and, what could he do at that point, he said, "That's stupid — of course I do."

Now he is in his chair, almost dying from getting into this situation. Alone. Joined by millions and zillions of people around the world who forever will regret not saying what they should have, not being where they should be, not being who they should be. Unless they do something. Which is what Dave is just starting to realize.

"Never is it necessary to give anyone bad news," *Palmistry for Beginners* advises. "We never know what harm we can cause. Your client's fate is his or hers alone, that particular life will have its shares of highs and lows. You will not help by informing someone there is no way to escape unpleasantness. Remember the cloud and its silver lining. Use this image to lift spirits, if you indeed read that trouble is ahead. And for the client who seems unconcerned about tomorrow, refrain from mentioning the topic if they do not."

Rosie waits and then says to Tina from ceramics and First Bank's Graphics Department, "Dave isn't feeling great."

"His nuts again," Tina overinforms. "Still does a Tae Bo video — on a VHS player from years ago. One minute he was doing a kick, next thing he was on the floor. They've never been the same."

"Maybe so. Maybe not."

"Ah, he'll get over it. I'm glad to know that's all it is. I gotta run. He's probably home by now. Waiting for me. Missing me. See ya next week!"

From her place on the couch, Rosie watches Scot, his back to her as he works on the details of his best-seller. She wonders if he ever sits and stares, like Dave. She knows Scot used to sit and stare at her, and she'd look up to meet his eyes and ask him what he was looking at, and he'd say something cornball like "Only the most beautiful thing I've ever seen." She wouldn't know the exact date, but she can't remember having that back-and-forth since, let's see, maybe since the end of the winter?

Maybe since Irene left town? Before that, for the three years they'd been together, Rosie had seen nothing but love from Scot. Love on a schedule, maybe. But love. A cozy evening could start only after the ninety minutes he assigned himself for working on his newest game idea. He'd listen to her troubles regarding a surly co-worker for only thirty minutes — more than that just added fuel to the flames, he said. Rosie was asked to e-mail him no more than twice a day (including forwards) — the Internet ate too much of his time, and simple "I love you" messages, while appreciated, were that many more minutes used in opening, reading and deleting. Rosie acquiesced, really — what was the problem with someone not wanting to have to read silly things all day? — but as she gave in to that request, she did recall how she and Dale used to e-mail one another in-cessantly, and just from across the living room — "Get over here!" "No, you get over here!" "Race you!" If Rosie were to look into her palm, she would see herself not only reliving that memory every time she wanted simply to send Scot a goofy e-mail, but a whole lot of other times he acted more like a secre-tary than the man she wanted until death did them part. But Rosie does not look into her own palm. The truth that lies there, Rosie does not say even to herself.

She saves truth-telling for others' realities. People who pay for it. Who fill her days. Who stand in line, waiting to be helped. To be told that the roofers left a string of very sharp nail-gun nails on your front lawn, to the right of the Virgin Mary, so don't go barefoot.

That it's Cushing's Disease. Old horses can get it. There are pills. She will live past your wildest expectations.

That it's a pilonidal cyst, not cancer. People get this, it is harmless but there will be surgery. However, you will live past your wildest expectations.

That a void is in her soul. Everybody has this at some

point. She will go for vitamins, thinking they will help. But in purchasing the vitamins she will meet the boy who will turn out to be the best thing for her, ever.

That your son will talk to you for the first time in two months when he asks you to go with him to the photographer next week to pick out his senior portraits. You will be so touched by this gesture that you will buy the most expensive package, including the big one decoupaged onto a half-circle of pine. The next week he will be back to not talking to you, but you will have that memory of going for the photographs, and of the photographer saying what a lovely son you have, and isn't he such a gentleman, too?

The last woman is weeping so much that she is one of the people for whom Rosie has to leave the half-circle cutout and come out through the door and give a big long hug.

Some mornings, Rosie finds customers in the hall when she arrives. Drinking coffees and looking at the morning paper and rolling little babies back and forth in multi-wheeled strollers. Once she raises the gate and unlocks the door and gets herself behind the half-circle cutout and moves the curtain for the first reading of the day, she is in her own world. Has no idea how busy the other tenants are. All she knows is that she is looking and seeing and telling non-stop, and that she is making money. And that even when her work is disturbing, as tough as the seeing and relaying sometimes are to be part of, it is helping somebody. She is giving information people really want and need, and she can feel good that she is not just making things up. No knock to Irene, whose name still hangs above the door, but Rosie is telling the truth. Yes, the boy in the coma indeed hears his mother singing that song about the boats that she always thought he enjoyed, but, more than anything, it gets on his nerves, and from deep within the cave of his silent world the boy tries his best to speak just so he can tell her to shut up.

If he could part the heavy curtain of the place where his mind is mired, and say anything to her, it would not be "Don't worry, I'm fine, I'm just very sorry that I went up on the roof after you told me never to again and that I would fall off, and that I'd end up dead doing that one day, which is just about going to happen.' It would be 'Will you stop singing that please?'"

What does he hear? What will she say? Why does she do that, and when will it happen next? Where Irene would maybe have told people fuzzy little stories — that they had a propensity for exaggeration or that they would be attractive to the opposite sex if only they got a decent haircut — Rosie is there giving the Web link for the ad that holds the dream job, or the blunt truth that illness is about to strike, so you should get to the doctor right away. Five months haven't changed things in one way — people are still asking about money — but now Rosie can, and does, give them so much more.

It gets doled out to everyone. Tenants. Relatives of tenants. Shoppers. Strangers. Sometimes, people she knows, and who know her, but aren't sure from where. They'll say she looks familiar. It is that whole thing about knowing someone only in the square feet of where you're used to seeing them. How, as a second-grader getting fitted for a new pair of Buster Browns, Rosie sat totally confused in the shoe store when she spotted her first-grade teacher browsing the pumps. That the teacher could exist anywhere but behind her desk, or at the show-and-tell table, or minding the line at the lavatory door, was mind-blowing. Many who come to the half-circle cutout have a version of the same reaction. They know Rosie's face from somewhere, only can't recall that it was another window, one at a bank. Where have they seen her? Does she have a sister? A twin? Everybody has a double. Has she ever worked at, what, the Grand Z? First Bank? No, if she had, what would she be doing here?

Some do recognize her, whooping, "Rosie Pilch I can't believe it!" Former co-workers: that college kid Jen who'd just started at the drive-up last Christmas, Antonio of the bilingual window, Stacey the receptionist, Mrs. Rossi in the western branch's vice president's office who had the back of her head shown in a TV commercial in which she was supposed to be applying for a loan from the western branch president, whose face was in full view. By the time they wander into Rosie's space, most of those former co-workers still are looking for a new place to work, but a few have moved on to another form of employment: waitress at Chili's, menswear clerk, UPS driver, something to do with First Bank's main office. They will tell her, "I can't believe you're doing this," and Rosie will answer, "Neither can I," and then after a few more lines of small talk and a promise to meet for a dinner she'll never have time to attend, will say, "Ten dollars, please," and then will ask for the wish that should not be for money.

Then she will tell them:

Your oil tank leaks.

Your cat is pregnant.

Your book is overdue.

Your lawn has moles.

Your fly is down.

Your pie will win.

Your woman will return.

Your promotion will come.

Your clematis will bloom.

Look tomorrow in the condensation that forms on your bathroom window, the shape of that, that is what the mountains behind your great-grandparents' home in the old country looked like to them, and you can afford to go there and finally see those mountains for yourself if you sell the electric guitar you bought when you loved the man who played the electric guitar. He used you, and you never used the guitar past that one lesson in which you learned the D chord, and you will get more from looking at those mountains in person than from looking at that guitar in person. You tend to beat on yourself in ways like that. Get the guitar out of the house. Get yourself out of there, too. And things will start to get better. Things often do get better, even when you think they cannot or will not.

She wants to add, "Take how it's been going for me." But by the time she lines the words up in her head, the woman who needs to sell the guitar and take the trip is far from space sixty-three. Rosie soon is, too. Not that far, but it seems so from way up there on the Orchard Mall sign, where she sips an Orange Julius and looks out to the hills. It is a baking August day, but the heat is welcome. Even a dead mall has overdone air conditioning, and for today's lunch hour, Rosie wants to sit in the sun. Doing so up at the sign had been Dennis's idea. If she wasn't afraid of heights, he'd said, he would take her to one of his most favorite places in the world.

Dennis feels he owes Rosie. But can't tell her that. Can't say what it means that someone else knows what Irene has meant to him and doesn't comment other than to just say kind things. Can't tell her what it means to hear about that figure on his palm. Someone waiting, not going away. Since Irene left, Bunny will pull Dennis aside and ask him what he is doing for himself these days. Will say exactly that: "Dennis, what are you doing for yourself these days?" in the tone of someone who knows he might need to be doing that. Dennis never knows how to answer. He shaves, he buys groceries, he saves his money. Is that what she means? He asks her that. He does not add that he also prays that Irene will come back. That she'll decide the elopement was a big mistake. That the man for her had been in front of her all along. Forty years. How could she have missed that fact? How could he have kept silent?

176

But when you don't feel you deserve what you really desire, you don't say a word. You just let the words of others, or one other, fill your head. Which is what Dennis too often does, allowing his father to remind him daily he doesn't deserve much of anything. How he'd managed to meet and marry Signy might seem a mystery, but realize that the father knew she wouldn't have been Dennis's first choice. The father delighted in the fact that his son had watched Irene head off from the half-circle cutout over the years with a variety of dates and love interests. The father delighted that none of them was his son. The father delighted over his son's having to settle, settling being one of the largest self-inflicted tragedies known. And the father danced all the more in Dennis's head when the union with Signy came to an end.

Rosie sees all these things just this morning, in the instant Dennis puts his hand out in a "ladies first" gesture at the foot of the ladder leading up to the sign. She has to stand still for a few seconds to register the new information, to further understand how large a part of Dennis's head is occupied by the dream-sparking love for an unavailable woman, and the dream-stomping comments of a dead man. She shakes her head at those sad facts, and Dennis asks, "Change your mind?" but she hasn't, and puts her hand on the first rung of the ladder that will take her up to the Orchard Mall sign.

A few minutes later, they stand on the walkway beneath the trio of exclamation points following the word "SCHOOL" in Dennis's latest message

STAY COOL
AS YOU SHOP
FOR SCHOOL!!!

and are silent as they stare at the full green hills. Dennis leans against the safety rail and watches his guest. He'd been up here with Larry Block, but that had been it for visitors in the forty years. There are rules and all that — he really isn't supposed to be allowing just anybody to climb the ladder — but who is going to complain? Realizing the answer, he quickly scans the now-busy parking lot for Mom, then looks back as Rosie takes a good long deep breath. He thinks of all the many times he'd wanted to bring Irene up to the sign. How often he'd imagined serving dinner there on the night of the day he'd write out their names on the same line, for all to see. He would have loved to have seen her reaction to the mountains, and the steeples, and the foreheads of the few tall buildings poking through the green far away. Even to having this vantage point for the parking lot. As they have been since the spring, cars and pickups and family vans and enormous SUVs are entering the lot at a regular pace. Entering and staying. For more than just to drop off film or pick up prints or take advantage of matinees or use the wide, vacant expanse of tar for the site of a teen's first driving lesson or to have a handy meeting place for carpooling or a safe place to attempt rollerblading. They are there to spend money, spend time. But, mainly, they are there to have their palms read.

Not for the next fifty minutes, though, as the movable hands of the "I'll be back at" clock on a sign inform those who approach the half-circle cutout. Irene had created the sign when she'd moved into Orchard Mall, but hadn't needed it for a good ten years. If she walked away from her space for a trip to the bathroom or a trip to lunch at the Pit, she wouldn't miss many passersby. If any. Only Dennis in his many, many daily trips past and through her door.

Rosie uses the sign for sanity, closing the curtain and placing the day's take in her purse and setting out the sign so she can take a walk, stop in to see Dervla or Ed or Bunny or Maria or the Russian girl, whoever is free in these days when few merchants are. She always is grateful for Dennis's company, but, as he doesn't have a store, she never can be certain where to find him. Running into him today as he exited the Tax Man's space was good fortune. She had just finished a string of innocuous readings — "Try sawtooth palmetto." "Switch to Paxil." "To cotton crotch." "To decaf." "To cordless." "To Tropicana." "To Tom's of Maine." "Refinance." "Reconsider." "Retire." — with the message "Don't be too delighted with this guy. He is a second chance, but also a second chance at getting your guts kicked in — he acts one way in public and will be another way at home that you don't want me to get into here, and that you don't want to get into at all. It is better to be lonely than to be with this person. Trust me on this. Please."

After a reading like that is when she most wishes Scot gave her occupation a whit of interest. She thinks of that very first person who appeared at the half-circle cutout, that woman Sheila, who Rosie hopes is right now watering the flower garden next to the green-sided house, the kind of flower garden Rosie had wanted to plant and that Scot had frowned on, seeing flowering plants, which you couldn't eat, as a big waste of money. Scot hadn't been in the area the day of that reading, and, in many ways, he hasn't been available since. He acts removed, as far away as if he were still on that island, on that wire, walking between the trees with his own accomplishments his only concern and goal. After a reading like she's just done is when she most needs someone for decompression. So when she'd spotted Dennis walking from the Tax Man's, and he offered a trip up to the sign, she reached for her own sign and closed the curtain.

Three little birds land in the branches of a nearby tree. It is something to be standing higher than where they are perched. To be out of the building. Away from the face of the would-be boyfriend in the same palm that the woman, if she does not heed Rosie, will one day soon have to raise against his punches. Rosie grimaces at the image, hugs herself despite the ninety-degree heat.

"Don't tell me you're cold," says Dennis, who is happy to think of something to say. They've been at the sign for maybe ten minutes without a word.

"No, just thinking." More silence. Then "Some of the things I see in people's hands, they're not nice."

Dennis says, "I bet," because he knows what he would see in his own hand, if he had any such ability. His head gets tangled as he runs through his mind the fact that he knows she knows what he thinks, what he wants, who he wants. He has no doubt Rosie knows. He'd never seen Irene's work as any kind of scam or sham or joke, even if she never was exactly able to tell you what you wanted to know. You went away with a good and hopeful feeling. In what might be the first negative thought he's ever had about Irene Cervelli, Dennis acknowledges that she'd still really known nothing at all when you considered the abilities held by Rosie. In two minutes on the first day they'd met, she instantly knew what he couldn't have. As he watches an ancient Accord and a shining smart Car vie for the same spot, he realizes this woman, this person, really knows him better than anyone ever has. He watches the smart Car win and feels a chill. What is stopping him from actually talking to her about the last forty years? Or how about just the last six months? Or maybe how about just these last few minutes, when he was standing there grateful that one person in this world had been to the inside of his heart and hadn't returned to laugh in his face? He takes as big a breath as he's seen Rosie take and turns from the rail to her. That's when Dennis says, "You know me. You really, really know me. I'm sure of that. Well, if possible, I'd like to get to know you."

20

Hannah Pomfret wants to do Halloween big. Years past, the mall had been a proper place for fright — all those dim and vacant halls, dark and dusty storefronts, that scratchy antique music flowing from somewhere overhead. But now that traffic has picked up significantly, she wants to use the occasion to increase it. Her idea is to have every shop distribute something to the trick-or-treaters invited to the mall via Dennis's sign.

"Whatever you can offer — candy, or something from your inventory, a great chance for some free advertising!" is what she writes in *Mall of Us*, which Hannah has resurrected over the summer. Part newspaper, part newsletter, all aimed at the Orchard community, *Mall of Us* has long been unnecessary. The number of tenants was less than two dozen, and anything one of them wanted to know about the others came by gossip that moved down the hall faster than Dennis on his motorized floor polisher after hours with no one there to mind his using the third and highest gear, zipping past the Orange Julius in a blur, iPod on the '80s hit "Take on Me" blasting through his headspace, Dennis feeling the excitement of it all. *Mall of Us* once had been relied on for official dispatches from down in Baltimore, for announcements of new stores, reminders of policies, pictures from retirement parties, and stuff culled from closer to home: recipes — Mary's Mexican dip, contributed by the lady who ran Pappagallo shoes, a Velveeta mix that called for the squishing of all ingredients with your bare hands; vacation pictures — the owner of the long-closed engraving shop standing with her mother and sister at the tiny little dock at Universal Studios in Hollywood that was used in the *Flipper* TV show; births — the mall's first in vitro baby, for instance, not really the mall's but belonging to the daughter of the woman who ran the store that sold living-room sets made from crates; and deaths — Dervla's first husband and the Affordable Attorney's cat and the Pit manager's half sister and the Russian girl's brother over in the old country — all of them going suddenly and unexpectedly and just like that.

"Now we're supposed to be giving stuff away — as if it isn't hard enough to make a living here" is what Mom is heard fuming when she scans her copy. She isn't any happier when she progresses to the end of the announcement, which encourages tenants to dress in costume.

"She's as crazy as you are!" Mom shouts over as Rosie is lifting her gate for the day, and Rosie just nods, whatever you say, fine. Despite the vase-appraisal advice that had resulted in the new car, Mom regularly hurls at Rosie the same abuse she used to aim at Irene. Hannah apologizes for this, though she has nothing to do with it. Bunny advises paying no mind. The Russian girl wants to teach Rosie a few foreign swears to pitch back at Mom. But Rosie really isn't bothered by her. She only feels sad for this woman — what could be so wrong in her life that she has to be so unpleasant?

Rosie doesn't wonder any of that aloud, of course. It isn't worth the oxygen. She has better things to use that on. Starting with the readings she'll give to the four people who are standing in her doorway.

Several of those in line are from the Orchard Walkers, the mall-walking program that actually had taken off back in the hottest days of August, when Hannah Pomfret asked Dennis to try again, another walking reminder, this one more detailed:

Suzanne Strempek Shea

"WALK IN 70-DEGREE COMFORT! STARTING DAILY AT 8 AM!" People desperate for any way to beat the heat began responding — people who wouldn't have responded before the word got around that Orchard — have you been there lately? — it's actually busy!

Nor would they have believed the reason. Orchard's rise is being credited to a woman's newfound psychic powers. Sure, the paper's business section has done a piece on the nostalgia vote, pointing out that the kids who'd shopped OM at its start now wanted to bring their own kids along. The local industry publication, *It's Business Time*, felt that mega-malls like Mountainside were becoming too expensive for the rental budgets of small to midsized stores. Television again showed up when the fountains of Town Common were turned on for the first time in fifteen years. And radio came to do an interview when Turn It Up moved in and started selling discs and a limited amount of vintage vinyl in the old Hit or Miss. Then radio stayed, WSPR-AM deciding to actually open a station in the mall and send its all-news, all-talk format out from the former Engraver's Touch space, the last shop at the end of Pleasant.

"Wouldn't you say the mall's new popularity is happening because you have a fine location, quality shops and a long history of serving the community?" asked Morgan Roberts, WSPR's 5:00 p.m. anchor, and Hannah Pomfret answered, "Yes, I would. But it's also because we have Rosie, the Queen of the Unseen."

Rosie Pilch is Miracle-Gro applied to a languishing garden. A fresh-air vacation granted to the impoverished inner-city kid. The half-time pep talk that contains all the right worlds. These things and more to a 856,212.85-square-foot behemoth of a building. To that, she can be a source of renewal. But to a two-hundred-pound, six-foot-tall near-fiancé with a briefcase of lists

184

and charts and journals and ideas, she seems to be nothing more than a source of ire. Why, he wonders, can't she listen to his advice, his ideas, his common sense? Why, he wonders, does she have to continue this job when he is so against it? It is harder to begin each day with the affirmations. "I am OK because he loves me," Rosie will remind herself every morning, even though she is finding this harder and harder to believe.

"I see great things for us, Rosie."

Unfortunately, Hannah Pomfret, rather than Scot, is saying this.

"Customer counts, weekly sales tallies, everything is up. New tenants. Steady increases across the board. Things are happening! Hey — that could be our new slogan . . . "

Hannah has come by for a reading, but she can't stop talking business. Rosie is ending a busy day. Once again, as she looks into the woman's palm, she sees swirls of change. Earthmovers. Cranes. Officials in hard hats. Millions of dollars being spent so millions more can be made. A house is no longer the best guess. She knows that Mountainside is planning an addition. Will Hannah be snapped up by them? Should Rosie ask if Hannah is interviewing over there? Or should she suggest it?

"Are you looking for a new job? You must be."

"I have it on the to-do list, I've made some contacts with friends in the industry, sure, but can you believe that in the past few months I haven't had the time?"

"I can." It seems just yesterday that Rosie had been stuck at her kitchen table in the little brick cottage at the edge of the municipal golf course. Now she barely gets inside her house to turn down another employment suggestion from Scot and collapse and wake and shower and change and head back to Orchard Mall. "But maybe you should be thinking ahead," she stresses. "There are big things awaiting you . . . "

Hannah cuts in, "Well, then they've got to be, right? Because you know everything. That's why people come here."

"Flatterer." Rosie smiles.

"It's true. You're it," Hannah says as backhoes roll across her Mount of Saturn. "This place is changing because of you. Look around. Look now. And that's what I'm here to talk to you about. We need to spread the word. That if people come here, they can get to talk to you, to find things out — and they can shop, too, of course."

Rosie isn't listening. She tells Hannah, "I see you on a trip." Hannah giggles. The line sounds so crystal-ballish. But that is what her palm now holds: Hannah on a plane. Row 14, Seat B, next to her a woman flying home on a bereavement discount, yet not looking the least bit upset. The deceased is a much older sister who in their childhood regularly had punched her in the stomach, even though her mother had said if you're going to punch her then aim somewhere else because don't you want her to have kids someday? The sister did all that punching and grew up and moved out to a commune of peaceniks. There are no fond childhood memories to mourn; this will just be a chance for her to get out of town and see after a very long time the other sister, the beloved one who never once punched her. Next to this woman, Hannah sits staring into the seat pocket and creating those two vertical lines at the inner edges of her eyebrows that secretary Laurie is always telling her could be erased by BOTOX. The source of Hannah's concern is Rosie's talk of her traveling to Baltimore. Work-related reasons, of course. She doesn't go to headquarters for a casual dinner.

"I see you on a trip," Rosie repeats. "Soon."

Bunny comes to the half-circle cutout that afternoon, just as Rosie is saying good-bye to a man she's informed that his parrot will never learn to talk, but that his teaching attempts are, for the parrot, a break from all those monotonous hours looking out the cage bars from its corner in the pantry. Bunny is holding a pack of postcards, the kind bound into book form, with perforations that allow for easy removal when you think of just the person you'd like to send one. The first card is the face of Princess Di, her eyes doing their trademark shy look upwards as she tilts her head down. Another shows Diana's brother in a little boat on a little pond, looking mournfully toward the little island on which his little sister was buried after she no longer was able to look up or down or anywhere else. The print on the back of that card says that the Princess's casket was encased in a lead box, a fact that makes Bunny shiver, imagining the lead-ish cold, and feel even worse for the dead princess. Bunny had been only a casual Diana watcher, but even so had set her alarm for 4:00 a.m. on the day of her funeral so she could rise in time to watch the coverage, feeling this was something she would not see again — not that she would want to actually see something like this again, of course. She ended up clipping from the next day's paper the transcript of the brother's impassioned eulogy, and later purchasing the cassette of Elton John's special song for Diana, the record-setting proceeds from which went to various princessly charities, so she felt like she'd done a good thing. But that's as far as it went for Bunny's interest, until she saw her distributor's offer of a great deal on a case of these Diana cards.

"Lookit these — didn't you love her?" asks Bunny. "People have been grabbing these — do you think she'll ever go out of style? I'm going to see if I can order more. I don't mean to make money off a dead person, but if they're selling, well, what can you do? Anyway, I've been so busy all day. Very busy. Thinking of Christmas — I might even hire some help this year. Imagine that. It'll be the last Christmas season here, but the best in a long while."

Rosie reaches for the pack of postcards and flips to the shot of the Princess with her red-haired sister-in-law. Rosie had held hope for Sarah's marriage to the cuter brother, but Sarah had ended up having her own string of troubles. Even so, according to what Rosie read, Sarah had stayed close to her ex, even living in the same home a few times over the years since their divorce. Rosie marveled at their ability to stay so amicable after the marriage was over. Hers hasn't even begun yet, and intimacy and caring already seem to have packed their bags and moved out. She shudders. Wonders what she can do even this very evening to start to regain what she and Scot shared in their first three years. She knows what she hadn't had in that time: this job. It has been made clear: get rid of it, and their old life will be back in an instant.

But get rid of that and what will happen to the mall and everyone connected to it? She takes in the compliments, but never says them aloud to herself, that what she is doing at Orchard Mall is not only keeping it alive but granting it new life. Bunny is in front of her now, talking about hiring help, and she's heard the same thing from many of the tenants. They need it, or soon are going to. Customers are verging on being an inconvenience, if that can be fathomed. It has been years since traffic like this. Years since the tenants have ended the day bone tired from concentrating on other people's wants and needs. For Rosie, one reading morphs into the next, making her recollection of the day's work a fuzzy chain of dreams, regrets, malaise, enthusiasm and hope, always hope. She has so much money in her zippered pay wallet at the end of the day that she regularly asks Dennis to accompany her to the night drop slot at the bank at the other side of the parking lot, past Pearle Vision. The night of the day that Bunny had come over with the postcards, as Rosie thanks Dennis, she hugs him out of nowhere. It has been a good day. She's told her customers nothing more amazing than that the set of keys one of them was looking for most of this year was in the pocket of the corduroy jacket he'd last worn in March, but it has been a good day. And she can't stop thinking how there are only seven weeks left until the end of a year that had begun so ominously. Just this afternoon Dennis had wheeled past her space the three giant structures that snap together to create Santa's cottage, which he'll set up tomorrow at the Town Common. Another village, to be set up within the one she's come to feel is home. On his break he'd asked her up to the sign. The day was a big and bright November one, the air the welcome liquidy cold kind you want to inhale until you feel every inch of your lungs bathed in it. Rosie sipped the air, and the hot chocolate she'd brought up, with an extra cup for Dennis. He was curious about the Thermos she'd brought up the ladder in a tote, saying he'd seen several like it at the flea markets, and with hefty price tags.

"My family never throws anything out," Rosie said. "My father carried this to the tire plant for decades. When he retired, my mother thought I could use it as a holder for floral arrangements. I took it home, then just started bringing it to the bank. Now I'm bringing it here." She looked at the silver canister, its sturdy ribbing dented here and there from its life in the factory, but still up for the task each day, heading to whatever is its next place of work, uncomplaining. She asked Dennis, "You ever think you'd be at the mall all this time?"

He watched a red-tailed hawk land on a light pole across Berkshire Road. Took in another breath. "Maybe it's hard to imagine, but it's been like a home for me. Does that sound corny?" He checked. Rosie shook her head. She did not laugh, and he was grateful for that. "The people here — the tenants — they were the first to ever really care about me. In my life.

Asked what did I need help with at home after I got the house? What was I doing at night or on the weekends after my divorce, and if I was sick did I need anything? When you grow up with nobody caring about anything that has to do with you, then have a building full of people remembering your birthday, it can be pretty strange, and then really nice. So nice you can't imagine life without them. I know I really, really can't."

Rosie didn't respond, afraid to sound trite if she tried to say what the mall had come to mean to her. She'd only been there a fraction of Dennis's time. But she knew what he meant. Irene had opened the door, both the one that got her out of her house and the one that got her into the mall and into space number sixty-three. And into this small world of tenants. Rosie stayed silent then, just refilled her cup, took the same leaning stance Dennis used as he rested his elbows on the safety railing, and soaked up just being there. When she hugs Dennis out of nowhere that evening at their walk over to the bank, it is because she can't picture her life without the mall people. Including him. Orchard is now her routine, its occupants a family that had come from nowhere when her bank one disbanded. And before her is a member who's unexpectedly come to be important. Someone for whom, she is happy to report at each of his readings, someone else is waiting. He'll see. It will happen. A new start. If she didn't see that in his hand, Rosie would have been very tempted to make it up, Irene-style, just so Dennis could enjoy the hope it gives that he might have a real chance at a real relationship, not just one he dreams about.

Dennis visits space number sixty-three more and more often since that first August day with Rosie up at the sign. Before that, she'd seen him and his palm at the half-circle cutout every single Monday, had seen the dark curled paisley of his inner life, which even just the tiniest prospect of seeing Irene once had cast with joy. Then the figure had appeared, waiting for him, and whatever it was translated to the first real hope Dennis has felt since spring. That last reading with Irene had been so regular and typical he couldn't remember any of the specifics she said, just that she'd worn a light-blue sweater. But he knew she'd reminded him, as she each time did, that there was hope. Always hope.

Now, since the figure, he isn't just being given the word, but feels all the possibility of all the four letters of the word. He talks about it often when he and Rosie share their breaks, which they do a few times a week, in the hallway near the Art Lane, or, when weather allows, up on the sign. It is a change of scenery for both and, for both, a chance to air out. Rosie needs that most days, as most days include scenes lots heavier than finding someone's long-lost car keys, and if Scot is there when she returns to the little brick cottage at the edge of the municipal golf course, he has no interest in hearing about them. She does not tell this to Dennis, as it really is no one else's business. And she's never been one to whine to one man about a problem with another. She talks about Scot in positives, tells Dennis of his great organizational skills, his foresight, his imagination that certainly one day will lead to his inventing a game that will captivate the nation. "Another Trivial Pursuit," Rosie had said up at the sign on a sharp October afternoon when the hills were newly painted gold and red. Dennis remembered playing Trivial Pursuit with Signy. Remembered he'd been awful at it. Wondered whose idea that game had been. Imagined the money that inventor had made. Thought about how successful Scot might one day become. And how such a windfall might mean Rosie would stay home, wouldn't need to come to the mall and work. Dennis quickly backed up. Both in his head, and physically taking the few steps backwards, bumping into the bottom of the sign as he surprised himself with the depth of his sudden hope that Scot's game proposals would continue to be flops.

According to *Palmistry for Beginners*, a reader must concentrate on the minor lines that link the head line with the heart line, which is not only a way to disclose personality, but to understand the soul. These lines normally start and finish within the Supernal Zone, a particularly spiritual area of the palm that is also called the Great Quadrangle. All of these sound to Rosie like destinations — you could pack a picnic basket and take a day trip to them. The Great Quadrangle, the book says, overlooks the Plain of Mars and is the field of the karmic pendulum, the great void between thinking and feeling, and, in the world of the palm, is directly linked with the soul. The area it represents is central to the whole human psyche, and, no matter who you are, all lines there are bound to carry great and deep significance.

The book reminds again that nothing is dependent upon the lines of the hand, that they are only symbols of a situation and not its cause or reality. But it notes that if you're going to bet on one thing when reading a palm, it's that if the Supernal line appears clear and true, the inner life — the human soul — will indeed be brought to full awareness during the subject's physical life here on earth. Karmic contents, perhaps from ancient times, have led toward this eventuality, this awakening. Sometimes the potential for the event can be seen in the left hand, the inheritance one. But other events may have prevented it from reaching its goal, which is true spiritual awareness.

Dennis has this potential.

And Rosie, who only recently read that portion of the book over a lunchtime mustard sandwich, points it out at the reading Dennis goes for two days after the visit to the sign. "You're a lucky man," she tells him. "Full awareness! How many people go through life with that?" The great news doesn't seem to register. "This is a really big thing, according to the book," she tells him. "And it's really a strong one. It has to mean something good."

Dennis squints. Draws his hand to his face.

"Don't see it."

"This. Here." She points. Her touch is the soft warmth of the electric blanket he'd used before Signy moved in and made him throw it out, worried they'd get cancer from the current.

"Oh."

"Think about it," Rosie says, trying to brew up some enthusiasm, poking his arm playfully. "This is rare. You are rare!"

"Ha." He has to add that on the order of his father, who is laughing now at the idea Dennis could be anything but ordinary. He does so loudly enough that the hall echoes with the one word.

"But you are," says Rosie, not as a cheerleader, but as what she truly thinks. There is a space here because those thoughts come through in the three syllables she's spoken. In the softness of her voice. In how she looks up from his palm, not unlike Lady Di on the postcards, glancing up through her eyelashes in that way. She lowers her eyes again and sees something else, something she also decides to say aloud, though she's known it since researching it after spotting the shape on Dennis's palm back in May.

"You also have an island in your heart line." Again the touch. "Here. This usually means there was a time in your life when things weren't normal. Got shaken up. The book says 'with emotionally painful results.'" She looks at Dennis's face here. He knows she knows, simply by looking into his hand, some of what he lives with. "It's like an injury in a war, in emotional combat. It can change the course of a life. Where somebody else's feelings might flow smoothly, yours met with this, this island. You had to travel around it. But you did. The thing is, you did."

No response.

"Look. Your hand says you did. You know you did. Better things are ahead. Waiting. I see it."

Rosie doesn't realize his hand is still in hers. She draws hers away slowly and, in making sure to keep them palms down once they are free, she spots her wristwatch.

"Hey, I gotta get back. I'll see you later, OK?" She smiles and turns, and Dennis watches her turn to start to close for the night. He turns his hands over in his lap. He says the word "Rare." But doesn't mean himself.

21

Hannah already was having a good day the morning two weeks ago on which Rosie saw the flight to Baltimore in her palm. She did not care about the future beyond that very night, when she would speak at a banquet of local business leaders.

"Chicken this month!" her contact had informed her, all gung-ho like some ten-year ban on poultry had just been lifted.

After the chicken, Hannah would stand at the podium and tell the members of the Pioneer Valley Business Society what it was like in this economic climate to see a place of business make a change for the extreme better right before your eyes. Yes, her mall appeared to have been dying — for how long had people called it the Dead Mall? — but it now was enjoying nearly nine months of an upswing when everything else in the local business community was swinging down.

Rosie had told her, "You're going to be brilliant."

"I know," answered Hannah, who was well prepared with a fourteen-page, double-spaced speech in large, easy-to-read font, hoping to give an impressive delivery. For something else to give during her visit, she and Laurie stayed late on a Friday to throw together a special fast edition of *Mall of Us*, containing all the press Orchard Mall had been enjoying.

"This is a time of great change." Rosie had told Dennis that at his last reading. But all on his own, Dennis had sensed that. Ten years since Signy had left. As many years without her as he'd had with her. He didn't know if he needed that allotment of time in order to be allowed another chance for love, but that was what he felt suddenly, that it had been time, specifically, for Irene. Oh, he'd been making his moves. Though Irene apparently had not seen them as that. Dennis always had been working on something somewhere in her day, or mopping up something on the periphery. So his being around maybe a little more than usual was nothing big. When he offered to vacuum for her twice in one week, she thought it was just for his lack of having much else to occupy him, not that it was Dennis's way of doing something special for her. When he stopped by in the mid-afternoon with an Orange Julius, she thought it was a chit for another palm reading, not a gift.

When Irene had told him over the winter that love was on the horizon, she'd been making that up. She thought, what the heck, she was happy with Sticks, and she wanted Dennis happy, too. With somebody. She didn't know who, but he was nice enough, and there had to be someone out there for him. She'd always thought that.

"There will be a winter, but then spring," Irene told him. "And then, you will know happiness as big as the mall parking lot."

Each time she'd said this back over the winter, Dennis had looked into Irene's eyes and nodded. He knew it would be true. He knew what was coming. Happiness. With her. For some reason it had taken this long to arrive, but who knows why things fall into place when they do? He wanted to take her palm to his eyes and tell her what he knew of the future — that whatever combination of lines and shapes and dips and rises he found there, they all translated to the fact that he was the one for her. But all he did was say, "Thanks," and lower his eyes and enjoy the warmth of Irene's hands until she gave him that final squeeze that signaled she was about to let him go for another week, and he shuffled off down the hallway to put a new washer in the dripping faucet in the Pleasant Street men's room, and took a good long look in the mirror, at the face bearing the smile of somebody who knew greatness was going to happen for him sooner than later.

"You think she wants you?" His father asked this and laughed. In the mirror, he was behind Dennis like one of those horror-show apparitions.

"You fixed the sink!" enthused the clerk from Fast Foto as he took his place at a urinal.

And Dennis had to ask, "Huh?"

Summer is over. Fall is almost over. Dennis sees just the long winter to enter and endure and emerge from before he'll feel any real warmth again. He is up on the sign this first Monday in November as into the lot on this morning rolls Bunny's car, the small four-door Chevette that gets her from home to the mall and back and that she does not ask more of. And then the Music Man arrives in his van, plum in color and with no writing on it because when he'd first had a van and had "MUSIC MAN ENTERTAINMENT" painted across the sides it had been broken into, and the police said he might as well have added the line "I GOT THOUSANDS OF DOLLARS WORTH OF EQUIPMENT IN HERE RIGHT NOW," so he had all the writing taken off, but did keep the vanity plate "MUSMAN" that costs him forty-five dollars extra every year, sort of a lot when you consider that, in keeping with the state's six-letter limit, it reads more like "muss." Then arrives the Affordable Attorney, who drives a sporty, squarish kind of wagon, blue as the eggs Dennis spots each spring in the nests built in the parking lot's ornamental trees, blue as the sweater Irene had on the last time he ever saw her. Then comes Mom. In that fancy, sleek, champagne-colored two-door thing she's been driving since June. If you get too close to this car, as Dennis has in an attempt to check it out, a sharp recorded voice asks you to move away, move away. Dennis, used to hearing sharp voices, ignored it and made an inventory of interior features to relay later to the tenants.

To the old tenants.

These days, that distinction is needed. Because, over the summer, for the first time in a decade and a half, new people have been moving in. New tenants. As opposed to the old.

Actual businesspeople asking to be directed to the mall management office, where they will inquire about lease terms and how soon can they secure a space. Despite there only being a couple months left in the year, actual businesspeople are painting and carpeting and refurbishing light fixtures and shelving and signage. There've been no new tenants since Bunny brought in her bargain cards. Absolutely nobody. But now, Orchard Mall is offering shoppers a relatively dizzying selection of shops to visit.

In the old Regis hair salon, now called The Magic Carpet, dozens and dozens of rugs have been unrolled and stacked like spare plastic capes once had been. At the new and blandly titled Sports Store, bold jerseys and mouth guards in all combinations of team colors fill the shelves that once held Radio Shack's twenty-four-hour weather radios and the miles of mysterious cord and plugs that had been its stock in trade. Lounging on odd little hammocks, a family of concerned-looking ferrets peers into the mall hall from their home in the enormous aquarium at the front of the new Animaland, located in the old Frederick's of Hollywood. Next door, the former Leather Shed is now an unnamed space offering discounted versions of the time-saving household gadgets advertised on late-night TV. Two women swath with yards of muslin the windows of what had been Anderson-Little, and Breathe becomes Orchard Mall's first and last purveyor of aromatherapy products. One of the men who brings his sports trading cards to the Saturday flea markets has enough confidence in the last months of Orchard to take over the former Piercing Pagoda and line the cases that once had held studs and hoops, piercing guns, rubbing alcohol and gauze with faces from the '78 Yankees and the '63 Chicago Bears and the '72 Bruins and any year of the Celtics.

At the same time arrived the carts. Not a fleet of them, but a wagon train long enough to have the old tenants standing in their doorways and marveling at the sight of Dennis rickshawing past them yet another of the fixtures that in better times had clogged the center of the hall, offering the lowest-rent option for those who wanted to get in on Orchard's good vibes, for a testing month or two, or an entire holiday season. The carts had dwindled in number as the mall had declined in popularity, the last one being pulled into storage in the early '80s, when the Cabbage Patch Kids craze ground to a halt, and so did any need for handmade dresses and jackets and hats to fit their big flat heads. In early August, a cart appeared in front of Experience Travel, and at a tall director's chair sat a woman ready to run a camera that would capture your portrait for immediate printing onto T-shirt, calendar page, coffee mug, tote bag. Then a cart was placed outside Cinemas I and III, its three little risers holding neat rows of empty milk bottles from the days when bottles of milk were delivered to your door by Day 'n' Night or Hillstretch or Morning Glory, collectors' items now picked from tag-sale table or estate-sale lot or backyard junk pile, sterilized and filled with a quart of Styrofoam beads to give the illusion of milk. Over by Lens is More, another cart was stocked with computer flotsam — mouse pads, copy holders, tiny vacuums to extract the graham-cracker crumbs from between your keyboard's *V* and *B*, and stick-on frames that make your screen a work of art no matter what you are doing. Then a cart was rolled near the medieval lights that mark the entry to the Flaming Pit, and to the mall itself. One look at the stock and the tenant for this one is obvious: "Orchard Mall: Main Street Recreated" reads the stitching on the fleece pullovers and corduroy ball caps and umbrellas that Hannah Pomfret has optimistically ordered, and offers at cost to any tenant.

"Just a way to keep the good feeling going!" she explains as she picks up her morning cup of coffee with two sugars, and Carla Agnello responds, "Great!" because that's what she thinks. Everything is great to Carla Agnello, who had given Orchard its own little Starbucks back in September, when she began serving coffees and teas and homemade baked goods where Papa Gino's had once doled out slices. "Great!"

One week into the venture that had Carla starting a second career after retirement from a job as a middle-school lunch lady, the café — she named it Carla's — was so busy that she lured the Russian girl into a similar enormous step, which had her leaving the Orange Julius and her familiar brown-and-orange polyester to wear whatever she liked as she helped serve and clear and earn any tips that were left in the hard-to-miss oversized coffee cup at the register.

No uniforms, no hot dogs, no loneliness for the final few months of Orchard's existence. Carla Agnello is funny and the age of what a big sister could be, and she helps the Russian girl, which was her name to the original tenants who'd come to know her when she was that, only now she is a little Russian woman, age fifty-seven, more of her life spent in America and at Orchard Mall than spent sitting in a crowded apartment in a row of boxish Cold War apartments and thinking how, far beyond the next one, and beyond that, and beyond that, America awaited. She'd come here alone at seventeen. Left her friends and her mother and even a boy who said he loved her very much and would marry her once he got the proper amount of money and once his grandmother died so they could have her bed in the corner of the front room. The Russian girl didn't want to wait. She applied for asylum with a church group somewhere in America she'd never heard of because, other than New York and Hollywood, she'd never heard of anywhere in America, and she ended up leaving them all. It was like dying, she would tell the tenants once she got hold of the proper words to be so detailed. Like dying, like ending an existence. Life here? A birth, certainly, but like most births, not a happy one. How many babies do you see arriving in the world laughing? Birth is horrifically difficult, a huge change, being propelled down a road uncomfortable and unfamiliar, leaving the known for the unknown — pain, suffering, but then there you are, there you land, and that is going to be your life, starting with getting picked up at the airport by a big bunch of people from a church two states to the north, being brought to an apartment, taught some English, helped with the currency system and social mores. What she would go on to do from there was up to her. And, of everything she'd been through, wasn't that the largest and scariest thing?

"Anything," her sponsors would tell her as she studied the visual dictionaries that depicted a street scene and the Russian and English names for everything there: shop, car, bicycle, road, policeman. "Here you can do anything."

"Anything," her boss at Orange Julius had told her when she landed the job because he went to the church that had sponsored her and also because he wanted somebody he could pay less than minimum wage and under the table.

"Anything," Carla Agnello would tell her over the counter she was decorating with a display of the beaded bracelets the Russian girl had made in her spare time but had never told anybody about until Carla admired hers and asked where could she get one, and the Russian girl told her to pick one. "Here you can do anything."

"Anything," Irene would tell the Russian girl so many times through the half-circle cutout window. "Here you can do anything."

And once when she went to Rosie, she got told exactly what that anything was.

Rosie saw the girl fishing. With the man who was her father. They were at the river's edge. The Russian girl was truly little at the time. Four, maybe. The father was telling her in Russian that Rosie could somehow completely understand, "Throw out your line and see what happens."

"Fish," Rosie told her. "Go fish."

* * *

"You said it. You said I would find just the house for me once I looked at the one with the old spoons for wind chimes. And I did. Goddammit, I did. I just came in here on a fluke. And you called it. Right on the nose. You said it would be the place with the old spoons hammered into wind chimes, and sure as hell I saw this house with a sign out front and went around the back and there were the chimes. Who'd believe that you would know it?"

Rosie shrugs again as she takes in the testimonial from the woman she can't remember ever seeing before at the half-circle cutout, but there she is, telling her that her words have come to pass, or that what she'd said — it was true. The house and the wind chimes. She'd once seen these images in this customer's palm, as she sees them in palms everywhere. The girl at the grocery held out her hand for Rosie's money, and there in the palm was the girl, now at the beach, being pulled by a cream-colored dog who had her arm. And there on the forearm was the dog-tooth scar, old, but still visible. The nun crossing in front of the convent waved as Rosie let her pass, and Rosie saw the first career as a baker of buns in a full-service grocery, big, puffy, turtle-shaped things dusted with flour and smelling of life, the not-yet-a-nun-teen forming hundreds of them at a worktable set in front of a big window through which shoppers could witness the birth of their dinner rolls. Now, this morning, in front of her, here in Rosie's rented space number sixty-three, she sees a woman who holds out her hand.

"Look at it again," she is asking. "I need to know more."

Rosie takes the bill and asks her to make a wish but not for money, even though she already has. Then she looks into the palm and says, "You will have one hundred and sixty guests at the reception, the color scheme will be black and white and silver, the menu will be prime rib, herb-crusted salmon or something called chicken Sorrento, the cake will be cream with cannoli-and-chocolate-chip filling, you will dance to 'Oh What a Night' by Frankie Valli because, he will point out, late September back in sixty-three is when you were born. That's not what the song is about, but you will find it meaningful nonetheless and he will arrange for the deejay to play it at some point in the night. Oh, and you will meet at the beach — your son will run into him and will drop his Popsicle in the collision and he will want to buy your son another and you will say your son can't talk to strangers, especially ones who want to buy him food. But you will let him buy the Popsicle. The Popsicle the boy loses will be orange. They will have only blueberry by the time the man gets to the stand. Your marriage will be happy and loving."

"She will let you in when she feels up to not only company, but your kind of company."

"It will be a red car."

"Tie the key to his pants with a long shoelace and he will stop losing it."

"The baby will grow outside the womb, I am sorry to tell you that."

"They will buy your company, but only for its mailing list. Everyone will be let go."

"Snow will fall before you get around to doing all the raking, or to arranging for a plow man."

"All she will leave you will be her button jar."

"You really should not be afraid to cook risotto."

"The furniture set you will fall in love with at a barn in Southampton will be a mahogany armoire with inlaid designs, a large half-circle beveled mirror with a single bottom drawer. They will ask $700 for it. You will pay by check and it will bounce, but due to bank error rather than your own."

"Use the good dishes, except for the tureen, which has a hairline crack that one night at a dinner party means the base will pop right off."

"Digital cable, in the premium class, will appear on your television a week after you order only the basic service."

"He has no license because of three drunk-driving arrests, not because, as he told you, he is so concerned about the environment that he does not want to be one more person driving a car."

"Raccoons are what you are hearing at night."

"Your brother will come from Greece and become a star on the radio here, in his native language."

"You should know that she doesn't remember, and, if she did, she wouldn't care anyhow."

"The religious people down the street are praying for you

even though you don't like that they are. You cannot stop them, so just forget about it."

"He will enlist just for the G.I. benefits, but then there will be an international incident, and he will really have to go and do something, and it will freak him out, but in the end his only assignment will be to sit at an airport far away from all the commotion and unload shipments of ready-to-eat meals and other militaryish things that will be needed where he is."

"You don't always have to be cleaning everything."

This last thing she tells to Ernest from the cinema. Another Orchard lifer, his first big event had been the 1975 *The Reincarnation of Peter Proud*, because portions of it were filmed in nearby Springfield. Jennifer O'Neill was among the stars, and was to appear at the mall for the first showing there. Dennis had been sent up to write out, "HOLLYWOOD IS HERE AT ORCHARD MALL!" The mall's second manager, a forgettable guy named Guy, rented a genuine Klieg light and brought out Orchard's entire stock of crowd-containing velvet ropes and posts, which normally would have been in storage until Santa Claus's Castle was unveiled the day after Thanksgiving. But a premiere — that, if anything, was a reason to pull out all the stops. Radio stations held contests for ticket giveaways. TV came to film Ernest instructing his ushers. Dress was fancy. Popcorn and champagne were served. The tickets were sold out. And up in the window of the projection room, Ernest impulsively grabbed projectionist Betsy in the kiss he'd been dying to deliver for the two years since the first afternoon she'd come in and filled out an application form for the job in which he had to instruct her. It was, fittingly, a movie kiss. Tight. Close. Lengthy. Movement of hands across cheeks and up through opposite heads of hair. A slow parting of lips bound by a string of saliva that added to the drama. Hearts like a pair of feet kicking an empty oil drum,

big booming sensations that blended with the sound of stomping from the theater below. The crowd — you might have been
able to dress them up, but you couldn't take them out — wanted the start of the movie *Peter Proud*. Ernest wanted all of Betsy.
And, it turned out, the feeling was mutual.

Their love story at Cinemas I and II and III ran through
Animal House, Rocky Horror, Rocky I, Rocky II and *Rocky III*, and
outran the existence of Cinema II, which closed in 1991 for
economic reasons — a pair of cinemas, rather than a trio, being
more than enough, and the second one being the largest. It
lasted through and past its immediate neighbors the Fireplace
Shoppe and Everything Velcro, through the exodus of Lerner
and everything else that once existed in the mall's north wing,
through the loss of Precious Child high-end children's wear and
Nut House snacks to go, of Planet Waves and its hippie clothes
and Ink, Inc. and its wonderful but ignored walls of writing in-
struments. Over time, Radio Shack left, too, as did Friendly's,
Koenig's Art Supplies and an Ava Gabor wig shop, Michael's
Crafts, the Waldenbooks and the CVS. The numbers of cine-
ma-ticket buyers decreased in corresponding measure, and
Ernest needed to take a second job. He became a teacher — of
film, of course. He didn't have a master's degree, so he only
ever reached the level of adjunct, but that was good enough for
him, allowed him to be called "professor," which he got a kick
out of, standing in front of a class of eighteen-year-olds attempting to translate the meaning of the original *Nosferatu* and
Seven Samurai, All Quiet on the Western Front and *Satyricon*.

As Irene had with everyone, Rosie always stresses to Ernest
there is hope. Because there is. No way to prove otherwise, really. But Rosie knows a whole lot more. And on Ernest's palm
she sees the white-gray screen of a laptop on which the three
acts of a screenplay are undergoing a revision. Rosie feels waves
of success emanating from Ernest's hand, as it if were a bed of

coals in a summer campfire. They are pleasing and welcoming and, aside from that, send rays clearly readable to Rosie as pride and self-esteem and passion.

"The story you're writing," she tells him, "you have to finish it."

Ernest's eyes shoot around the room, then back through the half-circle cutout, and he wastes no time asking, "How do you know about the story? Betsy doesn't even know about the story."

Another shrug. "It's what I do here."

"Yeah, yeah, but . . . "

"You have to finish it. Things will happen."

"Who told you?"

Rosie is honest again when she says slowly, "Nobody, Ernie, I just know it."

And she also knows the story will make a difference to Ernest and Betsy, and to a crowd she sees in his palm, which she interprets as being the enthusiastic audiences that one day will jam theaters to watch it unfold. Rosie hopes the film will be a love story. She has always enjoyed a good love story. Even if these days she feels far from being a star in her own.

At home, no Scot.

No messages from him.

No usual Wednesday-into-Thursday sleepover to make the weekend seem not that long off.

No decision-making for their first joint Christmas card, which is to contain the news of their imminent holiday engagement.

"I'm busy," his excuse.

"You're angry."

"You haven't listened to me since the spring."

"You've hardly talked to me since the spring, except to criticize."

"I just need to think about this."

"This what? Us?" Rosie has to add that last word. The problem might not be just her employment, or whatever strange skill she's acquired. "This isn't something that should be discussed on the telephone," Scot answers.

"So come over. Or I'll come there."

"I'm busy. I'll be in touch."

"I'm coming over."

Rosie is driving through the center of Indian Orchard before she realizes she never even asked Scot where he was when she'd managed to reach him on his cell phone just after she'd come home from work. Passing now through the quiet center of town, she sees the Tae Kwon Do mannequin dressed in a Santa suit. A decorated tree stands in the window of the state representative's headquarters. The Chamber of Commerce has run a string of fairy lights around the one feature in the window — the ever-present invitation to Picture Your Business in Indian Orchard. On this night, only a Dennis-shaped man — could that actually be Dennis? She notices too late to be sure — walks Main Street. Forty years ago, Rosie would have been dodging dozens of other shoppers as she followed her mother down these sidewalks as errands were accomplished. They'd visit the greengrocer for the fancy basket of fruit and chocolate that was the family's annual Christmas gift to Sophie from up the street. They'd pick up the massive circular raisin-studded babka they'd ordered at the baker's. There'd be a stop at the pet store — even her goldfish, Rosie argued, deserved a gift, maybe a new plastic frond? Her mother would run into Nan's Clothiers for a last-minute gift of an umbrella for whatever nun was at the head of Rosie's classroom that year and, always thinking ahead, she'd visit the stationer for a box of the thank-you notes Rosie would spend part of her Christmas vacation filling out in her neatest Palmer penmanship. A piece of pizza and an attempt at Tae Kwon Do are all she can purchase on these streets these days.

Scot's apartment is a few streets beyond what was Main Street's business district, a quick right after the building where a dentist once had yanked out one of Rosie's front teeth when tying one end of a string around the tooth and the other end around a doorknob hadn't worked. She is hoping this visit to the neighborhood won't be as painful, that whatever is ahead might be prefaced with the assurance "This won't hurt at all," even if it might.

And it does.

Scot is home when she arrives. She can see him through the window of the door she opens with the key designated from the rest of them on her ring by a heart she'd painted on with scarlet nail polish. He is sitting at his worktable, studying a set of papers before him, making quick marks, shaking his head, making some more. From the speakers where his iPod rests, a lecture on the raw food diet is being read by a man with an English accent. Scot had been intrigued by this method of dining since a night out a year ago at which one of his co-workers had instructed the waitress to bring him only a plate of uncooked vegetables, an order that mysteriously took longer to deliver than everyone else's well-done steaks.

"Our bodies have transformed due to our present diet — smaller teeth, shorter jaws, shrunken stomachs, and longer small intestines are among the results," the voice says as Rosie slips her key ring back into her bag.

She's not been at Scot's since — has it really been Labor

Day? Scot's landlady's picnic, Scot turning away her offer of a beer because boiling was part of how it was made, which led to a discussion about raw beer. That was Rosie's most recent nice day with Scot, the memory of how he forgot the wine he'd meant to bring to the picnic in the yard one floor below his place, and how he and Rosie went to retrieve it, then remained one floor up the entire afternoon, emptying the bottle, then its sister, purchased in the handy carton that held a pair of red and white. It was their first day together in maybe a month. It began awkwardly, but Rosie began to ramble about Hawaii when she wandered near the map he'd hung, blue pins noting the three places they'd stay, red marking the points of interest they shouldn't miss, green stuck through those they might want to fit in were there time. So they talked about Hawaii. Nothing else. The fresh-fruit buffet at the condo in Kihei, the deals to be had at the Maui Swap Meet, the naked beach in Hana to which a co-worker of Scot's had provided a map. Nothing was said about the here and now because it was getting harder and harder to talk about how the two of them just weren't fitting anymore. For a couple of hours they discovered they still fit fine while on the fish sheets, but there was something depressing about that cruise. Maybe fittingly for Labor Day, last call for amusement parks before they close for the winter, there was a final-ride feel to the one Rosie and Scot had enjoyed together that afternoon, as if they were nearing the limits of the age, height and weight requirements that would prevent them from ever again taking another turn on the attraction that one another once had been.

Even so, Rosie still drives herself to that same apartment, lets herself in, hears the voice saying that a diet is a choice, just like many other things. She chooses to not turn and leave when Scot doesn't hear her, just keeps making his marks on the papers. She chooses to say, "I'm here," though she has to say it three increasingly louder times before he looks up and directs a small clicker toward the iPod.

Scott pops on his faraway glasses. Adds to his face a flat smile. "You didn't need to come over," he starts, and Rosie runs that over with "But I did."

She slips her coat and bag onto a chair that holds Scot's laundry basket, its contents neatly folded in descending sizes of items, with squares of washcloths capping the stack. He's not come over to use her washer since maybe July. The label on the bottle of detergent she always had waiting for him — Cheer — further saddens her.

She walks to the worktable and glances at the papers. They make up a looping maze she knows he can see as a game board. The name "Plan B" is penciled at the top. Scot smells like the Fresh Linen that is the Cheer scent he likes and that Rosie, thinking it creepy that something out of a bottle is supposed to smell like something right off the outdoor line, does not like the idea of. But she has to admit there is something in it that reaches into her memory of being a kid playing beneath the clothesline, and now, of being an adult playing with Scot. She misses him, though he is right next to her, and maybe that is the worst thing.

"I'd like to talk about our future," she says. That is stiff, and sounds so, but it is right to the point. "I mean, we're supposed to be getting engaged, and we hardly see one another anymore. You don't like hearing from me, you're never around. What do we have together?"

"Don't you know?" he asks, looking up from his papers. "You're supposed to know everything." There is a playground taunt to the last line. Its surprise is sharp for Rosie, who responds in kind.

"One, I don't know everything," she snaps as, at a much lower volume, the voice talks about the value of the life force in raw foods. "Or I wouldn't be here asking you all this. Two, really, finally, tell me what is your problem with my work? I've never understood that. When I got my job from Irene, this is when we started to come apart."

She doesn't like the last two words. And maybe Scot doesn't either, because that's when he stands, and that's when he says with a softness she doesn't expect, "I really don't know. I can't tell you, because I don't know. But there's something about it from the start that I just did not like. I still don't. And I can't seem to change my mind. Will you bear with me?" Here's where he takes her hands. "Maybe it'll change. Maybe I'll change."

And that's when Rosie genuinely hopes he will.

22

"I'm listening," Rosie says. And the woman goes on: "The place was empty and old and had no atmosphere. It was like being in a jail. An apartment that could never be made into a home. I hated it. From the day I moved into it, I hated it. Five flights up. Would you just listen to me for a second?"

"I'm listening."

Rosie is. Because that is what enough of the people in her line want — somebody to listen. People want to know things from her all right, but they also want to unload. Rosie is far cheaper than a psychologist who might proclaim you nuts, as they did your Tio Hector, and certainly less expensive than a prescription, which your insurance would not cover. A session with Rosie calls for no recited prayer, unlike the actual church confessions you did years ago. Rosie knows the switchover point, where the reading moves from being just that to becoming a counseling session. When asked to make their wish but not for money, clients might pause — they've come here seeking news that money is coming. Now they have to think what else they might hope for. Or maybe the client will just ignore Rosie's request and start saying something like well, let me tell you what I've always felt, thought, been told about my future...

Rosie will nod or shake her head at all the appropriate moments. "You understand, don't you?" they'll ask, and she will say yes, even if she doesn't, because understanding is what most people are seeking — and who is she to deny them that essential?

"I'm not, not, what's the word — racist? I'm not."

"Wouldn't you have done the same thing? Tell me you wouldn't have."

"I'm sorely tempted now to say to her that I can't stay here, I have to get away. I want to yell, 'I'm going to get $30,000 when you die, could I have it now?' I need it fuckin' now for my sanity. She knows if I go down the road of asking, it will be for desperation. I have all these horror stories of my mother, and I keep putting them out of my head. They don't sink in. She looks fabulous. She looks fuckin' fabulous. Has a gorgeous room in that home. Tea's always made, and a radio. Everybody in the place has walls plastered with photos of their grandchildren, their family. My ma, she has two. One of my dad before he died. He looked like the devil incarnate. He had eyebrows that went up and out to here. There is one more photograph, she keeps it in her purse and that is the only thing in there because what does she need money for in that place? It's a picture of her — of my mother — at nineteen. When she was young she was very, very pretty. There's a reason for that being in there. That's how she sees herself. She never looks in the mirror. When she wants to look at herself, all she has to do is look in her purse."

Rosie looks deeper into the daughter's palm. Says what she sees, though she doesn't really need the visual: "She's not going to change."

"She might."

"She won't."

Rosie knows what she sees in the woman's palm. She thinks of last night, of almost grabbing Scot's and looking, and answering all his questions right there, but not making that move.

The daughter's rant, which maybe is all she really wants from her visit — to be able to say what she has to to someone who won't react — is much of what Rosie hears: I did that, these, those, all the demonstratives. How do these people not worry that she won't repeat, tell, record, publish? There certainly is enough material.

"Through time and experience, you will become sensitive to the mind-states of those who seek your ability to read," *Palmistry for Beginners* assures. "It will be clear that while a percentage will see a visit as entertainment or diversion, and others will be in positive anticipation of the future, there will be those who come to you at a sensitive and vulnerable place in their lives. Attempt to be careful of their feelings, do not relay feelings of sadness or depression. Your clients should leave their readings encouraged. The most important thing to remember: your clients should feel totally sure that you are dealing in full confidentiality. No gossip should follow, even with those closest to you."

There is that message from the book, but she wouldn't tell anyway. Rosie is who she is. Has no idea what her presence is like: a warm bath, the door locked securely behind, lights in the window and your favorite meal steaming on the stove, all comfort and understanding without a word uttered. A glow about her that, even if you never would believe such a thing existed, you feel she has it. Those who pay to sit in the half-circle cutout feel it, pay for it, again and again.

The woman whose mother is not going to change leaves the half-circle cutout, and Rosie returns her mind to the night before, and Scot's kind honesty. There is hope, always hope. Maybe he will change his mind about this one thing. This job and this place. Down the hall in this busier and busier mall, the Music Man sings. Loudly enough to be heard but at a level that is not deliberately showing off. The music of his era. Dire Straits. Jim Croce. Songs recorded by women even, in a lower key, if he is in the mood, Joan Armatrading, to whose music he'd made out with girls in college, down to the ground, down to the ground, and Joni Mitchell, whose songs he feels smart to play, they being so deep and architectural and storylike, drawing the map of Canada on a cocktail napkin in the blue TV-screen light. Some days when the mood strikes, he leans back into Carole King and sends down the hall and out into the world, "Will you still love me tomorrow?"

"Nobody knows about tomorrow," Mom shouts in answer from across the hall, and shakes her head in Rosie's direction.

23

But Mom is wrong.

Some people in Baltimore just happen to know what the next day will bring, at least as far as the future of Orchard Mall goes.

They have come up with the idea, therefore know it first. A big group of them, all in suits and ties, and the odd few females in similar getups minus the ties, sitting around a block-long conference table, deciding this big decision in mid-November.

Then summoning Hannah Pomfret, who makes her Rosie-predicted flight seated next to the not-at-all-bereaved sister, who studies the seat-pocket gift catalog and turns the corners of the pages containing a sleek, sterling-silver pocket perfume atomizer, a floating pool alarm shaped like a duck, a home clothing steamer of the type that retailers use to remove wrinkles, and a small safe that looks like a book. She ends up ordering none of these things. Simply enjoys the looking. It is part of the experience of a trip. Maybe her destination is different from everybody else's on this plane, less exciting, but she is going somewhere, and that is something in itself.

The not-at-all-bereaved sister has no clue as to where her seatmate is headed. Tries to guess from her businessy black-skirted suit and her fat leather bag of paperwork. Sees the OM logo on the top of most of the pages she studies, but this woman's eyes aren't good enough to make out the type that spells out Hannah Pomfret's painstakingly researched "State of Orchard Mall" report, one of the things she will be distributing this very morning at the meeting that has been described to her simply as both urgent and of utmost importance. Hannah hasn't had a moment to consult with Rosie in the two days between the call from Baltimore and the flight to Baltimore. She was too busy pulling together the report she hopes will show the mall's renewed life just as it is supposed to be dying.

Only once she is in their presence and aligning her report between the OM stick pen to its right and the napkin for her untouched cup of coffee to its left will the Board of Directors inform Hannah Pomfret of its decision.

"Orchard Mall has a fruitful future!" The board president, a guy who likes to be called Mac, even though his last name only begins with a Mc, announces this with an audible exclamation mark. "A bit of a joke there, but it's very true."

Hannah keeps aligning the things before her, now working to make the top of the report straight next to a horizontal line of grain in the wood table. She is not looking up; she is too afraid to move. Any movement would jar her awake, and she'd be back in her bed, Pancake's whiskered snout resting on her ankles, Rob's hand under her pillow like it belonged to him. Another hand, the left one of the man to her right, a first vice president, lights onto Hannah's shoulder. "Are you all right, dear?" he asks, because he is of the vintage that does not see the use of "dear" in the headlights of a modern boardroom to be improper. The hand is real, the room is real, and Hannah looks over to Mac there at the head of the table and knows he is real. As is his energy; his hands open broadly as he says how the recent huge upswing in business and new tenants have gotten them thinking, have stilled the swing of the wrecking ball. Will bring in other types of heavy equipment, the kind necessary to remake a mall. To give it new life. Rebirth. A new mall for a new millennium. "Hey," he laughs, "maybe ten years late, but still a good slogan?"

Hannah nods. She will agree with whatever he — whatever they — want. She loves her work. She loves her mall. She loves her tenants. She imagines whooping out this news, calling them together in the conference room to give all the details. What this will mean to them! The announcement will probably be the biggest moment of her working life.

"You'll hold a press conference next Friday, the day after Thanksgiving," Mac says, and Hannah reaches for her smartphone. "Santa will make his annual arrival and will present you with a letter from us to open in front of all the assembled crowd. It'll announce that Orchard Mall will be expanded and modernized, and will say how that will be the greatest gift to the surrounding area since the mall's opening forty years ago."

Hannah still has no words. She finishes keying in the words "press conference" — as if she'd need to remind herself — then puts down the device and looks at her hands, turning them over slowly to look at the palms where Rosie week after week has seen the earthmovers and other vehicles of construction. She feels joyously pelted by scores of thoughts: the mall will live, she will keep her job, the mall will live, new stores will come, the mall will live, the tenants can stay, the mall will live!

"Orchard can become the most fantastic mall ever," sings the female board member who has eyebrows like quotation marks. "We're hoping to attract several anchors that will give a definitely upscale tone. Who cares if there's a Sears — you can find that anywhere. But Bloomingdale's. Wouldn't you slam on the brakes for that?"

Hannah nods, because she would. She's been to the Bloomingdale's in New York City — and felt so New Yorkish the rest of the day, carrying her own Big Brown Bag full of Blooomie's merchandise. "It certainly can become the most fantastic mall ever," she agrees, "especially with such an anchor. Wait until I tell the tenants!"

The board members exchange glances, and the first vice president says another "dear," this one preceded by an "Oh."

"You may tell them the news of the mall's renewal," says Mac, tapping all the fingers of his right hand on the dark wood of the table, "but you must also tell them they will not be part of it."

It is like being kicked. "Excuse me?"

"We'll be starting from scratch. All new tenants. That will be one of the big promotional points. A full new slate of stores, from one end to the other. All the big names. Not that mom-and-pop junk — it adds nothing to a mall."

"How about heart?" Hannah croaks this out.

The second vice president, who's been using an unbent paperclip to inscribe patterns on a pad of paper, makes a smirky noise. "Heart sells on February 14. Rest of the year, it's brand names."

"But these, these mom-and-pop places, they are what have kept Orchard alive. And one business in particular really is what brought the customers back."

"And who would that be? Orange Julius?" The guy next to the paperclip person leads the laughing.

"Rosie. Rosie Pilch." Hannah tries to make herself taller in her seat. "The palm reader. I've sent you all the publicity. You got copies of the articles, the links to the TV and radio features. She's the reason people started coming back."

More laughter. Then a list of what the board sees as the reasons for the renewed interest — these from an official telephone survey of one thousand area residents: people were turned off by the size of Mountainside, missed their little neighborhood mall. Missed it, but, hey, if they had their say would want Orchard to be some version of bigger, more modern, to contain more of the famous chains, and to have some of the fancy stuff — canals for paddle boats, maybe, or a zoo of exotic — well maybe exotic but rescued — animals. After all, in this economy who can afford to travel far for entertainment? Staycations are the thing. Why not just go to the mall for a new experience? That's what locals said in the survey, and that's what they've been doing. It's all there on the monthly tabulations of what each business takes in. Going up, up, up since April. And Hannah has to say, really, the reason they've come back is this one woman.

"You — you did this!" This from the person two down from the paperclipper, Sid something. "You're the woman, Hannah —you don't have to tell us!"

"No. Not me. Rosie Pilch."

"Oh, yes," clucks the man who is third in charge. "The Queen of the Unseen. Your little palm reader. She's been there since the Ice Age. I never could figure out the attraction."

"The palm reader. She's the one who got everybody coming back to the place," Hannah says. "It's really nothing I did. You might not believe it, but it was all her. She — Irene Cervelli — was there for years. Since the mall opened, actually. She got married in the spring. Gave the shop over to her friend. Irene had no special skills at all. I don't know what you believe about psychics and things, but the woman who took over is amazing. You wouldn't believe the things she knows. She even saw me coming here today."

"I'm sure," says the woman with the tangle of cause-supporting ribbon pins on her lapel — pink, yellow, red, teal. "Here — here's an outline for the press conference. Mac and I will be present. We'll stay a few days. Groundbreaking will start December 1 so we'll be there for that, too. Some of the work will begin shortly after that, not really for any deadline, as it will be winter, after all, but to show the Christmas shoppers that we mean what we say. To start spreading the word of a bigger and better Orchard Mall."

Hannah nods, continues on her own track, "But the woman — Rosie — she's why everyone was there. Again, I don't know what you believe, but she's the reason for the business. They've been lining up for her since back in April . . . "

" . . . which is when business began to improve." The first vice president says this, and Hannah smiles at his assistance.

"No Rosie, no business," she says. "That's how I see it. She must be considered as a factor — named as a factor. She must be given credit. And, certainly, allowed to stay. With the others who are there now. They've been so faithful all these years. It's not right to throw them out."

"Right," says Mac. "Well not right. No, they're not staying." And then just as swiftly he says, "We'll see you the day after Thanksgiving." He rises, and everybody else does, so Hannah does, too.

Then she offers, "I'll e-mail you a new fact sheet on Rosie. It'll be a great story to include with the PR packet when we give the announcement. She loses her job, she finds ability. She gets shoppers coming in. She changes people's lives. She really does. She saw even this — she saw my flight here, down to why the woman in the next seat would be on a plane — I asked. I checked. And Rosie was right about the dead sister that woman didn't care about. She saw things that would be happening."

"Right," says Tom, and he opens the door that will send Hannah and the mall's huge news into the world. "We'll handle everything, don't worry. Credit will be given where credit is due. Just tell them to be out by January 31. All of them."

24

"Look! Look! Would you look?"

The words tromp big army boots through the lovely flower garden that is Rosie's dream. A peaceful seed catalog illustration, ethereal puffs of blooming lavender plants edging a soft path down which she walks, barefoot, relaxed, serene, dressed in the cap-sleeved sheath she'd spotted in *Modern Bride*, headed toward her groom. Then an urgent "Look, look, will you?"

A light.

Somebody shaking her.

Scot.

There.

Four-ten a.m.

The bus for New York City is to leave from the church parking lot this morning at six. There's been no alarm. Not on the clock, maybe, but another kind in Scot has just gone off.

His presence in the first place is a big enough event. After months and months of retreating from the life and routine he'd shared with Rosie for three years, he'd come by on Thanksgiving morning, the day before, just as she was leaving for her parents', carrying a tree-sized poinsettia and giving the reminder that they had the trip to New York City, to the Diamond District, the next day.

"You still want to do this?" Rosie had asked through the petals the florist had been inspired to dust with red glitter that seemed an insult to the plant's natural beauty.

"New year coming, new life coming," Scot said as he drew from a pocket the two tickets for the next morning's bus. The smile he gave was nostalgia. Rosie last had seen it so fully and genuinely back in another time. Back in the spring. She'd missed it. She'd missed him.

She let him in.

She called Bunny and got her machine, where she left a message asking her to hang a sign on Rosie's gate tomorrow. Yes, the day after Thanksgiving would be packed, but this was far more important. Bunny needn't call back; Rosie would be early to bed for the very early rising.

And she wakes very, very early, to Scot's voice. "Look, look, will you look — I need to know," he tells Rosie as she focuses and sees him seated on the bed, wrapped in the dark-blue fleece OM blanket she'd gotten from that new cart of mall-logoed merchandise.

"To know what?"

"Everything." The word isn't loud, but is large. "Everything."

"Huh?"

"Would you?" He snaps on the bedside lamp, is leaning toward Rosie now, extending his hands. "Look at my palm?"

Rosie takes this in. Takes it as a joke. A bit of long overdue romance on this very early hour of the morning of the day on which Scot is to give her the ring they will purchase in New York this very afternoon.

Slowly she reaches for his hands. "Ah, I see a beautiful future . . ." All this while focusing on the gray snowflakes printed on her pajama bottoms. She looks nowhere near his palms, keeping to her rule that, if you know the person well, you don't want to know what will happen to him. It might be good, it also might not.

"Look," he says. It is more of a plea. A new chill hits the

already cold bedroom as Rosie realizes he is serious.

"I thought you didn't like this sort of thing." Rosie stalls. She pushes the hands aside and sits up. "I'll start the kettle. We might as well get up, get ready for our day." She says this brightly, though it is clear things are only going to get darker from here on.

"Would you please look at my palm?"

Scot's hands are shaking. All of Rosie is shaking. Scot looks upset and offset and offput as he puts aside his mistrust for Rosie's talent and plainly, clearly needs to know what will happen in his life. He says just that: "I need to know what will happen in my life."

"They get like this." She can hear Tina from clay class and First Bank's Graphics Department. Nerves, jitters. It was understandable.

"I take this seriously, Scot. Because — and you know I have no idea why — I actually know things. If I do this, I will see without a doubt what your life has held, or what it will hold for you. Do you really want that?"

He nods nearly before the question is fully asked.

"Are you all right?"

He whispers something, and Rosie asks, "What?" and Scot answers, "No."

Rosie reaches for her robe. Scot tightens the blanket around his shoulders.

She inhales. Starts as usual. "Make a wish," she tells him slowly, "but not for money."

"I don't have a wish," he says. "I mean I do; I just want to know. Beyond that, I just want to know what you see."

"OK. Fine." She tries not to notice that he doesn't speak the wish of spending his entire life with her, or making her the happiest woman ever. None of that. He just wants to know what his life ahead holds. So she tells him.

In his right hand she sees the neat lines, boundaries, walls and fences that make up Scot's days. The one-ways, the no-returns. The roads down which he is to progress to get from one point to the next, one accomplishment, goal, destination, victory. Then, more into focus, she sees Scot. The center of him. His destiny. What she sees so often in every other palm — the true place he would dwell, both physically and in his soul. It is a room. Bright with white-painted walls and the uncomplicated lines of Danish furniture. Rosie scans the room but finds nothing that hints it is any part of the little brick cottage on the edge of the municipal golf course.

"You're not here," she says aloud. The image is not making sense.

"What?" Scot asks. "You can't find me?"

"I see you, but you're not here. In this house. You're someplace else."

"Where?"

And she says what comes to her without her having a millisecond to process:

"House. House with windchimes made of old spoons. House of the Human Services Director. The one with the blue dress on Mondays, always the blue dress on Mondays — it's Leah from the beach and the kid with the Popsicle incident, Leah who sometimes is irked that her parents long ago put the *h* at the end of her name, which causes confusion on forms and such, but other than that is adjusted and happy. As you are. Adjusted and happy. Then. With her. Finally."

The last word, like the others, just pours from Rosie. Like her mouth is a riverbed and the words are water that courses down it. She takes a breath, and this runs from her: "Finally. You are adjusted and happy. You have your job. And your health. And this woman with the blue dress on Mondays and the *h* that annoys her, and the skin problems that call for an expensive line of Fresh cosmetics that she has started to come to Orchard to buy at Breathe, which has added skin care to its inventory in response to customer requests . . . "

And she knows more about her.

Because Rosie and this Leah have met. In the mash of customers over the past few months. Rosie cannot recall her face. But knows what she'd said to her upon looking into her narrow little hand:

"You will have one hundred and sixty guests at the reception, the color scheme will be black and white and silver, the menu will be prime rib, herb-crusted salmon or something called chicken Sorrento, the cake will be cream with cannoli-and-chocolate-chip filling, you will dance to 'Oh What a Night' by Frankie Valli because, he will point out, late September back in sixty-three is when you were born. That's not what the song is about, but you will find it meaningful nonetheless and he will arrange for the deejay to play it for you at some point in the night."

The refrigerator makes some kind of clicking noise. A car goes past the house. Rosie can't take a breath, and with the rest of whatever is in her lungs she finishes with "You will meet at the beach, her son will run into you and will drop his Popsicle in the collision and you will want to buy him another and his mother — this Leah with the *h* — will tell you that he can't talk to strangers, especially ones who want to buy him food. The Popsicle the boy loses will be orange. They will have only blueberry left by the time you get to the stand. Your marriage will be happy and loving."

Rosie stops. She'd once swum too deeply in the shallow end of a pool, and her face had scraped the concrete. This is the same feeling. Knowing she can't go any farther. Knowing the hard fact of what is in front of her: "I'm not in there."

"Look closer."

"I'm not there," Rosie hears someone — wait, it is her own voice — saying. Then, "She is."

You could chalk it up to shock, this very next thing Scot says quickly: "Do you see me inventing a game?"

Rosie does the above, chalks it up. She herself is in another place, as if floating above the two of them on one of those near-death experience levels, and she answers with the truth again, "Nope."

"No game?"

"No game."

"Any books?"

"Nope."

"A book? Just one?"

"No book. A few articles in an inhouse newsletter . . ." As if it were written on his skin, she reads, "But you will have no enormous heartaches, no illnesses to speak of, no sudden tragedy. You will not invent a game, you will not write a book. But you will have love." It is getting harder to speak, which is the case when your throat is ready for you to cry but half of it is still being used for talking. "You will be happy. I can assure you that. Even without these things you want so badly. If you can imagine that. You will be."

Rosie keeps his hand in hers. Looks along his fingers and in between and on the backs and the fronts for any mention of her in his future life. Opens the fingers, searches crevices. Regarding that, she might as well be reading the palm of a total stranger.

A jealous stranger.

Play A Round had been rejected for being mindless and pointless. And, the very day Scot submitted his updated Game of Life, the department head had returned his idea rich with such modern pitfalls as anthrax in your mail, a recall of your cosmetic breast implants, having your retirement funds disappear via Bernie Madoff, and being outed. Most recently, the six-person series of famous vegetarian action figures had come back to his desk in similar swift fashion, seal unbroken, wearing a Post-it that read, complete with a name-typo that had especially irked, "Scott: Not looking at any more ideas for the foreseeable future, thank you."

In his palm, where her eyes remain as if fenced in there, Rosie suddenly sees Scot's envy — that she's never had one inch of a life plan and had been thrown off track yet managed to land on her feet and go beyond that to thrive. In his hand she sees him fuming over this. How she's managed to stand up and do something. All under her own power — whatever power that is. And Scot, with all his plans and dreams and knowing what he will be doing six years and one month and three days from today, has not a thing going the way he'd planned. You might add except Rosie, though this morning that fact is changing.

One last look. In his palm, the odd security-camera view of Rosie right at that moment sitting there on the bed, holding Scot's hand beneath the light of the little bedside brass lamp, telling him what he wants to know.

"I can't do this." He is looking away when he says this evenly, toward the window and into the dark of the very early late fall day.

And Rosie finds the breath to say, "I know."

25

Scot does not go to New York City that morning. He clears his belongings from the little brick cottage at the edge of the municipal golf course and takes one more step down the road to his destiny, to life with Leah, whom he is to meet at Point Judith the following Memorial Day weekend, courtesy of her rushing, Popsicle-bearing son.

Rosie does not go to New York City that morning. She goes to Orchard Mall and pulls down the piece of pink construction paper on which efficient Bunny has Magic Markered, "NO READINGS TODAY," complete with the addition of a scattering of stick-on stars, and sits at the half-circle cutout and, because this is how jokey life can be, first thing off, the first person who sits down asks the question: "When will I be married?"

Without missing a beat, Rosie takes the hand. "Make a wish but not for money," she requests, and the woman says, "I want to be married. Who doesn't?" Rosie knows at least one person, but stays silent. She looks into the palm. She sees this woman. And she sees a version of herself. She sees this woman not fitting in her relationship. But wanting to. Really wanting to. Being in love though secretly not sure exactly what that is, as Prince Charles got knocked for but had the guts to say aloud during his post-engagement interview. Asked, "Are you in love?" he'd responded, "Whatever that is." Whatever it is, was, can be, Rosie felt she'd had some version of that for Scot. Maybe a version isn't the ideal, but she'd thought it was better than nothing, and after all this time there was no sign that Dale was coming back. If she were perfectly honest with herself, "Why not?" is what it had come down to when Scot actually sank to one knee that night a few years back when he finished the plans for a card game involving edible playing cards ("Snacks included!") and asked if she'd marry him. The woman who extends her hand to Rosie this sad morning feels the same way about her life and her man. Rosie sees herself in that. Doesn't want to see herself, really doesn't, but does. The woman's man means well, but is molding her world into his — when hers is fine the way it is. It is a perfect thing, if you want to use that word. And in her need to be needed, she is willing to give up who she is.

"When will I be married?" the woman asks. "I need to know what to do."

And Rosie says simply, "Run."

That day she goes on to tell a man that his brother-in-law should have used two more support beams when he constructed the deck on this guy's house and it will be a miracle if it survives bearing the winter snows. She tells a woman who doesn't have a deck how much keeping her small backyard tidy when nobody else in her block bothers to do that means to the woman across the alley who has no backyard and imagines this neat one with the circle of always-dusted-off plastic chairs is hers. Rosie tells another woman that she worries too much, that situations take care of themselves, and she is only stressing herself out, and when the woman asks, "What'll I do if I don't worry?" Rosie is at a loss for words.

She continues to sit and field questions:

"Can I get out of my contract?"

"Will I be able to go to the concert?"

"Would she say yes?"

"Where can I find that one paper?"

"Who told her all those things I'd said, and when, and to who else because I have to stop this thing in its tracks."

"Why do I? Why do I? Why do I always want her?"

And Rosie answers:

"You cannot legally get out of the contract, but the thing you need to remember is that it is your life and your time, and you must do what is right for you if this work is making you crazy."

"You will not be able to go to the concert. Even though at first it will seem like everything will be perfect. Despite everybody in the world wanting one, you will manage to get the tickets, they will be forty dollars, no less, plus a surcharge for ordering them over the phone, and also state tax. You will be allowed use of the car for the night, and her boss will not give her a hard time about wanting the night off even though she will have just been out sick with a cold that sounded worse than it was so when she called in everybody was more than sympathetic. So you will have the tickets, and a date, and the car in which to take her to the show, and then just after you will have picked her up there will be a man running to the tree belt and flagging you down, and you will see him from the corner and you will at first think he has to be crazy, and you will just make a wide circle around him because he is now in the street, not just on the curb, he is waving and yelling something, and she is putting her hand around your arm, the first time ever she will touch you, saying, 'We have to stop,' and you will know that she is correct. You will spend most of the night with him in the emergency room, with this man who could not think of the three digits for 911 when his daughter couldn't breathe because even three numbers cannot be called to mind at a time like that. So you will not be able to go to the concert. No."

"She will say yes. But it will not be a full yes. She will say yes I will move in with you but it will be more from a feeling of — and I hate to say this — sympathy. She will feel sorry for you. She will move in because she will feel sorry for you. She thinks nobody else would. That is the type of person she is. And the type of person you are is somebody who puts that out in the world. The idea that you are not worthy.

"And she, she is the type of person who feels the same way about herself. So she would give her life away just because she feels sorry for you. Does that answer your question?"

"That one paper, it is in a carton marked Pat's Papers. There are smiles drawn in the top part of both of the capital *p*'s. The paper you look for, it is right on top of your art history essay titled 'Albrecht Durer: The Dissatisfied Master,' for which you got an A-minus with the only comment being, 'Why don't you leave more room in your margins so that comments can be made?' and it is beneath the instruction manual that was in the drawer next to the stove when you moved into the house. There are recipes in the back of that manual, and you actually made a few of them, and you know that sweet potato casserole from there? The one with the desserty covering of brown sugar and nuts and spices? The one your sister asked to copy down? She later submitted it as her entry to her church's fundraising cookbook and in the preface said, 'I came up with this recipe on a whim one day, when I wanted something that was both good for me, and that tasted like it wasn't!'"

"You are the one who told her all those things. You don't remember you had seven gin-and-tonics before you saw her there in the ladies' room coming out of the first stall near the door, the one your mother always told you never to go into because everyone in the world takes the first stall as they come in the door and there are just that many more germs. But this woman you told what you told, her mother never said any of that to her, the only warnings this one's mother gave about public restrooms was not to hang her pocketbook on the hook on the door, you know, whatever the color of people she was hating that day, she said those people go to Kmart to buy stickon plastic hooks to apply to the inside of doors and then they will reach over and steal. But that day in the ladies at O'Connor's there were no racial groups to watch out for other than white people, there was just also-white you and your red blood full of clear alcohol, and this other woman, the one you yourself told those things to, how you just found out that the old priest in the next town, the one who can barely speak English and has the size and demeanor of one of the little kindly saint statues up on the altar, this father, he is your father. And the woman you told went on to tell only her mother, and she only told her because what you told her was so unbelievable that she had to repeat it to somebody, but she is not a gossip, so she chose her mother, who is nearly stone deaf and didn't even know the daughter was speaking."

"You always want her because you don't have her. And when you get her, if you ever get her, you will want somebody else because people are much more perfect and lovable and attractive and right in fantasy than they are in reality, and she will make the same mistakes all the others have, and you will make the same mistakes you always do, including wishing you had somebody else, when you then will go on to do the same thing again."

"No, no, I won't, not with her," says this man. And Rosie says back, "Yes, yes, you will."

Because she knows everything. Unfortunately.

From down the hall, big applause. Some loud whoops of the type you hear at sporting events or concerts. More of a voice coming from a loudspeaker. Additional clapping, yelling. The switching on of Christmas music from the overhead speakers. Joy to the world, the mall has been saved. Saved!

And Dennis there, pushing through the line, walking the sixteen steps to the half-circle cutout and standing still and big-eyed for a moment before he asks Rosie, "Did you hear the news?"

26

L
O
O
K
A
T
U
S
N
O
W

Tusnow.

That's what Dennis reads.

Tusnow.

He needs more space between the words.

But he really doesn't care.

He is asking the world to look at us, but the us is no longer something he is part of.

Us is now Them.

Specifically, the New Visions Marketplace Conglomerate, a Phoenix-based firm that in the space of three weeks has taken over Orchard Mall as construction project manager and aimed the mall in a bright new direction, the likes of which have never been seen by shoppers in these parts. Cranes tower high over the shell of Sears. Surveyors scope out sight lines in the parking lot and mark them with sticks and with plastic ribbons that snap in the sharp winter wind. All along Berkshire Road flaps a bright green-on-white line of banners that read, "Future Home Of THE NEW ORCHARD MALL!"

You name the large or impressive chain found in every mall nationwide, it is — or soon will be — added to those banners, and added to Orchard. While so much is being taken away.

Hannah Pomfret had managed to say only about every other word as she stood before the December monthly tenants' meeting back on the first of the month and announced three pieces of news:

"I am being replaced."

It came out as "Am replaced," but everybody got the message, and if they weren't struck silent, they gasped or, like Dervla shouted, "No!" before they'd even realized they'd spoken.

"Yes," said Hannah, and "Why?" asked Bunny, and Hannah answered, "Baltimore has someone better for the job," and "There could be nobody better," called out the Music Man, and Hannah asked, "Anybody have a Kleenex?"

The second piece of news sent the box of tissues that Dervla retrieved from her desk around the room after Hannah read stiffly from a folder: "I also need to tell you that all tenant leases are to be renegotiated by January 31." Then she looked up from the folder and said, "I'm speaking in confidence here — you should know that it's pretty much guaranteed that the new rates will be way beyond what anyone here can afford."

Carla didn't mean to, but clanked her coffee cup against the leg of her chair as she set it on the floor, where any long-term hopes for her new shop also had just landed. The Russian girl stared at Hannah. The Tax Man checked his BlackBerry out of nervous habit. Mom, who'd rather ignored Hannah's first bit of news, straightened with actual interest. Dennis kept his place, leaning against the back wall, and focused a few feet away to the last line of chairs, where Rosie sat. She didn't have to wonder about her fate. It had been written on the note she'd found on her porch back in the spring — Irene had invited her to run the business until the mall closed. It wasn't closing now, but there was no way she could afford to stay.

"One last thing," Hannah said, and she read again that tonight, the extent of the new plans would be revealed. The names of the big-deal stores. There'd be a press conference at 6:00 p.m., timed so that, barring some tragedy, it could lead off the evening news. Cameras would zoom in on an artist's rendering of what would be renamed Orchard Mall at the Water's Edge. In the watercolor you would be able to see that the little brook along the far edge of the parking lot was to be widened, a bridge would span it and a gazebo would be built, as would a fenced children's play area complete with watchtower for a security guard. This was the water's edge. This was the new mall. This was the new world. One that would have no room for the affordable and the homemade and the unseen. Orchard, which had been so huge and then had fallen into nothingness and gotten resurrected, was suddenly so promise-filled that Baltimore wanted to turn it into its crown jewel.

"That's what it says here. Crown jewel." Hannah finished her last words, and only the sounds of her soft sobs and the hard whine of the ancient air circulation system followed. Dennis ran to shut it off for the remainder of any announcements in the meeting room, a rectangular space built to be just that — a space for community groups to utilize free of charge, just another benefit of coming to the mall when it first opened. The Russian girl looked to Ernie, who looked to the Village Stylist, who leaned into the shoulder of Bunny. "No chance for us?" asked the Music Man, and Hannah shook her head. "We've been here from the start," shouted the manager of the Flaming Pit, referring only to the business, as he'd just come to the mall seven years previously. But he was right. And there was a "Yeah," and a "He's right," and then Ed Horrigan, seated next to Mom, was jolted as she shot to her feet and snarled, "I knew it. I knew this would happen," even though the only person who'd had some clue was Rosie, who right now tried to look anywhere but into the palms of the Affordable Attorney as the Affordable Attorney stood and faced the merchants and put both hands up as if stopping a wall of traffic, then called out sharply, "We'll fight this! I'll do it — pro bono!" and Hannah mopped her eyes once again as she stood and said, "Maria, please, you're very kind but don't even bother. There's no chance. I'm sorry. There just isn't."

"The sudden and unexpected popularity of Orchard Mall has made us very enthusiastic for its renewed future," incoming Orchard at the Water's Edge Mall Manager Joan Connor told Channel 23 anchor Kiki Cutler on the live broadcast that night.

And when Kiki Cutler asked what Joan Connor might imagine was the reason for the sudden and unexpected popularity, Joan Connor said it was a renewed interest in the concept of Main Street recreated.

"People long for community. For what downtown used to be. We give them that," she assured with a hand set on Kiki's microphone-holding one. "We've been here for four decades, and we'll be here always. This is our holiday gift to the Western New England region."

"Returns not accepted." The Pit manager jabbed the clicker to silence the bulky, pre-flat-screen-era TV that sat on a shelf above the bar's selection of glassware. "Thanks for nothing."

The few tenants who'd gathered in the pub to watch on

television the announcement being made at the Town Common fifty yards down the hall had little to add. Only a few weeks were left at the place they'd called home for forty years. The barber and the stylist held hands. The Affordable Attorney typed hurried notes onto her iPhone. The optician removed his Italian frames and rubbed his eyes. Ed Horrigan and Dervla asked who wanted to stay for a drink. Ernest and Betsy did, the Music Man said yes, definitely, Dennis said maybe later and Rosie, way at the end of the bar, sat silent. The whole day was a mess. She was a mess. This wasn't supposed to be how this day went. Now she'd lost not only Scot but the mall, the people here, space number sixty-three, none of the future she'd dared to invite. She looked around and without spotting a palm saw looming unemployment or relocation for the mall tenants, most of whom in these final days would be headed to Rosie for a final reading.

She was in no rush to walk back to her space and decided to take the long way, down the hall and along the Art Lane to the exit by the cinemas, and a loop along the sidewalk for some fresh air before returning through the main door by the Flaming Pit. That's where she headed, slipping from the group at the bar, but in the next few hours, seeing so many of them before her at the half-circle cutout.

To each of them, even in this hopeless time, she told them their wish should not be for money. And that there was hope. Most sniffed at this. The Affordable Attorney said, "Only after a lawsuit, I don't care what Hannah says." And the Russian girl had started to weep. "I am too old for all this," sniffed the stylist, and the barber, standing behind her, nodded somberly.

"I was just getting started," Carla fumed.

"We were ordering new digital equipment," said the Fast Foto guy.

"I took on an assistant," said the optician, and that assistant said, "I quit a thriving practice to come here. To a mall that seemed to have something happening."

"Should I retire?" asked Bunny. "And if I should, how can I? I was just now starting to put money away . . . "

Rosie found no specifics in their palms, but one common denominator: "Everything's gonna be all right," she'd say.

"How?" they would ask.

"I don't know. But I see you working again. Sooner than you think. Same clients, and new ones, too."

"But that's what you told Bunny," they'd shoot back. "That's what you told the girls from the Pit. Don't just try to make me feel better. Tell me the truth."

"I am — I can only tell you what I see," Rosie would answer to those who thought she was just making it up. Which she was not.

"You will call her on the ninth anniversary of your father's death, as a gesture to say you are thinking of her, and she will say thank you, but she will not say back to you, 'I am thinking of you,' because she either isn't thinking of you, or she just cannot say that. Most likely, though, she is not thinking of you. She thinks only of herself."

"You can try and try and try all your life to get some approval from him but it will be like banging yourself in the head with a two-by-four. You can only please yourself, so that is the only thing you should attempt."

"Wait until February, there will be a two-for-one sale that will include airfare and car rental and six nights at the accommodations of your choosing."

"You are two months away from graduating, but the thing you have been studying will not be your life's work — you should know that, and I think you already do."

"He will lose his first job because he will be giving the groceries away to his friends."

"Your neighbor is having a lot better time than you think he is, no need to feel sorry for him."

"They will do a story on your daughter's time in the Peace Corps, and in that story is how you will learn she is engaged, though, I guess, since I've just told you that, you will really learn it first here. But you should still check the paper this Sunday."

"You will make the deal, but when you go to announce it at the big meeting, there will be a power failure in the building."

"There are deer in the woods that watch you when you stand outside at night to look at the stars. Two of them. Two deer."

"She will not be home for Christmas, but the local TV station will do one of those video hookups, and one night during the news they will play a greeting from her stationed over there in some place you can't pronounce, and you will think she looks thin, but that is only because she keeps her hair short now."

"You wish she would make the apology right now."

"You wish you could have lilac walls rather than hunter green, so paint them."

"You wish you'd said, 'Look both ways,' before he went to cross the street, but you didn't because that is something you tell a kid, and he was no kid, so you didn't, and along came the drainage company truck that could not stop because of the slush, and you should know that even if you had said to look both ways he would not have because he had the earmuffs on, couldn't hear you, couldn't hear the truck; it was not your fault."

Palms are being offered so fast, Rosie hasn't even looked to see whose this is before she greets and takes money and asks for a wish that should not be for money. She just sees the young man in the suddenly pink slush of the street and the drainage company truck driver kneeling next to him, no help at all. Then the screams. From Mom.

"What?"

The palm is hers — Mom's. As is the story about the young man.

Rosie has to find her next breath. By then, the palm is gone. Enclosed by the stubby fingers of the woman who one time in her life had actually loved somebody. And lost him — literally, right in front of her eyes.

"Um, I ... "

"You just shut up. And keep those people, those ... your freaks, keep them on your side of the hall. That's what I came in here to say."

She motions to the hall with hand closed, finger pointing at the many, many who are waiting for Rosie.

"Keep 'em away. Or else."

Rosie can only nod. She watches the back of Mom disappear into the crowd in the hall, hears the snappings of "Move it," and "Get away," as she makes her way back to the land of Welcome signs and reminders that the Holy Ghost is following you around constantly, so you'd better get used to it. Everything fuzzy-warm and cheery and reassuring, painted up and sold by a woman who has chosen to become anything but. Bad things happen. Life's path often is not your decision. What is your decision is how you deal with it. People go like that. Just like that. In bed, in the street, in a hospital, in a battle. On the day after Thanksgiving. Just like that they go. You can go with them, or you can go on, just like that. Mom had made her choice of how to deal with her tragedy nearly half a century ago, way back in the same month that Jacqueline Kennedy had to do the same. Now, JFK is dead, Jackie is now dead, the young man in the slush is dead, and Mom has been, too, for just as long. This is a parting gift for Rosie from Mom — answers to questions everybody's wondered but nobody's ever dared to ask her. Why she is so mean is simply because that's how she's chosen to be ever since her husband had died.

More people in a great wave. Seeking, wanting to know, asking, searching. Hoping. Always hoping. Will he come back? Has she ever read that letter? Will the procedure work this time? Why do they not want to hire me?

Rosie takes hand after hand of stranger after stranger. Sees truth upon truth. Tells as much.

Dennis is next. Suddenly there. Rosie takes the hand. It is smaller than hers, more worn-looking, like he's crawled to the half-circle cutout on it. She's seen it scores of times before, so that is nothing really to remark at. But what she sees on his palm today indeed is.

It makes her blink. Try to focus. Lean in. To see what she sees on the hand of Dennis. Which is skin. Just skin. The skin of a palm. Bearing lines, nothing more than that. No pictures, moving or still. No history, no present, no future, nothing but skin. Rosie looks at it. Blinks a few more times. Moves the palm closer. But she could pull it to where she would be brushing it with her eyelashes and there would be no doubting that Rosie can see nothing in the palm of Dennis but what had been there when he opened his hand.

After everything that has been fairly pouring from palms in these nine months — now nothing. Nothing. No future children, no past thievery, no yellow-and-black little bird hitting the window this morning, and you heard the *thock* sound and found it laying on top of the hedge just beneath the sill, and you could see the heart beating or lungs moving, whatever — something was moving, and you sat there hoping the entire bird would start moving, would pick itself up and take off and carry on, which in about twenty minutes it did, in a startled move of wing and tail and then a big flutter and then stillness, then it zipped off into the woods across the driveway, and you don't know how it did after that, but wouldn't it be wonderful if when you yourself had a big collision with something real and hard you would need only less than half an hour to recover and then fly off as if nothing had happened? No whining, no navel-gazing, no locating an insurance-approved counselor or joining a free support group, just flying off and carrying on?

But there are no birds in Dennis's palm. There is nothing. Nothing to add to the thousands of images Rosie has seen in palm after palm since that first day of spring. No flocked red Christmas ribbon to wind around the light post at your new condo. No weight gain from eating Rice-A-Roni too often once you got your own place. No job in the candle factory, which is fine because if you had been hired, you would have been laid off anyhow after the holiday rush. No tumor, no raise, no flat tire, no bat behind the curtains, no Clearinghouse Sweepstakes. None of that. Just skin and lines. All Rosie sees are the same things anybody else would see — anybody else who never had the ability to see the unseen.

Her own questions right then would have been the same as anybody's. She would have drawn the purple chair up to the half-circle cutout and extended her palm and asked, "Now what?" That would have been her only question: Now what? But she'd been chicken. And thought she'd have the chance to look whenever she liked. Like money in the bank. Now, all those chances are gone. Gone just like that.

So just like that, Rosie is as lost as anybody who has ever come to her. As puzzled about the future as the man who sits in front of her now, saying, finally, when Dennis dares to say something, thinking maybe that if Rosie had required any time to sink into a trance or whatever in order to do her reading, she has to be there by now.

"What do you see for me?" he asks.

"I don't see anything," says Rosie. The words arrive by barge, so slow, yet powerful, and she couldn't have stopped them if she'd tried.

"Nothing?" He is hoping that will somehow prompt the reminder that someone is waiting. On this day, it would be appreciated more than ever.

Her voice is small. "No."

Dennis knows when to quit. He takes his hand away slowly and says, "That's OK."

"But I don't see anything." Rosie is now looking into his eyes. Doesn't he get it?

"That's OK, Rosie. I understand." But he doesn't. She is either too upset, or whoever is waiting has lost patience, or both. He stands and he walks away.

Bunny is up to Words of Comfort, the category of cards that falls just after Get Well and just before Sympathy. Into these slots are organized the cards that inform others you are thinking of them, you are there if there is anything you could do, that everybody has bad days and you hope this message brightens things. The illustrations are florals, quiet meadows, and, for some reason, lots of teapots, like people in turmoil turn constantly to Lipton or Tetley rather than Jack Daniels. Right now, Jack sounds good to Bunny. Beer seems too picnicky for the circumstances. Wine too date-ish or celebratory. Whiskey strikes her as serious, tough, bad, something that could land you in big trouble. And this is a serious, tough, bad place she already is in right now, her business ending and no prospects for setting up elsewhere. She'd known the day was coming, but for months had been caught up in the spin of the line of customers, and, basically, the work she'd unexpectedly found she knew how to do. But huger and worse than all that, just the fact that all this is ending. That her days at Orchard are over. She opens the card decorated with comical honeybees. "I'll always bee here!" it announces. Bunny slams it shut. First, she is deathly allergic to bee stings. Second, she won't always be here.

Nor will Rosie, who walks in right then and takes Bunny's right hand, still holding half the card, and stares into it. Sees the same thing she'd seen — or not seen — on Dennis. Flesh. Lines. Creases.

"It's gone," she tells Bunny. "It's over."

"Everything's gone, everything's over," Bunny agrees. This is the immediate world right now, gone and over. Who knows what will happen next?

"It's gone," Rosie repeats. But Bunny doesn't get it. That Rosie doesn't have it. The thing she'd suddenly been given has been taken away just as swiftly. Just at the time when she needs it the most.

27

G
R
A
N
D
R
E
O
P

Dennis sees, "GRANDREOP."

It sounds like a procedure you'd send somebody a get-well card for enduring. Or a three-story-high B-movie creature that would tread the length of a city.

"I press this keyboard, and just like that, today's message." Joan Connor is telling Dennis this as she types out the rest of it, the "ENING!!!" Joan then steps back and puts her hand on Dennis's shoulder. "From here," she tells him, "I am going to inform the world!"

The "here" is her office — really Hannah Pomfret's, now Hannah Pomfret's old office, which now includes a computer solely to run the lights on the new Orchard Mall at Water's Edge sign. Sure, Dennis is still there, still has a job, but Orchard is not the mall he's known for so long. None of his friends are left. Even Laurie in the office is history, replaced by a male secretary who, his many desk photos attest, in his spare time rescues pugs and hosts many pug-centered social events.

"Get over it."

Dennis hears this in his head every time he passes Rosie's space. The echo has been there since the day two months ago on which he spoke his last question through the half-circle cut-out. He can't bear to look into what is now just a darkened alley, its metal security door papered with a sign boasting that, coming soon, is something called Pottery Barn Kids. Dennis had considered calling in sick on the thirty-first of January, hadn't wanted to see the final end of the mass exodus. The caravan of U-Hauls lining the curb to carry off desks, waiting-room chairs, racks, merchandise, would have been too much, and he didn't want to be there — not when he was still going to be there, at the mall, his job preserved because, after all, he is an employee of the mall, not a tenant. But he found the courage to show up on that last day, making scores of trips from store spaces and offices to cars and those rented trucks, with handcart, with rolling platform, with armfuls of the accumulations of four decades. Rolodexes, barber chairs, eye charts, developing machines, an enormous movie projector, everybody but Mom asking at some point for a little help, because everybody but Mom wanted the one last chance to do something together. Mom's stock was owned by the people who made it, and they'd adhered to the strict instructions ("Pick up your merchandise by January 31 or it will be incinerated") they'd been mailed. She threw into the Dumpster the forty-year-old shelving, so there was little more than the contents of Mom's counter to pack and bring to the car, nothing she could trust anyone else with, as there was no one she allowed anywhere near her still-new car. Eight months old and, other than Mom, it only had ever been occupied by the people who constructed it, those who drove it onto the train that brought it east, and those who drove it onto and off the eighteen-wheeler that delivered it to the retailer. Things weren't going to change on this day. Rosie and Ed Horrigan and Dennis were pushing old shopping carts full of travel posters, computer parts, and an ocean-liner model and a globe past Mom's car as she loaded a few small boxes into the trunk. One toppled onto the ground and Rosie, only on instinct, because if she'd thought she would have known better, asked, "Do you need help?" and Mom answered, "The only one around here who needs help is you. Professional help. Go and get some professional help." The slam of her trunk lid was the last word from her.

And it would stick in Rosie's head.

Rosie's trunk was slammed by Dennis's palm an hour or so later. He said, "Well, I guess that's it," and she nodded, because it was, it was it. The end of everything that had started with finding that envelope on her porch.

"I'll see you," Rosie said, though she'd already decided she didn't want to return to the mall again. Both Orchard Mall and whatever it was to become. So she wouldn't see Dennis at the mall. But she would see him somewhere else. Because, as she told him, and she meant it, "I'm just glad we met." Dennis wanted to say the same thing, but had never wept in front of anyone, which would have happened right then if he'd tried to speak, so he stayed silent. That's when Rosie reached to hug him and took in the warm autumn-leaves aroma that was there around him even in the frigid winter. Muffled in his down coat, Dennis's arms reached around her slowly, and there beneath the lights of the Orchard Mall sign, they hugged for just a little longer than either had anticipated. Rosie leaned into him because she just plain needed to lean into somebody. How long she stayed there in Dennis's hug she wasn't certain. It could have been three heartbeats, it could have been half the night.

The only thing that prompted her to step back was her worrying whether it felt as necessary to Dennis as it did to her. So she moved back, stepped back, nodded as if it were the conclusion of some kind of ceremony. Dennis nodded, too. For what, he wasn't sure, but if it was to agree that what just happened was the only thing to do at the moment, he was saying yes. Yes, it was. Because wasn't it that kind of day, emotions and all? They said nothing more to one another. Rosie unlocked her car. Started the engine. Gave Dennis a small wave as she moved from her parking space beneath the sign, up the hill and onto Berkshire Road and out of sight.

28

It isn't six yet. There had been talk of going for pizza after everyone was done clearing their space, but who knew when that was going to be? How it probably would be isn't as much of an unknown. More sadness, more reminiscing, more talk of plans, more of what Rosie wants to move away from now that she's moved out. She'll see the tenants again, probably at their new locations once those are secured, or at social events — Bunny was talking spring, and a picnic in her yard — so for now Rosie points her car north. There is no plan other than delaying her return to the brick cottage on the edge of the municipal golf course. She takes a detour off Route 91, thinking she'll treat herself to some costly organic groceries at that new place near the university. The Affordable Attorney has told her that when a sale there is completed, the cashier rings a loud bell. Rosie might go in just to observe that. Really, what else does she have to do?

That is the question on her mind when she sees the sign. Not just "PALM READER," but its preceding adjective: "PROFESSIONAL."

Mom's snappish comment flies through her head: "See a professional." And here, to her right, according to the big sign, is one. And one who might know her next step. Rosie turns just before she misses the driveway.

Two young boys run from the side yard. Rosie shuts off her engine and watches them frolic in the snow. They wear hats with earflaps that at once are like the old days and the height of geeky fashion. They are constructing some sort of fort and roll snow eagerly, collecting wet, fat layers. Rosie begins to shiver and knows that she either has to get into the house or drive off. She puts her hand out, toward the key. Then, quickly, she opens the door and steps out.

The first door at the house lets her onto a warm, glassed-in front porch. Three upholstered chairs are set in a circle around a small table bearing statues of one of those many-armed Indian gods, Saint Jude holding a huge club, a naked goddess-ish woman offering a tea light, a crystal ball the size of a tangerine, a deck of playing cards and a copy of *Prevention* magazine that belatedly promises you methods for getting the new year off to the best start ever.

Rosie shuts the door, and a rope of six or seven brass bells hanging from the knob announces her presence, but no one emerges from behind the blue cloth curtain to her left. Rosie can hear a television, Kiki Cutler somberly interviewing a cardiologist who is calling this type of snow a widow-maker. People who do no regular exercise the rest of the year try to shovel something of this weight and bam, they're dead. Over this is a phone conversation: "Get me the mu shu, and don't forget the sauce — that's the best part. And a coupla dumplings. Unless you want to split them? Ok, then, a whole order."

Rosie reaches back and jangles the bells on purpose. The TV goes silent. A few footsteps approach, the curtain moves aside.

There is no half-moon cutout. No wall. Nothing between her and this Coralie, which is the name above the professional palm reader line on the business card. Coralie sits in a folding chair with an embroidered tablecloth ineffectively covering its true identity. She regards Rosie for a moment in which Rosie can regard her. Coralie is about thirty but looks closer to forty. There is a hard look to her that the cotton-candy lipstick and blonde dye job in need of refreshing do not ease. She is very pale and very skinny and, apparently, very warm. Despite the season, wears a sleeveless pink T-shirt, soft orange leggings and bright orange flip-flops. Her exposed arms are strong looking, and the left one is barbed by a long T-shaped scar of the raised type that hints at incorrect stitching. "Now, I'm here," she tells Rosie, "What would you like, my darling? A reading? Two hands and face, twenty-five dollars. Tarot, twenty dollars, or twenty-five with hands and face. Spiritual consultation? Thirty. Now what can I do for you, my darling?"

Rosie hadn't expected to be given the menu details as if she were sitting at the Flaming Pit and being read the specials for the evening. And she doesn't expect the R-rolling accent from someone who isn't ancient and who isn't topped by a babushka. Rosie reaches for her purse, still unsure what reading she wants or what she is doing there.

"Not now, my darling," Coralie says. "First, my darling, make a wish." She leaves it at that, but the request is surprising enough. Rosie had liked the idea of wishing — that's why she'd asked her clients this. But she hadn't known it was proper reading etiquette. The absence of the reminder not to wish for money creates a space for Rosie, who keeps waiting for Coralie to add it. But then she realizes the space is the place for her to be wishing. It is like asking what was the last book she read or movie she watched — when put on the spot, it is like she's never read a word or seen one frame of a film. No wish comes to her. Then one does, but it is a question she keeps in her head: "What just happened? I want to know." And, as if she can tell it is the time to now begin, Coralie extends her hands, palms up. "OK, my darling."

Rosie sets hers into the woman's, palms up as well.

"Relax, my darling."

She tries. Coralie examines Rosie's left hand. Looks. Studies. Pushes into sections of fingers, stretches muscles, peers into wrinkles. Her hands are warm but not overly, like water that's just the right temperature.

"What just happened," Coralie says, "was what was supposed to happen."

Rosie's eyes shoot from Coralie's prodding fingers to her brown eyes. Rosie doesn't remember saying her wish, is sure she hasn't. She feels her pulse move past the speed limit. She feels what so many at her half-moon cutout had to have when Rosie had echoed what had been whispered only inside their heads. She is Sheila on that first day, she is Wireboy's mother. She is Dervla and Dervla's daughter. She is Hannah. She is Mom. She is Scot. She is Dennis. And now she is herself, hearing what she might have seen for herself, had she the courage to look back when she had the ability to see. "A set of keys. A hole in the wall. Things others wanted to know. A man. Things you did not want to know. A man." She stops. Looks at Rosie. Doesn't appear to know, or care, that she'd once been a competitor. She asks, "Does this make sense?"

Rosie nods. She doesn't know if it is proper to interrupt, but most people had always interrupted her. She asks, "But what just happened?"

Coralie turns her attention to Rosie's right hand. "An end. A beginning."

The last part sounds scripted. It could have been made up, said to anyone. At any time. Graduation, unemployment, death. Could apply to so many situations. Rosie might even have heard a version as she waited to say hello at the half-moon cutout, Irene saying, "I see an ending. And a beginning."

"Sorry." Coralie now. "I was wrong." Rosie hears it, the *G* of the last word hitting her temple. "I said 'a' man twice back there." She nods to the left hand. "There are two. I mean there were two. One's gone. The other" — now she runs a finger past the little triangular island in Rosie's lifeline — "the other is still there. I ask you, what are you waiting for?"

Rosie finds her voice. "I didn't know I was waiting for somebody. I wait most days for something. A change. A new direction. A new job."

"Nope. It's somebody. You've been waiting for somebody. But you just said good-bye to him." She closes Rosie's hands now, as if shutting her shop door for the day. "Unless you want more," Coralie says, "that's twenty-five dollars. Cash."

29

As the new year — and new mall — begin, Dennis decides to begin spending more time at the other end of the building, emptying the trash and sweeping the floors of a whole different neighborhood, one he's always skimmed just so he could savor cleaning near the space that had been Irene's. The one that last had belonged to Rosie.

Rosie. It has been just over a month since he's seen her. And there hasn't been a day she hasn't taken up a good part of his mind. Since he'd spent part of his New Year's Eve parked outside the house for sale across from hers, working through all manner of lines that would explain his unexpected presence at her door, a presence he never made happen, therefore never had to decipher, he could see himself making a big mistake for the second time. He misses Rosie like the song Muzaked into the old sound system, violins that sang, "Don't it always seem to go, you don't know what you got 'til it's gone?" Since March, Dennis had Rosie's presence, her warmth, her patience, her ear. Only when she isn't there does it dawn on him fully that he wants to have everything else about her. "You're an idiot," he hears in his head. "Mope over this one for another forty." He moves quickly away from the voice, walking the empty hall all the way to the other end of the mall, arriving just as a crew of men with sledgehammers begins to level the Orange Julius to make way for an interactive computerized map of Orchard Mall at the Water's Edge.

He gives directions to the architects who've come to scope out the interior of Fast Foto, which will be turned into an annex of the gift shop of the Boston Museum of Fine Arts. He sees the *S* being pried from the wall so only *EARS* is left. Other letters eventually will come along: an *M* and an *A* and a *C* and a *Y*, then an apostrophe and an *S*. But *EARS* is what Dennis sees each day when he comes to tend to a new end of the mall, where the Russian girl gives him his black coffee for free. The Orange Julius is gone. Carla's is gone. But in what seems like an afternoon, a Starbucks has materialized in its place, the Russian girl now behind that counter, refusing Dennis's money as she always has.

He takes what she's pointed out to him is called a venti-sized cup of his black coffee up to the new fancy electronic Orchard Mall sign up by the road. He's been given the instructions for access but has been told there'll be little reason to have to climb up there. Maybe to give it a power-wash twice a year, the installer crew's chief had said as he handed over the keys to the box that holds the crank that Dennis is now rotating soundlessly, causing a shiny new ladder to fall into place, awaiting his ascent.

From the sign, he looks down at the massive space the mall occupies: sixty-seven point six acres all told, including building, parking lot and ring of ornamental trees selected for their timed flowering in a long string of spring weeks that right now, in the early part of February, are only a cruel rumor. Dennis takes in the new air and the view, the gentle rounded white backs of the mountains to the west, the row of snowy pointier ones up north, and, to the south, the hard edges of downtown's less than handful of high-rises. To his right, cars turn into the parking lot that already is heavy with vehicles floating on the once-quiet asphalt sea he used to look out at with Rosie at his side.

Across the street, a McDonald's is taking shape at a fascinating rate of speed. Some of the construction workers are trying out the slides in the glassed-in playground, and Dennis wonders is that part of their job or are they, as is he, just killing time and getting paid for it. Beyond the McDonald's, the former Zayre department store, closed since Dennis's grammar-school years, is getting whacked by a wrecking ball sending out big, flat, hard noises. A Cornucopia natural foods grocery will be put in its place. Upscale baby spinach for the upscale crowd that Orchard will woo. Beyond the crane, another sign: Pier 1 is to be built in the woods there somewhere. Pillows and baskets and plates shaped like fish, all made somewhere very far away from woods that grow somewhere very far away, coming to this woods right here. The woods that run for a stretch into a neighborhood that runs for another stretch into what once had been the center of this town, where three streets converge at a triangular green once edged with all the necessary shops: pharmacy, bank, greengrocer, butcher, baker, clothing store, cobbler, office supplies, pet store, barber, dentist, doctor, most of the people and services that Orchard had long ago sucked out of existence.

For decades, Dennis's route to work has taken him past the storefronts empty for decades. He has driven over the bridge and past the little town common that marks the official entrance to downtown Indian Orchard, and onto a Main Street once edged with pharmacy, bank, greengrocer, butcher, baker, clothing store, cobbler, stationer, pet store, barber, dentist, doctor — most of the people and services and stores that Orchard had long ago sucked out of existence. But on this morning, the state representative's office had been dark, but somebody already had been by to raise both the American and POW flags. A few empty storefronts down, the mannequin in the Tae

Kwon Do studio's window had fallen over, or maybe was posed as the victim of some successful attack. This morning, the door of the pizza place was taped with a large piece of white paper on which somebody had hand-lettered, "EAT HERE OR WE'LL BOTH STARVE." From the small space in which the cobbler used to reattach the loose tongue in your dress shoes, the tiny Indian Orchard Chamber of Commerce invited passersby to "Picture Your Business in Indian Orchard!" As he had every day, Dennis had shaken his head. Asked himself a sad "Who'd be crazy enough?"

On this day, just as he looked at the sign again, he'd asked the same question, and heard, as he normally did, "Well, you'd know crazy," machine-gunned from an invisible form in the backseat. Dennis swerved to the curb, to one of the many vacant parking spaces, and spun to scan the backseat. He saw only a stack of the Orchard Mall canvas bags that Hannah had pushed into his arms in lieu of the good-bye she had been unable to voice. He saw the bags and nothing else. Because it came to him in this very second that nothing else — no one else — was back there. There never had been, just as there never had been anyone behind him stomping on any good thing or progress or idea or person that crossed Dennis's path. They'd been nothing more than age-old echoes of a long-dead man who no longer figured in Dennis's reality. The only person in the car was Dennis, who shut off the car and opened his hands, backs to the steering wheel, and stared.

He thought about all he'd been told by Irene over those years, by Rosie over most of the past one. There was hope, Irene had told him so many times, always hope. And now, somebody was waiting. He'd given that message a good long thought each time Rosie had delivered it. He couldn't begin to guess or suppose who it might be, and there in his car in the parking space in front of the space that once rented formal wear and that closed in the early 1980s, back when its claim to fame had been the prize of a twelve-inch color television to any groom with a wedding party of twelve or more, he turned to the storefront. An old mirror was the only thing on display, and in it Dennis saw himself looking back. Nobody in behind him, he was happy to admit, nobody beside him, he noted with resignation. But there indeed was someone there. Himself. And like the time the giant plywood monarch butterfly suddenly came unglued from its decades-old perch on a window box over the mall's old Main Street and fell flat onto his head as Dennis washed a fake window on a fake wall below, he felt slammed by something he hadn't expected — this time the idea that he'd been the one who'd been waiting. Waiting for him to do something. He watched the lights flicker on in the Chamber of Commerce office, and something lit similarly inside his head. He checked the mirror. He looked no different: the khaki jacket, the graying curls he enjoyed keeping on the long side, the searching eyes that could stop looking. He'd found what he needed. And in the second daring move of his day, in a car now silent but for the many and great possibilities audibly bouncing from his brain to his heart and back, he reached for a pen with one hand, and opened the other, palm up, and began to write.

Up at the sign this afternoon, watching the renewed mall grow at his feet, Dennis feels his enthusiasm surge, a big flood of hope, the dancing type he hasn't felt since he'd last spotted Irene in her half-circle cutout. Can it have been almost a year? That had been an ordinary day, that last one before she left for good, for that guy Sticks, for Canada, for a life that would never include him. If nothing else, it was proof that you never know what an ordinary day will bring. Both bad and good.

More proof: right here, right now, on this day, Dennis slowly takes out his cell phone and more slowly takes off his glove and ever so slowly opens his right hand and looks into the palm that gives his future. A few hours earlier on that deserted Main Street, using a pen emblazoned with "Orchard Mall at Water's Edge: Main Street Recreated," he'd written across his meaty line of fortune the phone number that will allow him to do some recreating of his own. Here, up at the sign, he looks at the number, then at his palm, and he begins to punch the numbers.

30

"But remember — nothing in this world is dependent upon the lines of the hand. They are only symbols of a situation and not its cause or reality. However — if you're going to bet on one thing when reading a palm, it's that if the Supernal Line appears clear and true, the inner life — the human soul — will indeed be brought to full awareness during the subject's physical life here on earth. Karmic contents, perhaps from ancient times, have led toward this eventuality, this awakening. Sometimes the potential for the event can be seen in the left hand of inheritance, but other events may have prevented it from reaching its goal — the attainment of true spiritual awareness, which is far and away the most valuable form of uncommon sense."

Rosie has that line, and it appears clear and true. She stares at it there at the kitchen table of the little brick cottage on the edge of the municipal golf course. She is back to sitting, just as she had been before she'd found the envelope from Irene. She skips the mantras prescribed by the therapist in the zip-off pants — they no longer apply. She no longer fusses and dresses as if she were headed to the bank, or even just the mall. She only throws on some jeans and a sweater and waits for the paper, for the mail, then for *The Young and the Restless* at 12:30 because, she's found while re-indulging in the soap for the first time since high school summer vacations, whatever is happening in her life, the people in Genoa City always have it worse.

Over in Genoa City, Nikki or Victoria, Phyllis or Lauren — or even the late Katherine Chancellor in all her long years in the serial and the planet — none of them has gone through the drama that Rosie has starred in for the past year. The loss of the job. The sitting around. The finding a job. The finding of some strange ability. The marriage plans. The unhappiness from the future groom regarding the strange ability. The dissolution of the engagement early on the morning the ring was to have been bought. The dissolution of the strange ability. The closing of Irene's space. The message from the professional palm reader regarding not one but two men, the second in particular. The landing back in the kitchen at home, where she sits this morning and stares into her right hand and wishes she'd done that ages ago. Back when she truly could see things. Scot had been smart to ask when he'd had the chance to find out. What might Rosie have learned about herself? Where might she be now if she'd seen all this coming?

She envies her old clients, whom she imagines as being brave enough to maybe go out and do something after taking her words into consideration. Maybe they did just march the sixteen paces to the door and reconnect with their shopping parties at the Flaming Pit and laugh about what they'd been told. Maybe they laughed off any information, went right to a trim at the Village Barber and by the time the backs of their necks were being dusted by that giant powder-scented brush, they'd forgotten about any specifics they'd been told. Maybe. But most of them did not. Rosie can't know this because, however it sounds, she no longer knows anything. So she cannot know that so many of them actually listened and acted.

They bought the cheaper birdseed.

Studied their calculus.

Pulled up their flies.

Stopped thinking negatively.

Let him make his own meals.

Just went and bought the necklace.

264

Invited the new people over.

Decided to quit after all.

Turned in at the cardboard sign advertising Saint Bernard/Newfoundland pups.

Finally opened the IRA.

Let her have her space.

Headed south. Found the green-sided home with the sister who was waiting. Stayed. Would not, would not, would not be a victim again.

All that, but Rosie won't know this. Can't know this. Just as she won't know how what she saw in so many palms set in motion so many changes.

The foreign woman actually lets the phone ring a few times when she calls. And Ed Horrigan picks up. And she says she is different now. Mature. She pronounces it "matoor," like the surname of that old actor Victor. She says she is matoor. And grown up enough to realize Ed is a very nice man. One who she hopes is not taken after all this time.

Now that he has more spare time than ever, the cinema's Ernest gives it to his screenplay, enough time that he feels confident enough to finish it and think about getting it into the world.

The tax man and the wealthy woman he met in the grocery aisle six that day fall in love and pool their investments and make an offer to Ernest to fund some portion of the production.

And two days after Rosie finally sees a professional, as she had been advised, the man the professional said she is waiting for drives to the brick bungalow at the edge of the municipal golf course and rings the doorbell.

31

To be clear, that last action was not exactly sparked by something Rosie saw in Dennis's palm. She never once had looked at his hand and seen him driving through downtown Indian Orchard on the morning of February the twenty-third and spotting the Chamber of Commerce's sign and taking it to heart. If all that were in there, Rosie had missed seeing how he dialed the Chamber from up on the sign, climbed down, got into his car, drove through that same downtown and past the Chamber sign seen anew that morning, then to this street and to her driveway, where he sits for a few minutes, swatting away the "What the hell are you doing here?" and "You think something like this is going to work?" that still somehow, despite his earlier revelations about their not being really heard, machine-gun constantly from an invisible form in the backseat.

Dennis's car is maybe fifteen feet from the door of the little brick bungalow at the edge of the municipal golf course, and that means he is fifteen feet from an action that could change his life. He turns slowly. Scans the backseat. Sees only the canvas bags. He sees the bags and nothing else. Because nothing else — no one else — is back there. The only person in the car is Dennis, who, making the second daring move of his day, and the most daring one of his life, opens his door and walks toward Rosie's home.

Rosie doesn't see ahead of time how he wavers between knocking on the metal storm door of the porch or pressing the doorbell, doorbells always so startling, and he does not want to startle her on this morning — not in a bad way. She doesn't know before it happens how, just as she is watching Maggie Yee pull a sled loaded with twins across the putting green of the snow-covered fourth hole, the doorbell will ring, always so startling, and she wonders, as we all do, who could be out there? Not before she opens her front door and sees, five feet ahead of her at the storm through which, nearly a year ago, Irene had dropped her key and the letter saying she was running off to be married, Dennis.

There is a line of things she does not see before they happen, but here is what she is present to witness and feel and take in: the wall of cold air that hits her when she opens that storm door. How Dennis doesn't move, take a step forward, just stands on that top step until she finally says, like the fact it is, "Well, you have to come in." How he walks into the living room and over to the pellet stove that she has never figured out how to feed or use or buy pellets for — that thing had been Scot's idea because even though it was brick, which people always say retains heat so well, he'd always found too chilly for his liking the little bungalow at the edge of the municipal golf course, and had gone out to buy this monstrosity and paid for the hole to be broken through the wall, and the chimney vent to be put into the hole through the wall, saying the savings on oil were going to be enough to fund maybe a solar panel in a few years. If you were going to go through all that fuss and planning and purchasing, wouldn't you maybe have stayed around? Maybe. Maybe not. In Scot's case, not, so the stove is cold, a surprise for Dennis as he nears it, hoping to warm up. Rosie is present for that, for the waving motions he makes with his hands toward the top of the stove, the hands that are angled away from her, and despite that, and despite the fact she can no longer see anything in anyone's palm, she looks away, out the window, to the greens topped with white, and to Maggie now replaced by the lone cross-country skier chased happily by some hairy black dog with clumps of snow attached to the feathers on his legs. Rosie is present to watch Dennis cross the living room to the kitchen and join her in gazing at the skier and the dog just as a light snow begins falling.

"I'd like to," Dennis says, still turned to the kitchen-sink window. And Rosie says, "I have a pair you could use," because she knows that the skis Scot had bought at a tag sale and never even tried are still in the garage. And Dennis says, "No, not that," so Rosie asks, "What?" and Dennis says, "I'd like to do something different," and Rosie asks, "What?" because there is no way she can know, not in the way she used to know things, what different thing he means. And Dennis says, "With you," and Rosie says, "Huh?" and Dennis says, "Because you'd have to be there if I went and did this." Rosie asks, "Where? What?" and Dennis says, "There," and he points out the window, and Rosie says, "You want to go skiing?" and Dennis says, "No," and Rosie says, "Golfing?" and he says, "Not golfing," and she says, "I'm lost," and Dennis says, "You don't have to be," and Rosie just tilts her head in confusion, and Dennis just settles his into a nod that without words says, "It's going to be OK." And he reaches for her hand and asks, "Wanna get outa here?"

32

A little green plastic manatee hangs from Dennis's rearview mirror, a souvenir of a visit to the mall a few years back by a Sea display of undersea wonders that was nothing more than a video of what you could see if you actually went to the park. Rosie has never been in Dennis's car, but she remembers once seeing the manatee as an image in Dennis's hand, moving like it is now, swinging purposefully forward, slightly back, then ahead again as the car moves, now over the bridge, and then slows at the little town common that marks the official entrance to downtown Indian Orchard.

The palm-image of the manatee comes to her now, as does the one she is seeing next, and once had seen in his palm at the half-moon cutout, how he pulls to the right, into the very first space after the common, the first in a very long line of empty spaces at the start of an empty Main Street once edged with pharmacy, bank, greengrocer, butcher, baker, clothing store, cobbler, stationer, pet store, barber, dentist, doctor — most of the people and services and stores that Orchard Mall had long ago sucked out of existence.

Rosie looks over to the state representative's office, its walk neatly shoveled and dotted with blue-hued ice-melt. A few empty storefronts down, the mannequin in the Tae Kwon Do studio's window remains knocked over, but from that position still is able to kick a leg toward a big glittered snowflake hanging from a length of fishing line. The pizza place wears a sign that wants you to "Try Our New Pie," and she is wondering when they'd starting baking, then remembers that some people refer to pizzas as pies, though she never has, and all that observing and reacting and thinking gives her something to do while Dennis remains as silent as he's been for the whole trip over.

The manatee is still moving once the car is parked. Rosie looks the right, to the Chamber's hopeful "Picture Your Business in Indian Orchard!"

"Every day, I come through here, I read that sign," she says without turning to Dennis, "And I think 'Who'd be crazy enough?'"

When he doesn't comment, that's when she turns, and that's when Dennis says, "Me."

In the pizza place's corner booth, they order the first pie of the place's day, and they sit there until it is time to order another one for dinner.

"I have some ideas," is how Dennis starts. "Because I have some money."

Rosie nods. She imagines he does, living alone for a lot of his years, pretty simply, from what she gathers, but he hadn't been paid a ton at Orchard Mall — that is another thing she imagines, and doubts he is getting much more from Orchard Mall at Water's Edge, the khaki Dickies shirt of which she spotted for the first time, with a little nostalgic turn in her gut, when he'd removed his parka after they'd ordered.

"Money is good," she says.

"You don't get it," Dennis says. "A lot of money." He says this in a sort of whisper as he takes a napkin from the dispenser. He pins it under a forefinger and spins it as he tells Rosie, "There was a guy at the mall, Lawrence Block. The first manager ever. And before he left he gave me a raise. I put aside every penny of it."

"Must have been a good one if you have lots of money," Rosie says, but she is hearing Dennis's words over Coralie's. And now, seated across from Dennis, is seeing him with new eyes and that fresh feeling of arriving somewhere you've always really wanted to be. She watches the spinning napkin, and it is how she feels, out of nowhere, right now, turned around and around and around. The feeling is so fast and strong that she pulls her head back suddenly, just as Dennis is saying something about the Tax Man. Dennis takes the gesture as surprise over the news that the Tax Man, who in his sometimes for-those-who-trusted-him-enough role as Investment Counselor Man, has been cultivating Dennis's Lawrence Block raise so fruitfully over the decades and also had the foresight a few autumns ago to suggest he yank his money from the stock market until further notice. And then there was the crash that ruined so many. But not Dennis.

Rosie hears Dennis, and still is hearing Coralie. Still is considering what she said. And what she is feeling. All she needed was to be seated across from Dennis to get that feeling of being where she's always dearly wanted to go. And she didn't even know she'd been waiting for such a trip until he showed up today and took her here. To downtown Indian Orchard. To this seat across from him. She hadn't been doing much of anything. Moping. Playing again and again in her head the message the professional palm reader had given. Sitting at the kitchen table, reading the paper, making lists of people to call back, people who left messages reporting on what they were doing since shutting down their shops at the mall. Bunny phoned from Rhode Island, where she was selling her cards at a small space in a small hospital where her sister helped people with their insurance difficulties. The Affordable Attorney was working from home, still working on a way to get back at Baltimore — she'll do it, mark her words. The Village Barber had joined his brother's shop nearly an hour's drive south. The Music Man had applied to teach at schools, sending his version of an application — cover letter, resume, CD, a portion of which he played on his twelve-string. And on Rosie's answering machine. Dennis was, well Dennis was at the mall, was OK. Just was calling again to say that, and to hope she was, too.

She recognized the Music Man's Pachelbel's Canon in D-major, which, before he'd clued her in last summer when she complimented him on it, she'd known only as the theme song to a television commercial for imported pasta. She never returned a call to anyone, but played the Music Man's message a few times a day, and Dennis's right after it, each time. They took her back to the mall, and she tried to imagine her life there, but it was as gone as the ability that had kept her busy for all those months. That same ability had shown her again and again a presence in Dennis's life. How often had she told him, "Someone is waiting for you"? Now, as if she were back in Cinema I or III and the red velvet curtain that Ernie mechanically raised to signal the start of the night's feature were in front of her eyes, she realizes that waiting for Dennis is what she's been doing since the final time she pulled down the gate for space sixty-three. Today, here at the table, awaiting a pie that is a pizza, the waiting is over.

"So I called the Chamber." Dennis is still talking. He is seated across from the person who has been waiting for him, and he is talking about the Chamber. But you can't fault him — he doesn't know right now that Rosie is that figure Rosie herself has seen many, many times in his hand. He is talking about calling the Chamber. And about money, and about saving a lot, and about being spared the financial crushing most everyone else had suffered, and that's when Rosie snaps awake. It is that whole banking mess that had caused her to lose her job. That had stranded her at home. That had put her in Irene's mind when Irene had needed someone to take her place. That had put her at the half-circle cutout. That had unveiled to her an ability to see things, to tell other people things, that early one morning showed her fiancée that his destiny was not seated across from him on the bed in the little brick bungalow on the edge of the municipal golf course. That had put Dennis's hand in hers. That somehow put her here, across from him, in the pizza place. Here, which makes her say, "There's nowhere else I'd rather be." Aloud.

Before he can react, Dennis has to take a few breaths and a sip from the red marbled plastic cup of Coke he'd ordered with no ice because it's always too cold that way. He has to wait to speak, because how often does what you really, really want to happen actually happen?

He looks at Rosie and thinks about her all the things she would never dare think about herself. Puts to her all the words she would never apply in a row beneath her own name. Destiny, destiny. He thinks about how this is what life does — brings you to the halfway point and teaches you to open your eyes and gives you the person you truly should be with.

He lets go of the cup, and he opens his square hands, the type that belong to a person who is practical and rational, who can be relied upon to do exactly what he has promised to do, and on time. These sorts are persistent and sometimes success-ful, and no touch of a scandal will ever come near them. Rosie closes her eyes, lowers her head, and then looks into Dennis's hands. She sees the muscled Mound of Venus, his calm, nearly lineless Plain of Mars, the little star down near his wrist that Irene had always told him would light the way. She sees the dramatic plunge from Jupiter to Mercury that hints at one or more over-dominant parents and a feeling of inadequacy. Both his Jupiter and Mercury are set low, indicating the need for affection, a fact that flashes back to Rosie, and even if it hadn't, she would have been helpless then to not take her hands from the warmth of her pockets and place them into the heat of his, moving her rounded fingertips over his spatulate ones, which both Irene and she had always noted were the ideal, showing both enthusiasm and confidence, even if until today it has been difficult for Dennis to embrace those qualities in himself. The reminders are there. As are those in his fate line, showing communication and promise. Always promise.

For the first time, Rosie's hands are in Dennis's, rather than below and cradling them, as they had so often at the half-moon cutout. He is not a client at her window, though right then she indeed is getting a glimpse of the future.

"I know it sounds very strange," Dennis is starting, as he looks at the reality of her hands held in his. This can't be happening. He continues as if it weren't. "I'll say it again: I want to bring this place back to life. This whole center of town here. Bring it back to what it was before the mall. Give it some energy. There are six vacant storefronts for sale right now. I'll start by buying those. And getting everybody back together."

Another image, though nothing more prescient than the rest of us might conjure in our heads: Main Street truly recreated. It makes her smile. Then the vivid blues and greens of the foliage-edged Orchard Mall at Water's Edge logo blare from Dennis's shirt, and Rosie has to say it: "What about the mall?"

"It's not going anywhere. I know it'll attract a ton of shoppers, but why wouldn't they come here, too? A sweet but sensible made-over downtown that could almost be a destination in itself. Taking them back to the old days. I made my wish. Like you asked. It wasn't for money, and for a long time, it was for someone I couldn't have. Today, I realized, I got what I wanted — an idea. This here, this is what I really want to do. Put some real stores down here. Get the Music Man and Bunny's and the cinemas and the Affordable Attorney — get everybody here. Starting with you. Your own place, designed any way you'd like."

Rosie smiles. "I don't do palms any more. Remember? Whatever I could do, it went away."

Dennis considers this for the time it takes the guy from behind the counter to quickly deliver the refill of Cokes. He says, "Maybe your work was done. Maybe you told everybody what they were supposed to know."

The ice in Rosie's cup settles with a crack. In the silence that follows, she leans forward and says, "But there's still one more thing I have to tell someone."

Dennis waits, wondering the recipient. Dervla? One of the high-school kids who lined up every Saturday evening? Rosie answers his question with his name. "Dennis," she says, "I don't know how you're going to take this, but I'm the one who was waiting for you."

33

In the office of Main Street, Inc., Hannah Pomfret's portrait is the first photo on the wall. She stands before an earthmover, wearing a gray pantsuit and a battered hard hat and muddied Wellingtons, face beaming lighthouse-strong with the pride you might expect from someone who's the new — the first — manager of the effort to reclaim a neglected, once-vital and soon-to-be-vital-again part of a city.

In real life, she stands before the picture, which has been printed in black and white, an effect she finds rather dramatic and is considering asking the photographer for a copy to hang in her own home, a condo in a stone building three doors down, just above Bunny's Card Nook. Kiki Cutler stands next to Hannah, extending a microphone, and Hannah has to refocus from the rather stunning image of herself to respond to the statement that Kiki feels she must repeat, having sensed Hannah's distraction. "Ms. Pomfret — look at the crowds on Main Street tonight! Who would have thought that downtown Indian Orchard could ever be revived?"

"Who could have predicted it?" Hannah asks back with a smile, using her favorite inside joke of a response, and she winks toward the woman who did, who more than a year ago saw in Hannah's palm images of her in those same boots, that same hat, near that same type of equipment. The setting wasn't clear at the time, but Hannah, of course, had assumed it would be the mall. And such equipment eventually did arrive at Orchard Mall — sorry, Orchard Mall at the Water's Edge — at the same time Hannah was asked to depart, her job taken by a manager fresh from that much talked-about shopping complex that was part of the new football stadium across the state where the Patriots play. Hannah soon accepted the curious invitation to meet Dennis at the pizza place in downtown Indian Orchard. After a period of astonishment, accepted his generous offer to manage the project he was starting. The one that would reunite the tenants of the mall — and include anyone else they could land. The one that on this first day of fall is being unveiled.

Rosie winks back at Hannah, then glances around the room and excuses herself from the group of well-wishers availing themselves of the wine and cheese spread that has been set up in the office. She passes through a back office, then opens the door to the fire escape and begins climbing the metal stairs.

She finds him at the top. She knew he would be there. At the sign. His sign. Well, the sign for Main Street, Indian Orchard. But, really, Dennis's sign. It is about a third of the size of the one back at Orchard Mall, but it still has impressive height to it, and you still have to climb another story once you get to the roof in order to spell out whatever message you wish. Today's message, a simple

WELCOME BACK TO MAIN STREET!

glows against the white board in sharp black Times New Roman letters lit by a set of solar-powered lamps. The words are lined up perfectly, have been since Dennis hung the letters upon assemblage of the sign two days ago — a crane-requiring event that made for more great press — yet he is up here again, using a long pole to fiddle with the pair of *E*'s. Rather than the coveralls he continues to wear daily, even though he technically is CEO of Main Street, Inc., a company that owns fourteen of the twenty storefronts edging the central part of the neighborhood, and that has its eye on three buildings housing the other six, Dennis wears a dark-blue, double-breasted suit that is the first purchase ever recorded at Downtown Clothiers, located between Riverside Weavers craft gallery, and Lens is More. The Clothiers and the Weavers are among the eight new businesses Hannah has attracted to Main Street in the seven months since she met with Dennis and, over a pizza that she never before had thought of as a pie, heard his plan. Up at the sign, Rosie doesn't disturb Dennis. She stands at the platform's edge closest to the street and looks down at the stretch of glowing storefronts below. Because they'd wanted to be in the same lineup they'd known at the mall, there is the Music Man's, then his brother's, that blessed Tax Man and sometimes Investment Man. Across the street from them, the Village Barber, with the Village Stylist next door. Just after a small stand of ochre-leafed real-live maple saplings shading a concrete bench, and just past Experience Travel and Bunny's Card Nook is the one large shop shared by Lens Is More and the Affordable Attorney, who now is back where she came from. On Main Street. New home of Fast Foto (Your Digital Specialists), Carla's Coffees and Teas, the New Flaming Pit, and the Russian girl's first business venture, a window at which lines form for orders of the fish and chips unlike any other. To find the place of all knowledge, enter the next doorway past hers. The one across from Bethany Colrain, Weaver of Wearable Art. Turn in at the sign for Coralie, Professional Palm Reader. A woman who really knows what she's doing.

It was Coralie who'd put the two and two together, the two being Rosie and Dennis. Didn't so much put them together as, on the day that Rosie's palm-reading ability meter had run out, gave the crucial information Rosie might never figure — that she was the one waiting for Dennis. Crucial information that now seems the biggest and most sense-making truth Rosie has ever known. When she told it to Dennis that day at the pizza place, he blinked. Blinked again. But the only thing in his eye was the reality of Rosie saying, "It was me, Dennis. The person waiting. It was — it is, me." She didn't go away when he blinked. And she will not. Ever.

"Tell me that again," he'll say, and she'll repeat it, and the odd time he is alone, in something he hasn't done since he was a kid, he'll get on his knees and say a prayer of thanks that hers is the only voice that now echoes in his head.

There at the sign, on that first day of fall, she says, "Great view up here," and Dennis stops his letter-tweaking and walks over to say, "It just got better." Rosie leans into him, and he is as solid and assuring as that night in the parking lot, the night she left him only to find out she'd be spending the rest of her life with him. The ring on the fourth finger of her left hand, white gold with a small hand shape bearing a tiny ruby in its palm — specially made to Dennis's rough design by the jeweler who back in May took the storefront next to the state rep — is the latest reminder. As is the condo they are furnishing across the way, just above My Back Pages, the new little independent bookstore and newsroom that you'd think anybody would be nuts to open in this day and age of the big-box store and the online store and the reading from an electronic tablet held in your hand, but, hey, you never know what the future will bring.

Rosie once did. Had she taken a look, back when she could see things in her palm, she would have seen Dennis in her future from the day she was born. Just as if those images of Irene, then of the waiting figure, hadn't been all that was taking up Dennis's mind, she would have seen herself there in his. From

Day One. From the perch at the sign, she looks down at the pizza place where all this came together, the small office next to it where her therapist with the zip-off pant legs now rents a space. He stands outside on this night of open houses, distributing to the many passersby his business card and a list of ten ways to find peace. Included is his suggestion of making the list of why you are OK. Rosie thinks back to her many mornings at the kitchen table, reciting hers over and over again, as if it then would be real to her, as if it would make them all the more true. There is no need for her to reach for a paper to remind herself of the love she now has. There's no need to remind yourself of a fact that is as present as the lines on your palm skin.

Inside Main Street Cinema — at seventy-five seats no comparison to Cinema I or II or III but just big enough to cater to the crowd interested in the independent, the foreign or those with local ties, that last category being the one into which the attention-getting little movie made from Ernest's screenplay falls — the Music Man's sweeping theme song swells. In their third-row seats in the newly reupholstered former Star Theater, Dennis takes Rosie's hands in his. She runs a forefinger along his Supernal line and remembers that, if you're going to bet on one thing when reading a palm, it's that if the Supernal line appears clear and true, the inner life — the human soul — will indeed be brought to full awareness during the subject's physical life here on earth. Karmic contents, perhaps from ancient times, have led toward this eventuality, this awakening. And to this moment here in the Main Street Theater. So full, yet easy to spot so many familiar faces —Ed Horrigan and his foreign soon-to-be-American-citizen woman to their left, Bunny to their right, the girls from the Pit, Ernest and Betsy up in the projection booth watching Ernest's story shown for the first time, a story set in a place not unlike the one in which they'd all met and parted, now being played in the new home that Dennis made for them all. At the center of it, he and Rosie sit with palms together. Stories together, pasts and futures together. The lines meet, one heart, one head, one life. Venus, Mars, Saturn, and then Jupiter, the seat of the soul. Even if you had all knowledge and power in the world, you couldn't have seen this coming.

"We arrive bearing what we are born with," a woman's voice tells us over the first scene, that of a huge and massive shopping mall somewhere in America, parking lot empty, a lone figure rushing across patches of snow and to its door, to word of her future.   "Our lives are what we make of those things," the voice continues as the camera zooms to her hand on the door, her steps in a vacant hall, her turn into a small space where a woman sits waiting behind a half-circle cutout. "We can choose. Joy or anger. Love or hate. Settling or change. Desperation or hope. Make your life. Make a wish."

And that is how the story begins.

Interview With the Author

What was the inspiration for the story?

In the mid-nineties, my husband Tommy Shea and I were walking in New York City's Lower East Side and in front of a sparsely furnished storefront spotted a sign reading "Palm Readings $10." I thought, "What can you get in New York City for ten bucks that's legal?"

Inside, we were greeted by a young woman with an Eastern European accent who took my hand and said "Make a wish but not for money." I don't know what else she told me — she could have given me that night's winning lottery number but all that stuck with me was her request. I already was thinking what a great title it would make for a book about a palm reader. When I started the actual writing, I didn't know where I'd put her booth. A trip to the movie theater at the "dead mall," which is what everyone in my neck of Western Massachusetts used to call a particular withering (and now demolished) shopping mall in Hadley, got me thinking how affordable one of the empty spaces in such a place might be, and how my fictitious palm reader indeed could be working there. And as unemployment became a fact of life for so many over the time I was writing this story, I thought I'd give my main character that jarring reality, and the need for routine.

Was your first palm-reading experience in a dead mall?

It actually was over the river from that dead mall, in Northampton, Massachusetts, where a psychic fair used to be held one Saturday a month. A hall just off Main Street would be filled with a variety of psychics, and you'd pay per reading. I attended in 1991 with the idea that I'd gather information for a story to sell to a magazine or newspaper. I don't know why I chose to start with the table of a palm reader named Art, but I did, and he took my hand, knew that I was a writer, knew what material I was thinking about working on, gave me the first name of the woman who would become my mentor, and the surname of the woman who would become my first agent. I'd say Art knew his stuff.

Are you a fan of shopping malls?

I enjoy browsing as much as the next person, but tend to do most of that while in a city on business or vacation, so most of the malls I have visited aren't near home. Plus, not unlike some of my characters, I prefer to shop in an actual town, rather than one recreated inside an enormous building. A huge mall is located half an hour from my home, but I go there only for one store — the Apple shop that helps me with the computer on which I'm writing this. The size of that mall is too much for me — almost depressing in a way. Most recently, I spent time in the United Arab Emirates when Tommy was working at a newspaper there. There in the 110-plus heat, I used them as walking tracks, and saw how malls there, too, are a town center, these drawing so many every day and night with their necessary air conditioning, dazzling array of very-high-end shops, and more-dazzling inclusions of ski hills and ice rinks.

You write both fiction and nonfiction. With which genre are you more comfortable?

I like writing both, I like being able to switch gears after a long project in one genre or the other, making all the decisions in fiction — should the poodle be pink or white? — and following the facts in nonfiction. I'd suggest that all writers try a stretch into another genre.

Reading Group Discussion Questions

Rosie Pilch's life changes with the loss of her job. Describe what you imagine her life would have been had Irene not left the note and key on Rosie's porch.

Has the loss of employment ever been a positive experience for you? If so, who was your Irene in that case, and how did she or he work magic in your life?

Have you ever taken a new job you weren't certain about and been surprised by how well it suited you?

When was the last time you had an Orange Julius?

This story is set in a dead mall. Does a living mall hold a place in your own life story? Does it hold a place in the culture of your community?

If you have a mall in your community, how has it affected the area over time? Does the book's first description of a down-and-out Main Street in Indian Orchard sound familiar?

If you have a dead mall in your community, what's it story? Were you there at the opening? What was its heyday? What caused its decline? Is there any hope or effort for its future?

Rosie is not at all qualified for her new job. What are your thoughts on how her ability becomes clear?

Have you ever gone to a palm reader? What were you told? Did the predictions come to be?

The mall shopkeepers comprise their own community. Who was your favorite or least favorite character, and why?

What are the future of malls in a world in which online shopping is so prevalent – any predictions?

Some Other Books By PFP / AJAR Contemporaries

a four-sided bed - Elizabeth Searle
A Russian Requiem - Roland Merullo
Ambassador of the Dead - Askold Melnyczuk
Blind Tongues - Sterling Watson
Celebrities in Disgrace - Elizabeth Searle
(eBook version only)
Demons of the Blank Page - Roland Merullo
Fighting Gravity - Peggy Rambach
Girl to Girl: The Real Deal on Being A Girl Today - Anne Driscoll
"Last Call" - Roland Merullo
(eBook "single")
Leaving Losapas - Roland Merullo
Lunch with Buddha - Roland Merullo
Music In and On the Air - Lloyd Schwartz
My Ground Trilogy - Joseph Torra
Passion for Golf: In Pursuit of the Innermost Game - Roland Merullo
Revere Beach Boulevard - Roland Merullo
Revere Beach Elegy - Roland Merullo
Taking the Kids to Italy - Roland Merullo
Talk Show - Jaime Clarke
Temporary Sojourner - Tony Eprile
the Book of Dreams - Craig Nova
The Calling - Sterling Watson
The Family Business - John DiNatale
The Indestructibles - Matthew Phillion
*The Winding Stream: The Carters, the Cashes and the Course
of Country Music* - Beth Harrington
"The Young and the Rest of Us" - Elizabeth Searle
(eBook "single")
*This is Paradise: An Irish Mother's Grief, an African Village's Plight and the
Medical Clinic That Brought Fresh Hope to Both* - Suzanne Strempek Shea
Tornado Alley - Craig Nova
"What A Father Leaves" - Roland Merullo
(eBook "single" & audio book)
What Is Told - Askold Melnyczuk

Made in the USA
Middletown, DE
25 April 2021